WILDFIRE

Ralph Cotton

A SIGNET BOOK

SIGNET
Published by New American Library, a division of
Penguin Group (USA) Inc., 375 Hudson Street,
New York, New York 10014, USA
Penguin Group (Canada), 90 Eglinton Avenue East, Suite 700, Toronto,
Ontario M4P 2Y3, Canada (a division of Pearson Penguin Canada Inc.)
Penguin Books Ltd., 80 Strand, London WC2R 0RL, England
Penguin Ireland, 25 St. Stephen's Green, Dublin 2,
Ireland (a division of Penguin Books Ltd.)
Penguin Group (Australia), 250 Camberwell Road, Camberwell, Victoria 3124,
Australia (a division of Pearson Australia Group Pty. Ltd.)
Penguin Books India Pvt. Ltd., 11 Community Centre, Panchsheel Park,
New Delhi - 110 017, India
Penguin Group (NZ), 67 Apollo Drive, Rosedale, Auckland 0632,
New Zealand (a division of Pearson New Zealand Ltd.)
Penguin Books (South Africa) (Pty.) Ltd., 24 Sturdee Avenue,
Rosebank, Johannesburg 2196, South Africa

Penguin Books Ltd., Registered Offices:
80 Strand, London WC2R 0RL, England

First published by Signet, an imprint of New American Library,
a division of Penguin Group (USA) Inc.

First Printing, July 2012
10 9 8 7 6 5 4 3 2 1

Copyright © Ralph Cotton, 2012
All rights reserved. No part of this book may be reproduced, scanned, or
distributed in any printed or electronic form without permission. Please do
not participate in or encourage piracy of copyrighted materials in violation
of the author's rights. Purchase only authorized editions.

Ⓞ REGISTERED TRADEMARK—MARCA REGISTRADA

Printed in the United States of America

PUBLISHER'S NOTE
This is a work of fiction. Names, characters, places, and incidents either are
the product of the author's imagination or are used fictitiously, and any
resemblance to actual persons, living or dead, business establishments,
events, or locales is entirely coincidental.
    The publisher does not have any control over and does not assume any
responsibility for author or third-party Web sites or their content.

If you purchased this book without a cover you should be aware that this
book is stolen property. It was reported as "unsold and destroyed" to the
publisher and neither the author nor the publisher has received any payment
for this "stripped book."

ALWAYS LEARNING   PEARSON

A DEADLY TRAIL

Why had they ridden into the fire?

Because they had laid out their escape route before ever riding into Phoebe, he answered himself. Somewhere up ahead, they had fresh horses waiting for them. That was all it could be. When he worked out the miles from here to Phoebe in his head, he realized they wouldn't have attempted to make it as far as Bagley's Trading Post without a change of horses. The trading post was still a twenty-six-mile ride from here, most of it over dry, rocky, leg-breaking terrain.

Fresh horses? Good enough. He'd stick with that notion until something proved otherwise, he decided, staring up along the rocky, winding trail. He had their tracks. He'd catch up to them and take them down. He only hoped none of the fire had jumped across the chasm and rekindled among the pine woodlands in front of him. It was the season for wildfires, he thought, dry, hot, deadly—there was nothing he could do about that. His work had to go on, wildfires or not. He cradled the rifle in his arm while the horse stood drawing water beside him.

For Mary Lynn . . . of course.

PART 1

Chapter 1

Arizona Territory

Wildfire raged.

The young Ranger, Sam Burrack, sat atop a rust-colored barb on a bald ridge overlooking a wide, rocky chasm. With a battered brass-trimmed telescope, he scanned beyond the buffering walls of boulder and brush. Long, rising hillsides ran slantwise heaven to earth, covered by an endless pine woodlands. He studied the blanketing fire as it billowed and twisted its way north to south along the hill lines. He watched flames the color of hell lick upward hundreds of feet, drifting, blackening the heavens.

Through the circle of the lens, he spotted four wolves sitting next to one another along a rock ledge, winded and panting. Their pink tongues a-loll, they stared back at the wall of smoke and fire as if numbed, overpowered by it.

At the bottom of the hills, where the woodlands came to an end at a chasm, Sam saw a large brown bear stop in its tracks, turn and rise on its hind legs. The large beast stood erect with its forearms and claws spread wide and raged back at the fire, ready to do battle. Yet even so powerful a beast looked helpless and frail beneath that which lay spoil to its domain. At the end of its roar, the bear dropped back onto all fours as if bowing in submission, and loped on.

The Ranger shook his head, noting how little caution the other fleeing woodland creatures paid the large beast as they darted among dry washes and gullies and bounded over brush and rock with no more than a reflex glance in the roaring bear's direction. Even the barb beneath him paid no mind to the bear's warning until a draft of hot smoke swept in behind it. Then the horse skittered sideways and chuffed and scraped a nervous hoof.

"Easy, now . . . ," the Ranger murmured, tightening on the reins and collecting the animal. "We're not going to get you cooked." He patted a gloved hand on the barb's withers. "Me neither, I'm hoping," he added, closing the telescope between his hands. He looked down at the sets of hoofprints he'd been tracking for three days and gave the barb a tap of his boot heels.

But the barb would have none of it. Instead, the animal grumbled and sawed its head and stalled back on its front legs.

The Ranger picked up his Winchester from across his lap. He gave another, firmer tap of his boot heels, this time reaching back with his rifle and lightly striking the barrel on the barb's rump.

"Come on, pard, we know our jobs," he said.

This time he felt the barb take his command and

step forward onto the down-winding path toward the rocky land below them. But even as the animal did so, he gave a chuff of protest.

"I know," said Sam, "I don't like it either. . . ."

Four hundred yards down, the meandering dirt trail hardened into rock and left the Ranger with no sign to follow other than the occasional broken pine needles where one of the four men's horses had laid down an iron-ringed hoof. But that gave him no cause for concern—the old overgrown game trail lay down the rocky, deep-cut hillside. And now that the fire had moved in across the thick woodlands, there would be no other logical way north at the bottom of the hills except to follow rock chasm to its end.

He knew the bottom trail would stretch fourteen miles before coming to water—twenty-six miles farther before reaching Bagley's Trading Post. By then, the men he followed would need fresh horses. They wouldn't rest these horses out before riding on. That took too much time, he told himself. Men like Royal Tarpis, Silas "Red" Gantry, Dockery Latin never wasted time when they were on the move. Out in the open this way, these men instinctively moved as if someone was on their trail, whether they knew it to be a fact or not.

Men with blood on their trail . . . , Sam told himself, knowing there was a younger man leading the gang these days. That man was the Cheyenne Kid, and he was known to be ruthless. But now the Kid was wounded, bleeding. He'd shot and killed two men in Phoebe, a bank teller and the town sheriff. The sheriff had managed to put a bullet in the murdering young outlaw before falling dead in the street. Sam had picked up the men's trail the following day, and he'd been on it ever since.

Sure, they knew someone was coming.

Sam drew the barb to a halt at a break in the trail and looked to his left, across the chasm where the fire roared, smoke filling the sky. He took off his left glove and felt the barb's withers. The horse's coat was dry—hot to his touch. So was his own left cheek, he thought, raising his palm to his face, feeling the prickliness of his beard stubble, noticing the stiff scorched sensation along his cheek line, the dryness in the corners of his eyes as he squinted them shut for a second, gauging the heat.

Untying the bandana from around his neck, Sam fashioned a curtain of it beneath the brim of his sombrero and draped it down his left cheek. It would help some, he thought.

"I hope I didn't lie to you, pard," he said to the horse, recalling his earlier words to the animal.

He picked up his canteen hanging from his saddle horn, uncapped it, swished a mouthful of water around in his mouth and spit it out along the left side of horse's neck. He leaned forward in his saddle and poured a thin stream of water down the horse's muzzle and along its left side, taking in his own leg and back along its flank. The horse shuddered and chuffed and reached its tongue around to lick at its side.

"That's all for now," Sam said.

He capped the canteen and rehung it. All right, it was hot, but he'd expected that, he reminded himself. Three miles ahead of him, give or take, he saw the fire had waned on its push southward. In the wake of the billowing inferno stood a few bare and blackened pine skeletons.

But he and the horse were safe. He had calculated the risk before putting the horse forward onto the trail. Had the wind made a sudden shift and blown straight at them before they'd reached the trail's halfway point, he would have turned back and raced to the top again before succumbing to the heat. Halfway down the trail, he'd realized there was an end to the fire a few miles to the north—the direction he was headed in. From that point, had the wind changed suddenly, he would have raced down the trail.

Whichever way, they'd make it.

And oddly enough, he thought, owing to the rise of heat, it had been hotter atop the trail than it was here below. Still, it had been risky, said a cautioning voice that often admonished him at times such as these.

Yes, it had, he admitted. *But . . .* He let out a breath of relief.

"'Life is naught without its risks,'" he quoted to himself.

Who had said that? He shrugged as he nudged the horse forward. He didn't know. Probably some obscure penny dreadful author who had stood, or *imagined* himself to have stood, on just such a trail as this.

He started forward along the lower end of the trail, where he knew the heat would be less intense. As he rode he shook his head. Leave it to men like these to ride into a wildfire, he thought.

Why had they done that?

But as he asked the question, he had to remind

himself that he had followed without hesitation—so closely that he'd had to water both himself and his horse down to keep up his pursuit. What did that say about him? He didn't want to think about it right now.

He rode on.

Four miles farther down along the chasm trail, he felt the heat on his left begin to wane. A mile farther the temperature had subsided enough that he was able to take the bandana down from his face. Beneath him the rusty barb rode at a stronger gallop. Along their left, beyond the buffer of boulders, dirt and shale, the woodlands lay blackened and ruined, smoke still rising. It was slower now, less intense, but nevertheless engulfed them in a gray, suffocating haze.

Now he had another problem.

He stopped the horse and stepped down from his saddle. He listened to the barb wheeze and choke, its labored breath rattling deep in its lungs.

"Easy, boy," he said, rubbing the horse's muzzle. He stepped back to his saddlebags, rummaged out a shirt and shook it out.

He tied the sleeves up around the horse's head and made a veil of the shirt. The horse resisted a little and whipped its head until the Ranger took the canteen and poured water down the horse's face and threw the shirt onto its parched muzzle. He held the wet shirt in place, letting the animal breathe through it. When the horse felt the good of what the Ranger was doing and settled, Sam took his hand off its muzzle.

"Good boy."

He poured water onto his bandana and tied it across the bridge of his nose. He led the horse forward by its reins, feeling the thickness of the smoke with every step.

"I make it . . . seven, eight miles to water," he rasped, as if the winded horse understood his words and took comfort in them.

Three miles farther, he noted the smoke had let up, enough that he could make out the blue of the sky. Underneath him the horse breathed easier; so did he. Stopping, he took down the warm canteen and lifted the shirt from the horse's muzzle. He kneeled in front of the horse and took off his sombrero like a man given to a vigil of prayer.

"You need this worse than I do," he said, pouring the water into the upturned hat.

The horse lowered its muzzle into the sombrero and Sam let the wet shirt fall around the ensemble.

When the horse finished the water and tried chewing at the hat brim for more, Sam stood and pulled his wet sombrero away and placed it atop his head. Canteen in hand, he climbed back into the saddle and gave the horse a tap of his heels. On their left, among boulder rocks and dry washes, antelope, deer, coyote and an assortment of smaller creatures still skirted in the same direction, slower now that the threat of death inched farther into the distance.

"It's up to you now," Sam said to the horse as the barb galloped forward, the air, the ground and the atmosphere already turning cooler around them.

For the next five miles he gave the barb its head, the horse keeping up a strong, steady pace, moving farther away from the raging fire. With the wind in their faces, even with the lingering odor of pine char and brimstone in the air, Sam felt the horse surge with a renewed energy when the scent of water managed to reach into its nostrils.

The last few hundred yards he had to rein the barb down to keep it from bolting toward the rock runoff tank lying below a steep hillside to his right. The barb muttered and blew and shook its head in protest, but it followed the Ranger's command.

Thirty yards from the water, Sam saw a panther and two cubs begin to slink back from the water's edge. Grudgingly, with a large-fanged growl, the big mother cat crept backward to the shelter of boulders as the Ranger stepped the horse forward. He noted the upper half of the mother cat's left ear was missing. Dried blood caked down her neck and shoulder. Mimicking its mother, one of the cubs raised its back toward him and let out a hiss—showing its small and helpless fangs. The Ranger smiled sadly, nudging his horse forward.

Across the water Sam saw the rumps of a small herd of elk move away into the growth of pine and juniper mantling the rock chasm still running alongside his trail. A moment earlier a young bear had stood up on its hinds and looked at him and the horse, then dropped and turned away as the Ranger scanned the rock tank from fifty yards.

Odd, he thought, elk, mountain lion and bear, all watering within less than thirty feet of one another. Yet odder still was that all three species had cut short sating their thirst at the glimpse of man. The only animals to remain as the Ranger rode closer were birds of all size and variety. They sat along the rocky water edge, preening themselves of the smell of smoke, and drinking fearlessly, as if knowing that in an instant they could be up and gone should man try any of his dark shenanigans.

A few of the smaller birds fluttered up and away as the Ranger and the horse filed past them at less than fifteen feet. But the larger birds only stared and squawked and continued attending to themselves.

"Don't mind us," he murmured, riding past.

When he had looked all around the water hole and satisfied himself that he and the horse were the only ones there representing their species, he swung down from the saddle, rifle in hand, at the water's edge. The larger birds sidestepped away from him, making room for him and the horse, but giving up no more of their spot than they had to.

Where he stepped down from his saddle, he saw the hoofprints of the four horses in the sandy dirt among the rock. On one of the half-sunken rocks, he saw spots of dark blood and he stooped and took off his glove and touched his fingertips to it while the horse lowered its muzzle and drank.

All right, Cheyenne Kid, how far ahead are you? he asked, rubbing his fingertips on the spots and then examining them for any sign of red moisture.

"Bone dry," he murmured aloud, as if any of the creatures of the wilds were interested. He stood and looked back and forth along the trail, first at the smoky distant trail behind himself, then along the rocky, winding trail ahead. Now to the earlier question he'd asked himself, he thought.

Why had they ridden into the fire?

Because they had laid out their escape route before ever riding into Phoebe, he answered himself. Somewhere up ahead, they had fresh horses waiting for them. That was all it could be. When he worked out the miles from here to Phoebe in his head, he figured they wouldn't have attempted to make it as far as Bagley's Trading Post without a change of horses. The trading post was still a twenty-six-mile ride from here, most of it over dry, rocky, leg-breaking terrain.

Fresh horses? Good enough. He'd stick with that notion until something proved otherwise, he decided, staring up along the rocky, winding trail. He had their tracks. He'd catch up to them and take them down. He only hoped none of the fire had jumped across the chasm and rekindled among the pines woodlands in front of him. It was the season for wildfires, he thought, dry, hot, deadly—there was nothing he could do about that. His work had to go on, wildfires or not. He cradled the rifle in his arm while the horse stood drawing water beside him.

Chapter 2

Red Gantry climbed down from a lookout spot atop a large boulder where he'd been perched like a hawk for the past hour. He walked to the shack, his Spencer rifle across his shoulders, his gloved hands draped over either end.

A steely-eyed gunman named Dockery Latin sat on a short empty nail keg out in front of the shack, dealing himself a hand of solitaire in the dirt between his spread boots. Seeing Red Gantry coming, he looked up from beneath a wide-brimmed slouch hat.

"No sign of anybody?" he asked, putting down a card.

"Not a soul, not a sight, not a sound, Dock," Gantry said. He grinned and stopped beside his fresh horse at a short hitch rail. Three other fresh horses stood there, hitched, saddled and ready to ride. In a lean-to shelter farther across the small clearing, their four spent horses stood resting.

"Hmmph," Latin said, with a distrusting scowl. He turned over a card in his hand and studied it.

"I think we're in good shape," said Gantry. He swung his rifle down and shoved it into a saddle boot. "Sometimes you've got to relax and appreciate your good fortune."

"Relax, huh?" said Latin, staring at him.

"That's right," said Gantry. "We've got away *clean*. Let's be glad of it."

From inside the cabin came a painful moan.

"Ask Cheyenne how *clean* we got away," said Latin, nodding toward an open window. "See how *glad* he is."

"This long-riding business, you're bound to lose a man now and then," said Gantry, "even if it is the boss." He grinned again. "You might say it sweetens the pot for all of us."

Another moan resonated from the window, this one sounding less painful.

"I'd like to know what that little gal is doing to him," Gantry said, staring at the window. "I might want to moan out loud myself."

Latin gave a dark chuckle, pitching another card down on the dirt between his feet.

"Wait until Cheyenne tells her she ain't going with us," he said. "She'll make him moan, sure enough— she might even make him holler out loud."

"He was wise to wait until she gets his wound cleaned and bandaged," said Gantry.

"Yeah, the Kid's no fool," said Latin, "at least not when it comes to looking out for himself."

Gantry eyed him. "Are you saying you're good with him shooting the sheriff and the bank teller down, making sure we've got a hanging coming to us?"

"Naw, I can't say I was happy with that," Latin replied in a lowered voice. He fell quiet and studied the deck of cards in his hand.

"Neither am I," Gantry said quietly.

Royal Tarpis, a bearded, heavyset gunman, stepped out onto the porch wearing a long yellow trail duster and a dust-streaked derby hat.

"I can't take it no more in there," he said, stepping down off the porch and over with the other two gunmen, a Winchester rifle in his gloved hand.

"All the moaning and bleeding got to you, did it?" Latin asked, turning over another card and studying it in his hand.

"Moaning and bleeding . . . ? No," said Tarpis. "I'm talking about watching the fine little gal frisk around like there ain't an eye in the place on her."

"Hell, Roy," Gantry said to Tarpis in a lowered voice, "there's nothing stopping you. Unless maybe Cheyenne puts a bullet in your ear."

The three gave each other a look.

"Nothing stopping all three of us, far as that goes," Latin said. "It's a *free country*, is what they always say."

Finally Royal Tarpis said, "Boys, I'm sided with Cheyenne, at least for now. I couldn't do something like that to the boss's gal."

"She's not his gal," said Gantry. "He's made that clear enough."

"That what he says now, but still . . . ," said Tarpis. "I couldn't do that."

"Do what, Roy?" said Gantry, again with a teasing grin.

"You know . . . ," said Tarpis, embarrassed. "Jerk little Gilley's britches down, Cheyenne lying right there." He shook his big head. "It ain't in me."

Gantry chuckled and looked back and forth between the other two men.

"I bet you wasn't raised that way, was you, Roy?" he asked secretively.

"Come down to it, no, I expect I wasn't," Royal Tarpis said proudly.

"But that's today, you wasn't," said Latin, himself giving a grudging grin, flipping a card into the dirt. "Hang around here a day or two longer, see her flaunting that pretty little rear end around the dinner table, bending over the cook stove. Sooner or later your *raising* will fly plumb out the window." He turned over another card in his hand and studied it. "I know that I wouldn't trust myself too much longer if we were to overstay—"

"That's why we're leaving here right now," said the Cheyenne Kid, cutting him off. He stood stiff and shirtless in the open doorway, his trunk wrapped in strips of dingy white bandage, from his waist all the way up under his arms. A big Colt horse pistol hung from his right hand.

"Hey, Cheyenne," said Latin, taking on a cautious look, "I meant no harm, anything I was saying. We was all just play-talking. No offense intended."

"None's taken, Dock," said Cheyenne, staring coldly at the older outlaw. "If it was, I would have walked out here shooting." He gave Latin a hard stare. Then he turned from one man to the other. "Did anybody hear me say we're *leaving*?"

"What about Gilley?" Gantry asked in a lowered voice.

"What about her?" said Cheyenne.

"You said she wasn't going with us," Gantry said, almost in a whisper.

"She's not," said Cheyenne in the same guarded tone. "She met us here with fresh horses. I'm done with her."

"That's all well and good. But I hate leaving a sore-headed woman behind," Gantry cautioned. "If she's mad enough at you, there's no telling what she'll say to whoever comes by asking about us."

"Who's leading this bunch, Gantry, you or me?" Cheyenne asked flatly, his hand tightening around the big Colt.

"You are, Cheyenne," Gantry replied quickly. "I'm just stating the way—"

"Gilley's not telling anybody anything. I'll take care of her once and for all before I leave here," Cheyenne said, cutting him off. "Don't you worry about it." He nodded down at the knife handle protruding from his boot well.

The three men looked at each other with a slight nod of agreement.

"We're good," said Gantry.

"I'm *real glad* to hear that," Cheyenne said with sarcasm, stepping down off the porch, his movements stiff. "Now get some horse under you and ride on ahead. I'll take care of Gilley and catch up the next mile or two." He reached over and pulled a bag of chopped tobacco from the shirt pocket behind Latin's brush-scarred trail duster.

The men looked at each other again.

"*Well . . . ?*" said Cheyenne in a raised voice. "What the hell are you waiting for?" He took the rolling paper that Latin handed up to him and began building himself a smoke.

Inside the shack, Gilley Maclaine hurriedly jerked seven paper-bound packets of bank money from inside Cheyenne's saddlebags—his share of the bank robbery in Phoebe—and pitched them under the bed.

Kill me . . . ? That son of a bitch!

She'd show him, she thought to herself.

Moments earlier she'd gone out the rear door and picked up an armload of kindling for the cook stove, thinking they'd be here at least for supper. She'd made her way around the side of the house to the front door to announce that she'd be boiling some beans when she'd caught the words being passed back and forth in a secretive tone.

That son of a bitch! she repeated to herself, retying the saddlebags and laying them back on the chair beside the bed where Cheyenne had kept them. She'd done everything he'd asked of her. She'd brought horses for him and his gang, risked getting both her and the horses roasted alive coming down from the high trail while the wildfire still raged out of the north. She'd slept with him! Anger flared in her eyes, on her face. She'd tended his gunshot wound! She was nobody's nursemaid—*that son of a bitch!*

Kill her? *Huh-uh.* She didn't think so, not if she had any say in the matter. And why was he doing this? she asked herself, slipping over to the front window and peeping out, seeing him smoking his cigarette, staring off in the direction the others had taken. Just to cheat her out of her share—money he'd promised her for bringing the horses. He wasn't worried about her keeping her mouth shut. She'd never given him reason to think he couldn't trust her. She'd been straight with him, as straight as any man he could have hired to do the job.

To hell with him, then. . . .

She snatched up a pile of scrap bandage, a riding blouse and a pair of dirty underwear she'd left lying on the floor by the bed, and stuffed them all down in the saddlebags to fill the void left by the money she'd taken.

Now it was time to go, she thought, turning, heading out the rear door. As she reached for the door handle, she heard Cheyenne's boots step up onto the porch. Inside her head she listened to a voice telling her to hurry, make a run for it before it was too late. All right, that was what she needed to do.

But she stopped with her hand on the door handle. No, she couldn't just turn tail and run this way. Even though he intended to kill her, she had to take some measure of satisfaction for herself.

This is crazy! the inner voice warned her. But she refused to listen. She turned from the door and walked calmly forward, meeting Cheyenne as he stepped inside the shack and stood with the big Colt shoved down into his waist.

"Everybody's gone," she said, as if surprised. "I was going to fix some supper."

"Not tonight, Gilley," Cheyenne said, facing her, his

feet spread shoulder width apart—a gunfighter's stance, she reminded herself. Did he think she was dumb enough not to see he was up to something? Or did he think it didn't matter, that there was nothing she could do about it anyway? She stood a little over five feet, lean, not skinny, certainly not big enough to handle a big, strong man like him.

"Then, we're leaving too?" she asked. "I suppose it's time you give me my cut?"

"Yeah, about that . . . ," said Cheyenne. He paused and smiled; she saw the handle of the knife in his boot well. "Come closer, Gilley, let me look in your eyes."

You must be out of your mind! the voice said to her.

"Sure," she said, smiling, stepping forward. She knew she should turn and run, but she wasn't going to. She stopped three feet from him and smiled, looking up into his eyes as he reached his left hand out and placed it on her shoulder, his right hand free to reach down for the knife.

"I've got to do something and I wish I didn't have to, Gilley," he said. She felt his hand tighten on her shoulder.

Here it came, she told herself, seeing his right hand ready to reach down for the knife, moving a little stiff and slow owing to his side wound.

"Oh? So do I," she said, cocking her head slightly, still staring into his eyes like some moonstruck schoolgirl.

He gave her a curious look and almost stopped to ask what dreadful thing she had to do. But before he got the chance, the hard, pointed toe of her boot swung up with all of her anger, fear and fury and buried itself like a hatchet high in his crotch.

"There, *you bastard!*" she shouted. "Try and kill me!"

She sidestepped out of his way as he rose onto his toes and jackknifed violently forward, his mouth agape, toward the floor.

Cheyenne gagged and staggered, his left hand coming away from her shoulder. He grasped himself tight with both hands up between his legs.

"Oh? Does that hurt?" she said mockingly, as a long string of spittle swung from his lips.

"Plea-*please*—" he groaned, staggering, bowed, struggling for breath as she reached down and jerked the long knife from his boot well.

"Is this what you had in mind for me?" she said, holding the knife blade down where he could see it though a watery veil.

"No—" he rasped. "I wasn't going to—"

"Don't lie to me again," she hissed, pressing the tip of the knife against the back of his neck hard enough to draw blood. "I heard every word you and your buzzards said out there. To think that I trusted you—gave myself to you!"

In spite of the wound in his side and having been kicked in the groin, Cheyenne summoned up his strength when he felt the sharp steel bite into his neck. As Gilley spoke, the bowed gunman swung up and around suddenly. His arm knocked her away from him; he made a quick, desperate grab for the Colt on his waist. Gilley hit the floor; the knife flew from her hand. Seeing the Colt come into play, she knew there was nothing for her to do but scramble away and out the rear door as a bullet whistled past the side of her head.

She raced away zigzagging across the small clearing, bullets spitting into the ground, nipping at her feet, causing her to alter direction wildly until she bounded into the shelter of tree and rock and stopped long enough to look back.

In the doorway of the shack, Cheyenne stood, still bowed, holding on to the door frame for support. Firing the last bullet in his Colt, he held the empty gun up smoking in his hand, scanning the pine woodlands for Gilley. Remembering what Red Gantry had said about leaving an angered woman behind, he calmed himself, gathering his breath and his reasoning.

That crazy bitch, he thought, knowing he'd have to get her back here and kill her.

He swallowed his anger and some of the pain in his groin and called to her in a strained voice, "Gilley? Gilley, *sweetheart*? Listen to me. I don't know what just happened here, but I'm sorry. Hear me? I'm truly sorry."

He waited, lowering the smoking Colt and listening toward the woods. He reached around inside the doorway, took a bandoleer of bullets down from a wall peg and hung it over his forearm. He dropped the spent shells from his Colt onto the porch and replaced them with fresh rounds as he spoke.

"I hope you weren't hit, darling," he called out. "God, I'd never forgive myself if you were."

Gilley watched from cover, also catching her breath, checking her body to make sure she wasn't hit.

Cheyenne finished loading the Colt, spun the cylinder and cocked it. "I don't know what I did to cause you to kick me, but you come on out now, you hear? Whatever's wrong, we'll fix it, you and me, together." He managed a weak grin toward the woods, fresh blood spreading across his bandaged side.

Gilley saw Cheyenne turn the cocked Colt quickly toward the sound of a bird rising from the woodlands floor. Seeing it was only a bird, he lowered the Colt an inch but kept it ready.

"Mercy, but that was some little spat we just had," he said, his voice growing stronger. "But no harm done, eh? It's nothing we can't sit down and talk over, is it?" His grin widened. "They say making up is the best part of these little lover spats."

In a pig's eye! Gilley told herself, turning, creeping farther away into the rugged shelter of rock and woodlands.

Chapter 3

The Cheyenne Kid turned back from the doorway and straightened up, more of his strength coming back. He managed a dark chuckle of appreciation, thinking about how much guts it took for Gilley Maclaine to make such a stand for herself. Most women, hearing what she heard, would have made a run for it and never looked back. Not her, he thought. She didn't wait for it to happen. She didn't shy back from a fight. She saw it coming and brought it to him—you had to admire her for that.

Still, he'd have to kill her before he left, he reminded himself, thinking about Gantry and the other two, what they would think if he let her get away. He almost felt bad about it now that he saw how she'd handled herself. She was a petite woman, svelte, but seasoned and hard, the kind of body this land sculpted a woman into if she stayed alive long enough.

He found his bloodstained shirt and put it on, keeping an eye out for the woman through an open window. A Winchester rifle stood in its saddle boot. Would she slip in and make a try for it? He'd see. . . .

He gave himself a slight smile as he buttoned the bib of his shirt and stuffed its tails down into his trousers. He winced as he stooped, picked up his knife and shoved it into his boot well, his wounded side feeling stiff and sore, his crotch still throbbing in lingering pain.

He had to admit there was something he liked about her kicking him that way. He picked up his saddlebags without checking them and draped them over his shoulder. Not the kick itself, he corrected himself quickly, walking to the open doorway. That certainly wasn't something he *enjoyed*. A man would have to be twisted in his brain to enjoy getting kicked in the sack. But the idea that she didn't hesitate for a second to let him have it? *Yeah*, something about that he liked—he liked his women tough, he decided. What was wrong with that? He continued to ponder these thoughts as he made his way over to his waiting horse and un-hitched its reins.

Stepping up into the saddle, he drew the Winchester rifle from its boot, checked it and laid it across his still-throbbing lap. Gilley hadn't fallen for the rifle bait. *Now what?*

"All right, Gilley," he called out in a no-nonsense tone to the surrounding land, his voice echoing a little, "this is your last chance to straighten things out between us." He looked at the tired horses still standing a few yards away. "No reason we can't put this behind us . . . saddle you up a horse and ride out of here together."

Deep in the shelter of the woods, Gilley watched Cheyenne from around the edge of a large boulder. She listened, but she dared not reply, even though something cried out inside her, wishing that things between them could have turned out different. Maybe things had just gotten out of hand for a minute there. In the heat of the moment, him and his men running from the law, maybe he had lost sight of how he felt about her—

Don't be a fool! she told herself, the voice in her head admonishing her for even considering such a thing. *Jesus, he tried to kill you!*

That's right, he did, she thought, taking the side of good reasoning. *Once they try to kill you, it's pretty much over,* she resolved.

Anyway, she hadn't come into this thing looking for a man, she thought, watching Cheyenne look back and forth, then nudge his fresh horse over to where the tired horses stood. She had come into this for the money, pure and simple. Sure, she had slept with him. That was always expected with men like him. Cheyenne would never have allowed a woman into his fold had she not first submitted to him. It was the way things were done. Luckily, he hadn't shared her with the others—*not yet anyway*, she thought.

But all that aside . . .

She allowed herself the faint trace of a smile, watching him lean down enough to loosen the tired horses and shoo them away, shouting and waving his rifle barrel. He hadn't killed her. She would get her money— and then some, as soon as he rode away and she could slip inside the shack and gather it from under the bed.

She would almost give a portion of that money just to see the look on his face when he opened the saddle-bags and looked inside.

"All right, Gilley," Cheyenne called out. "I've tried to reason with you and make up—gone as far as any man can go to straighten things out." He paused and listened, hearing no reply from the rocky woodlands. "I've been more than fair, and understanding."

She could tell by the calm way he'd acted coming out of the shack that he hadn't yet checked the saddle-bags and discovered his money was missing.

"Once I leave, you'll be left out here by yourself," he called out. "You better think about it real good before it's too late—a woman out here all alone, no horse, nobody protecting you. There's still wildfires sprouting up everywhere."

The son of a bitch.

How stupid did he think she was? She slumped against the big boulder and kept watch around the edge of it until he chased away all the tired horses, then turned his fresh horse and rode away alone the trail. Even when he was gone out of sight, she stayed put for a while longer, playing it safe until she was certain he wasn't sitting somewhere watching, waiting for her return.

In the middle of the hot afternoon, the Ranger had seen the black wall of smoke boil up over the pine-covered ridges and hilltops to his west. Streaks of orange flame licked upward within the churning blackness, as if the whole of it arose from a deep porthole to some lower nether realm. Beneath him the rust-colored barb

chuffed and grumbled under its breath as the smell of
char wafted across the rock chasm still flanking their
trail. The Ranger patted his horse's withers with his
gloved hand.

"I know," he said to the animal, as if horses both
heard and understood what was said to them. "It looks
like hell's not through with us yet." He raised his fingertips and idly touched the damp bandana tied
around his neck. He looked down at the hoofprints in
the rocky dirt. He didn't like turning away from them,
but it looked as though that was the wise thing to do,
for now.

He nudged the horse forward, off the trail and
upward along a thin elk path into the rock and woodlands, not wanting to get caught on an open hillside
should an increase in the wind push the fire to them
any faster than it was already traveling.

Nothing between us and the devil, he told himself as if
not wanting to frighten an already skittish horse with
talk of their dire prospects.

An hour later, in spite of their climbing higher up
off the trail and farther away from the black distant
smoke, long looming gray streaks of it weaved into the
woodlands and among the rock around him like ten-
tacles searching him out. The Ranger pulled the bandana across the bridge of his nose and rode on. He
reached back into his saddlebags and pulled out the
damp shirt he'd wrapped around the horse's muzzle
earlier, having it ready just in case.

But as they climbed higher up the steep game path,
he saw the gray smoke still lying beneath them, spread
like a gauzy shroud over the rugged terrain, not rising

to engulf them. *Not yet anyway*, he told himself, nudging the horse on.

When they reached a higher trail and he stepped the barb onto it, the Ranger saw a lone horse standing bareback, facing them from less than twenty feet away. He saw a length of lead rope hanging from the horse's muzzle to the ground.

"Easy, now," he whispered as the barb walked toward the horse slowly. When the barb sidled close enough, he picked up the dangling lead rope with his left hand and drew the horse over beside him. In his right hand he held his Winchester rifle as he looked around warily, knowing he was closer to the men he was tracking than he might have been had he stuck to their hoofprints and ridden through the encroaching smoke.

Putting the barb forward, he rode along the trail at a walk, lead rope in one hand, rifle in his other, until he came upon another horse standing facing him, this one in the middle of the trail. Instead of gathering the tired horse and continuing on, he stepped down from his saddle and stood watching and listening for any sound or sign along the trail in front of him. Somewhere nearby the gunmen had changed horses. These were the horses they had used to ride here from Phoebe.

As he watched the trail before him, Sam put both horses on the lead rope and looked them over good before leading them and the barb forward quietly. When he found a path filled with fresh hoofprints that wandered off into the rock and woodlands to his left, Sam hitched the horses to a pine sapling and traveled forward alone. Climbing over boulders and picking his way through trees and rock crevices, he crawled, at length, atop a rock ledge overlooking a shack situated in a small clearing.

There were no horses anywhere around the shack, Sam noted, yet he still waited, rifle in hand, poised and ready. Within moments, from atop his rocky perch in the waning afternoon sunlight, he saw a single figure wearing a long riding duster and wide-brimmed hat walk into sight from beneath the porch roof. Sam noted the canvas bag draped over one shoulder as the figure moved across the clearing onto a narrow rocky trail and disappeared into the shelter of tall pines. With his rifle still poised, Sam waited and watched long enough to satisfy himself that no one else was coming out of the shack. Then he lowered the rifle and scooted back across the rock ledge.

Time to go, he told himself. When he knew he was out of sight, he stood up dusting the seat of his trousers and walked back to the horses. Knowing where the thin trail from the shack led out onto the main trail, he hurriedly gathered the horses and took cover behind a rock twenty yards from where the two trails intersected.

When the lone figure walked into sight, the Ranger stepped out from behind the rock with his rifle cocked and aimed at chest level.

"Stop right here," he said in an even tone. "Get your hands up where I can see them."

"Don't shoot!" the figure said.

The wide hat brim hid her face in the thin evening light, but Sam could tell it was a woman by the sound of her voice.

"Please, don't shoot!" the woman repeated, letting

the bag on her shoulder drop to the ground behind her. She raised both hands shoulder high and spread her fingers wide apart for him to see. "I'm unarmed! As you can tell." She wiggled her fingers a little for good measure.

"Lift your hat, easylike," Sam said with a curious turn in his voice. "Let me see who I'm talking to."

The woman lifted the hat back off her head and let it fall by its string down behind her. With her hat off, her hair fell to her shoulders.

"A woman," the Ranger murmured.

"Thank you," the woman said. She stared with apprehension on her face—not scared, but concerned, wondering who this was, where this was headed. "Are you the law?" she asked hesitantly.

"Yes, ma'am," Sam said. With his left hand he held open the lapel of his duster, revealing the badge on his chest. "I'm Arizona Territory Ranger Samuel Burrack. Who are you?" His question was not harsh or demanding, yet firm enough to compel a prompt reply.

"I'm Jillian . . . Jillian Hodges," she said, lying about her last name. "Folks call me Gilley." She glanced around as if it suddenly dawned on her that she wasn't sure where they were. "Is—is this still Arizona Territory?"

"I don't know," Sam said a little briskly, almost cutting her off, not about to start answering her questions—at least not until he had enough answers of his own. "Where's the others?"

"What others?" Gilley asked, testing the situation, seeing what position she might jockey herself into, what gains she might make for herself.

"Are you sure you want to play it this way?" the

Ranger asked flatly, stepping forward, sounding indifferent to whether or not she told him the truth, as if he already knew her whole story and was only verifying it for himself.

She just stared at him, her hands still up, a warm evening wind sweeping through the air, whipping a strand of dark brown hair across her face.

The Ranger returned her stare and held her eyes for a moment almost against her will.

"It could go easier on a person who only provided horses, especially if that person *helped* the law do its job," he said.

Gilley thought about it, biting her lower lip a little, taking a chance on reaching a hand over and pushing the hair from her face.

"What about . . ." She paused, then started again. "What about a person who provided horses, but had no idea they were going to use the horses to escape the law?"

He'd better watch this one *real* close, the Ranger told himself, his eyes still fixed on Gilley's as he stepped in closer, lowering his rifle a little.

"I can't speak for a jury," Sam said quietly. "But I've gone as far with this as I intend to. Where are they headed? How far ahead are they?"

Gilley let out a breath with a slight sigh.

"Can I lower my hands, Ranger Burrack?" she asked. Before he could answer, she lowered her right hand, testing him.

"In a minute," he said, raising the rifle barrel and gently but firmly guiding her hand back up with it.

She looked a little surprised by his move, almost

hurt or offended that he could think she might be up to something.

The Ranger reached out and held her duster open, looking her up and down. He saw no gun tucked in her waist, no sign of any gun bulges beneath her clothing. He stepped around behind her, patted her waist, but stopped there.

"What's in the bag?" he asked, standing behind her, toeing the canvas bag with his boot.

"Only everything I have in the world," Gilley said in a humble, even voice. "My personals, a pair of trousers, a skirt . . . You can look for yourself, if you don't believe me."

Sam thought about it. Why would she even invite him to *look for himself*?

"No guns? Nothing sharp inside?" he asked. As he spoke, he picked up the bag and squeezed it here and there, recognizing the stiffness of stacks of cash.

She shook her head and said, "No, you have my word there's no weapons, if that's what you're looking for. Is this what you mean by *helping* the law do its job?"

Sam picked up the bag and laid it in front of her on the ground.

"If you're telling the truth, yes, that's *helpful*," he said. "Empty it. Let's see how *helpful* you're being."

She sighed again.

"All right, Ranger," she admitted, "there's money in the bag." She quickly added, "But I wasn't lying to you. There's no gun, no knife, nothing like that."

Sam nodded to himself.

"Just money," he said.

"Just money," she repeated.

"Money from the Phoebe bank robbery," Sam said.

She stalled, as if making sure she wasn't giving up anything on herself, then said, "It's money they gave me for the horses," she replied. "I can't say for sure where it came from." With her hands still raised, she looked around at him and asked, "Is that still being *helpful*?"

Sam didn't answer. Instead he said, "Go ahead and empty it."

"Right there, in the dirt, my clothes?" she asked.

Sam took off his sombrero and pitched it onto the ground at her feet.

"You can lay your belongings on my hat," he said.

Watching her upend the bag and empty it onto his dusty sombrero, Sam thought to himself, *Oh yes, I'd better watch this one real close.*

She sighed again, this time in resolve, knowing there was no way she could avoid him seeing all the bound bank money.

"Okay, Ranger Burrack," she said, "can I just be honest with you?"

"By all means, please do," Sam said quietly.

Chapter 4

While Gilley Maclaine separated the paper-bound stacks of money from her clothing lying atop the Ranger's sombrero, she told the Ranger as much as she could without openly admitting her role in the bank robbery. The Ranger listened more closely than he let on as he picked up the stacks of money and held them in his hands.

"So," she said in conclusion, "I agreed to bring four horses up to the shack and have them here waiting for him and his men." She shrugged. "It was stupid, thinking back on it. But it seemed all right at the time."

"This is a sizable amount of money for *four horses*, ma'am," the Ranger said, holding the money for her to see. He eyed her suspiciously. "You'll have to do better than that."

She stared at him for a moment.

"I stole it from the Cheyenne Kid's part of the bank money, all right?" she said finally, a little resentful that he wasn't fooled by her initial explanation.

"You *robbed* the robber," said the Ranger.

"If you put it that way, I suppose so," she said. "The fact is, Cheyenne tried to get away from here without paying me for the horses. I saw a chance to get what was mine and I took it. Can you blame me?"

Sam didn't reply. He only stared at her critically, as if he knew there was more to her story.

"He tried to kill me," she said flatly. She watched the Ranger's face to judge the effect of her words.

"Tried to kill you . . ." He gave a slight nod as if he found it reasonable to believe.

"I heard him tell the others what he was going to do once they'd left," she said. "So I took the money from his saddlebags and hid it under the bed. I was ready for him when the time came. . . ."

Sam listened as she gave him an almost blow-by-blow account of the fight.

When she'd finished telling him everything, she looked at the money in his hands with regret.

"And now you're taking my money and keeping it?" she asked. Her tone didn't hide the fact that she felt she was being unfairly treated in the matter.

"No," said the Ranger. "First of all, it's not your money. It belongs to the bank in Phoebe. Second of all, I'm not *keeping it*. It's going into my saddlebags—back to the bank, just as soon as I get this thing settled."

"Meaning, just as soon as you kill Cheyenne and his pals?" she asked.

"I'm taking them back," the Ranger said. "If killing them is the only way to make it work, I expect that's what I'll do."

"Can—can I be honest with you, Ranger?" she asked.

There it was, *for the second time,* Sam reminded himself.

"Sure, why not?" he said.

She looked at him for a moment, catching the trace of cynicism in his voice.

"All right, here it is," she said, as if unburdening herself of some heavy weight on her conscious. "I was having relations with the Cheyenne Kid."

Sam just stared at her.

"We were *lovers,*" she said with emphasis, as if he might not know what she was talking about. She studied his flat poker face for a moment, then said, "Do you understand what I mean?"

"I think so," the Ranger said.

"Well, we were." She shrugged. "So there. I know how bad that sounds, but it's the truth."

"Let me get this straight," the Ranger said. "You had sexual relations with him, and afterward he tried to kill you?"

"*No!*" she said indignantly. "Not *right afterward*. I mean, we were having relations before I ever agreed to bring the horse up here."

"I see," said Sam. He paused in thought for a moment. "So, you and Cheyenne *knew* each other as lovers. He asked you to bring him some fresh horses up here. Him and his gang rob a bank, come get the horses and leave you behind."

"And attempted to kill me," she interjected.

"But you robbed him. He left, and had no idea you'd taken the money from his saddlebags."

"Yep, that's the whole of it," she said. "Have I helped myself any, being honest with you?"

"With me, yes, a little," Sam said. "With a jury? I don't know. Either way you look at it, you had the stolen bank money on you when I found you striking out on foot. You did bring these gunmen some fresh horses. The only question is whether or not you knew they were going to rob something."

"If you were the jury, Ranger, what would you think?" she asked anxiously.

"Sorry, ma'am," Sam said, shaking his head. "I'd think, guilty as charged."

"What if I helped you catch them?" she asked quickly.

"That would be helpful," Sam said.

"I mean, I do have a good idea where they're headed," she said.

"So do I," said Sam.

"You do?" She looked curious.

"Yes, ma'am," Sam said. "I expect as soon as the Cheyenne Kid opens his saddlebags and sees what you've done to him, he'll be headed to wherever he thinks *you* are."

"Oh . . . ," she said. Her tone revealed that the possibility hadn't yet occurred to her.

"Until he finds out," Sam said, "I'm sticking to their trail. I want to be somewhere between you and him, when him and his gang comes looking for you."

"But don't forget, there's four of them, Ranger," she said.

"I'll try not to," the Ranger said in an even tone. He gestured toward the two horses on the lead rope. "Pick yourself one. If there's a blanket inside the shack, we can go back and get it, something for you to sit on until we can find you a saddle—"

"There's one back in the shack—a saddle, that is," she cut in. "A bridle too. It's over in a corner. It's old and dried out, but it'll do for now."

"Good," said the Ranger. "Let's get it and go. These horses are both tired, but we can rest one while you ride the other."

"All right," she said, sounding agreeable to setting off onto another adventure.

Sam saw her eye the money in his hands, then look away from it quickly. But not quick enough to keep him from seeing that she still had designs on it.

"Should we wait until morning?" she asked. "Because there's beans and some coffee in the shack too—"

"We're leaving right now," Sam said, cutting her off. He nodded at the distant wall of black across the rock chasm below them, the gray creeping smoke rising like slow floodwater among the valleys and wooded hills. "By morning we could be trapped here, roasted alive, or choked to death in our sleep."

"Oh, the fire . . . ," she said, looking out and down with him. "*Lucky for me*, I'm not what you'd call *concerned* with wildfire."

Sam looked at her.

"*Lucky for you*, I am," he said.

The Cheyenne Kid caught up to his gang on a winding high trail where the three had stopped and stepped down from their saddles to rest their horses. When Cheyenne spotted them and rode forward, they turned from looking out across the rock chasm at the blackened terrain. Countless spirals of smoke still curled upward here and there; stubs of charred timber with burnt, spiked branches replaced the plush green pine canopy that had existed only hours earlier.

"We were starting to wonder about you," said Gantry as Cheyenne reined down among them.

"You never have to wonder about me, Red," said Cheyenne in a short tone. He stared out across the valley and rock chasm at the scorched land. He swung down from his saddle and pushed his tired horse on its rump. The horse stepped away and stopped alongside the other three horses.

Dock Latin caught the horse's reins and hitched it to a short juniper.

"You took care of everything?" Gantry asked Cheyenne.

Cheyenne just stared at him coldly.

"I'm asking for all our sakes," Gantry said evenly. "I mean no offense."

Cheyenne jerked a thumb toward the full saddlebags on his horse's back.

"I gathered my gear and got out of there," he said, hoping to change the subject quickly. "There was another fire blowing in. I gave her four shots before I left."

Gave her four shots . . . ? The three gunmen looked at each other.

"So, you *did* kill her before you left?" Gantry said, not letting go of the matter.

"We tussled," Cheyenne said coldly. "She managed

to get away from me and run out the door. Like I said, I fired four shots at her. I'm satisfied that at least a couple of them hit her."

"You walked her down—saw her body, made sure she was dead, then?" Gantry pressed.

"What is this, Gantry?" Cheyenne asked, staring hard at the seasoned gunman. "You doubting my word?"

"No," Gantry said, without backing an inch, "not if you're *giving it*." He paused before adding, "So give it."

"You don't tell me to give my word I killed her, Red," said Cheyenne. "That's the same as saying I'm lying." He took one short step backward and put his hand on the butt on his Colt.

"All he's trying to do is pin you down, Kid," Latin cut in, speaking in a calm, quiet voice. "To tell you the truth, I'm not clear myself whether or not you killed her."

"Neither am I," said Royal Tarpis. He and Latin spread out a little, facing Cheyenne.

Cheyenne kept cool and shrugged.

"All right, let's not make a shooting deal of it," he said. "I saw my bullets hit her, so I didn't walk her down. I figured she ran until she dropped, then bled out there—like a deer might do."

"Except this one *deer* can get us all hanged if she didn't bleed out," Gantry said, still pushing the matter.

"He's right, Kid," said Tarpis. "Not to crowd you, but why didn't you walk her down, pop one in her noggin?"

"The looks of that fire coming, I figured it wise to get out while the getting was good," said Cheyenne.

"Besides, I chased off the horses. If she didn't bleed out, I left her stuck there. She'll be roasted to a turn by the time anybody comes upon her."

The three considered it.

Finally, Latin said, "Roasted to a turn . . . I wonder how that would taste, a sweet little woman like that, young, tender . . ."

"Jesus!" said Royal Tarpis with a dark chuckle. "Stay away from me, Dock, you depraved man-eating sumbitch."

"Not a *man-eater*, Roy," Latin said, raising a finger for emphasis, making himself clear. "That *would* be depraved."

"So would eating a woman," said Gantry. "Eating any kind of human flesh is a crime against nature, roasted to a turn or otherwise."

"So is having congress with a pet heifer," said Latin, "but them who've done it swear by it."

The others looked at him.

"Or so I've heard," he said in a waning voice.

"I'm not going to stand here talking about eating human flesh or fornicating with a cow," Gantry said in disgust.

"Neither am I," said Latin. "I was only saying . . ."

"Anyway," said Tarpis, gazing off across the chasm and back in the direction of the shack, which now lay miles behind them. "Once that fire gets through with Gilley, she won't be fit to eat. When the heat rises up from the valleys, it'll burn anything on the hillsides hard as stone."

Latin grinned at Cheyenne.

"So, Kid," he said, "I hope you had a good time with her while it lasted."

"You can bet I did," Cheyenne said boastfully. "She said nobody ever made her feel—"

"*Whoa!* Look at this," Tarpis said, cutting him off, gesturing down across the rock chasm, where a black oily wall of smoke rose quickly into sight, roiled throughout with orange-red flames. As they turned and stared back at it, the smoke and flames loomed higher and wider in the sky, pushed in their direction on a hot, strong wind.

"Lord God," said Gantry, as if in awe as they had to stare straighter up at it. "Where in the living hell is all this fire coming from?"

Seeing the monster inferno climb and block out the late evening sun, Dock Tarpis backed away toward the horses.

"Damned if I know where it's coming from," he said, his eyes darkly a-glitter in the high, licking flames, "but I know where it's headed. It's headed this way."

The others backed away with him, as if retreating slowly to keep from stirring some raging dragon.

"It won't cross the rock lands down there," Cheyenne said, unhitching his tired horse while the others did the same.

"You mean it hasn't *yet*," Gantry said.

Cheyenne just stared at him as all four of them swung up into their saddles. In the distance across the chasm, they heard a low, billowing roar.

"Wherever the hell it's headed," said Latin, "I hope it's headed where I'm *not*." The four turned their horses to the trail and rode away as the gray smoke rose up the hillside from the valleys, gullies and rock chasms as if seeking them out.

"These winds keep changing back and forth," Dock Latin called out to the others above the pound of the horses' hooves, "it's going to burn this whole damned world down!"

"It better not," Gantry shouted, "not before I spend all my bank money!"

"*Yee-hiii!* I'm with you on that!" Royal Tarpis shouted, riding hard behind him.

In the rear distance the fire raged and billowed on the wind. Silvery-black ash blew in like snowflakes. The riders felt the scorching, overheated breeze creep up onto their backs and shoulders as they rode on.

Sitting atop a stolen horse, looking down on the four riders as they galloped away ahead of the encroaching smoke, a young man named Segan Udall watched from a high, rocky perch. He breathed deep, a look of satisfaction on his face. His eyes glistened with tears. Below, gray smoke spread slowly along and across the rock chasm, filling the low spots and reaching upward. Segan looked farther back and across the land, seeing pockets of brown-black smoke that appeared to outline his trail for the past two weeks.

"It took, Caroline," the broad-shouldered young man called out to his wife, who sat in their open wagon a few safe yards back from the jagged edge of the cliff. "So help me, God, they've every one took!" he said in a grateful, bliss-filled voice.

The woman sat quietly, her hands folded in her lap,

holding the reins to the team of tired wagon horses who stood with their heads bowed in the afternoon heat. She watched her husband of three months turn his horse and ride back to the wagon.

"Did you hear me?" he asked, sidling up close to where she sat in the wagon seat. "They all took." He smiled at her expectantly, wanting her to share in his joy. Yet, as usual, she noticed that his smile looked tight and troubled.

"I heard you, Segan," she said flatly, cautious not to say anything to get him agitated.

"Well, is that all you can say?" he asked, his smile melting from his face. "You *heard me*?"

"I'm—I'm happy for you?" she said hesitantly. "I just wonder if it's the right thing to do."

Over the past three months of their yet-to-be-consummated marriage, almost since the moment he'd slipped the ring onto her finger, she'd watched her husband turn from a sweet, kind, caring young gentleman into a brooding, hot-tempered, easily vexed madman.

Madman . . . ? she asked herself. Was that being a little harsh? No, she decided quickly, it wasn't. She didn't like admitting it, but there was no use in denying the truth any longer. Her young husband's mind was no more reliable than a broken watch.

"It *is* the right thing to do, Caroline," Segan said. "When I think about another man's hands on you, it's the only thing that keeps me from going *killing crazy*."

She saw his hands tighten on his horse's reins just thinking about it.

"He—he was my husband, Segan," she offered meekly. "It was with God's blessing—"

"I don't care," said Segan, cutting her short "I can't abide it. I can't block it from my mind." He raised his knuckles to his forehead, squeezed his eyes shut. "It's killing me!" he half sobbed. "All's I see is him and you together . . . his hands, his mouth all over you—all the rest of it!"

His shoulders shuddered with his anguish.

She reached over and laid a hand on his bowed back, attempting to console him. But he shoved her hand away.

"Don't touch me with your shameless hands, not when I'm seeing something like this!" he sobbed. "It's taking all I've got to keep from stripping you naked and wearing out a switch on you, right here and now!" He raised his tortured face and looked at her through flooded eyes. "I hate wanting to do something like that . . . switching your naked bottom so bad that it's red and welted, and throbbing with pain!"

She winced a little thinking about it and stared at him for a moment.

"Would—" She halted, then asked as if considering it, "Would that help you get over it . . . my being married before?"

"I just don't know," Segan said, shaking his head. "All I know is I hurt so bad, I feel better when I see this world burning to a damned cinder."

Caroline stared out across the distance at pockets of looming smoke.

"Because, if I thought that would help . . . ," she murmured under her breath.

"I can't say, Caroline," Segan said, clenching his fists tightly, squeezing his eyes shut. "I only know if I'm not setting something ablaze, I'm hurting something awful."

A switching . . . my God, she thought with dread, gazing out across the blackened sky. He was serious; and it wasn't the first time he'd mentioned it either, she reminded herself. Oh yes. He had spoken of taking a hickory switch to her more than once or twice. In fact, he'd even mentioned her taking switch to him! See? He was a madman, no doubt about it, she resolved.

Lord, what kind of mess had she gotten tangled into?

Chapter 5

———◆———

Cheyenne and his men pushed their horses hard for the next hour, widening the distance between themselves and the encroaching smoke. For the next hour they rode at an easier gait, but kept watch over their shoulders, making sure the fire stayed far behind them in spite of the buffer of rock land separating them from the heart of the flames. It was almost dark when they stopped along the trail where a stretch of woodlands reached out flat for a half mile before pitching upward onto a long, steep slope.

"You need to pay attention, men," Cheyenne said, nodding back toward the distant gray haze and the brown-blackish smoke beyond it. "This is what hell's going to look like when you get there." Deeper inside the turbulent smoke, orange flames become visible in the darkening evening light.

Gantry let out a laugh and jerked his horse around beside Royal Tarpis.

"If you ask me," he said, "hell is going to have to heat up some to get itself hotter than this—"

"Quiet, Red!" Tarpis said, cutting him off. He looked around at the others, then off into the trees. "Anybody hear that?"

"Hear what, Roy?" said Gantry, not liking the idea of being interrupted.

"I heard it," said Cheyenne, lifting his rifle from across his lap. "Sounded like a wounded panther crying out." He looked at Dock Latin. "You hear it, Dock?"

"*Shhhh . . . ,*" Dock Latin said. He sat listening intently, his hearing piqued toward the woodlands.

The other three followed suit, listening in silence.

Finally, Gantry said, "That's no panther, that's no wounded panther . . . that's a *wounded woman.*"

A short, shrill cry resounded from the woodlands. The men looked at each other.

"Dock, I think you're right," Cheyenne said quietly. "Not too far in either." He swung down from his saddle, rifle in hand. The others followed suit.

"If it's a woman, we get to keep her, don't we?" Gantry whispered in excitement.

"Split up," Cheyenne said without answering him. "Find where it's coming from and circle around it." He started walking into the trees and whispered, "Be careful we don't shoot each other."

"What does he think, we're a bunch of damn fools?" Gantry whispered to Royal Tarpis.

"That would be my guess," Tarpis said matter-of-factly as they moved out into the dense pine woods.

As Cheyenne walked deeper into the forest, he heard the sound of short gasps of pain continue for a few minutes longer and then turn into muffled sobbing. He looked all around and saw his three men closing in with him on the cries. But just before they got ready to move in quickly, they heard another voice rise above the woman's sobbing as a man cried out as if in agony, "I can't do it, Caroline! I just can't do it!"

"It's all right, Segan," the woman's voice replied, filled with tearful pain. "We tried! And we'll try again."

In their wide circle, Cheyenne and his men gave each other curious looks as they moved in closer.

In a small clearing in the waning light of evening, Segan Udall had walked away from Caroline and tossed a long, thin pine branch away. He stood staring at the ground, his wide shoulders slumped, his eyes shut against a well of tears.

"It's never going to work for us, Caroline, no matter what we do," Segan sobbed. "I have taken a switch to you for nothing. These terrible things I see are just too much to live with. I'll never consummate this marriage!"

"Maybe I can help!" Red Gantry called out, stepping into the clearing, a crazy grin on his flushed face.

"What the hell is he doing?" Cheyenne growled to himself, seeing Gantry jump into the clearing.

Segan turned quickly toward the sound of Gantry's voice. Caroline snatched a wool blanket up and pulled it around herself with a fearful gasp.

Seeing the stranger's eyes on his wife before Caroline managed to cover herself, Segan flew into a blind rage. With a loud bellow like that of a bull, he raced across the clearing, head down, and plowed into Red Gantry before the startled outlaw could get his Colt up from its holster.

"Help—me—!" Gantry pleaded to the others as the

big man seated himself on Gantry's chest and batted his face back and forth between his big fists.

"We should let him kill you," Dock Latin said, he and the others stepping into the clearing, dragging Segan back a few feet by his boot heels. As the wild-eyed—still bellowing—young man tried to rise to his feet, Royal Tarpis reached down with his rifle butt and gave him a sound thump on his forehead. It wasn't enough to knock Segan cold, but it was more than enough to stagger his senses for a moment.

"Oh God! Don't hurt him! He's my husband!" Caroline shrieked, seeing Segan melt onto the dirt.

"Don't hurt *him*?" Cheyenne said, stepping over to her and pulling her to her feet. "Look what he did to our pal." He gestured down at Gantry, who lay struggling to get to his feet, his face battered and bloody. With no warning, Cheyenne jerked the blanket open before Caroline could try to stop him. "Hell, look what he's done to *you*."

"I'm all right! Please!" Caroline said, snatching the blanket closed across her naked breasts, covering the countless red marks Segan's switching had left up and down her naked body.

"You don't look *all right* to me," said Cheyenne, allowing her to keep herself covered.

"Let me see," Gantry said, staggering to his feet with Dock Latin's help.

"Get away, Red," said Cheyenne. "This is between the two of them."

"Like hell! I deserve to see anything she's got," Gantry insisted, "after what this loco sumbitch done to me."

"Get away from my wife!" Segan shouted, coming around from his dazed condition.

Gantry went for his gun, still hazy from the beating he'd taken. But as the Colt came up from the holster, Cheyenne grabbed it from his hand and stepped in between him and Segan Udall.

"Calm yourself, mister," he warned Segan, his Colt coming out, arm's length, cocking only inches from the young man's forehead. "I will make your wife a widow."

"Stop, Segan, for God's sake!" cried Caroline. "He'll kill you! I know this man!"

"You do?" said Cheyenne, stunned.

"You do?" repeated Segan, a strange look in his already crazed eyes.

"Yes, I do," said Caroline. "You're George Anholt, the Cheyenne Kid." She gave him a nervous smile. "It's me, Caroline Darby. Don't you remember me?"

George Anholt . . . ?

Royal Tarpis and Dock Latin looked at each other.

Cheyenne looked closer at the woman.

"Caroline Darby?" he said. "Yes, of course I remember you. I'll never forget that you and your husband saved my life." His Colt came down from Segan's face. Segan stared at his wife as she spoke.

"How have you been, Cheyenne?" she said.

"I can't complain, Caroline," said Cheyenne. "How about yourself?"

She gave a slight shrug.

"As you can see . . . ," she said.

"I was real sorry to hear about Herbert," said Cheyenne. "I never really heard how he died."

"He was killed in his sleep, Cheyenne," Caroline said, a look of remorse coming to her face. She drew the blanket tighter around herself. "They never found his killer."

"Him and I were staying the night at a public house," Segan put in. "Somebody wrung his neck."

"Oh . . . ?" Cheyenne said, looking the powerfully built young man up and down.

"This is my husband, Segan Udall," Caroline said.

"I see," said Cheyenne. Without so much as a nod toward Segan, he looked back at Caroline, gestured toward her blanket and said, "Why don't you get dressed? We'll talk some later."

"Yes, thank you, Cheyenne," Caroline said. She started to turn and walk away.

But Red Gantry called out, "Wait just a damn minute. I have designs on this woman. I'm the one found her first."

Cheyenne just stared at him for a moment.

"Red, she and her husband once saved my life when I was shot bad," he said.

"So?" said Gantry. "Her dead husband saving your life don't change what *this husband* done to me. I'm making demands here." He pointed at Caroline standing naked save for her blanket. "She's already undressed. What's the harm?"

"Jesus . . . ," Dock Latin whispered under his breath. He shook his head.

Segan started to step forward toward Gantry. But a look from Cheyenne stopped him cold.

"Look at me, Red," Cheyenne said in a demanding tone.

"What?" said Red.

"If you lay a hand on this woman, you will be dead before you hit the ground," he said firmly. "Do you understand me?"

Gantry looked at Dock Latin, then Royal Tarpis, then back to Cheyenne, seeing the same warning expression on each of their faces.

"Yeah, I understand," he said meekly. He rubbed a knot that stood out red and throbbing on the side of his head. Blood ran from a cut under his eye.

Cheyenne turned back to Caroline. He wanted to know the story, why she was out here in the wilderness, her new young husband taking a switch to her. But this wasn't the time or place to hear it, he thought. He looked over at the wagon and horses standing at the edge of the small clearing.

"We're heading away from the fire to a trading post nearby, Caroline," he said. "Why don't you and your husband here accompany us?"

Segan started to speck, but Caroline didn't give him a chance.

"Obliged. That is kind of you, Cheyenne," she said, sounding suddenly relieved. "I'll just get myself dressed and we'll be on our way."

But as the two spoke, Royal Tarpis had gotten nosy, walked over to the team of horses and examined the wagon bed. *What the hell . . . ?* His eyes rested on a pile of burnt torches. He picked one up and looked at it curiously.

"Cheyenne," he called out, "come take a look at this." Next to the torches stood a tin of coal oil and a pile of rags. Rummaging quickly through the rags, he pulled up a box of long wooden matches.

"Keep your hands out of there!" shouted Segan. He started to head toward the wagon, but stopped as Cheyenne leveled the Colt back at him.

"Settle down, *Segan*," Cheyenne said, speaking to the young man as if he were a foolish kid who would need constant correcting. He turned a short smile to Caroline Udall. "I can see how your new husband here might take a little getting used to. Is he always this way?"

Before Caroline could answer for herself, Segan cut in, his big fists clenched at his sides, saying, "Don't answer him, Caroline!"

"Please, Segan . . . ," Caroline said quietly, trying to calm her young husband down.

But Segan would have none of it. "Never you mind how I am, or how I ain't, mister," he said to Cheyenne.

Cheyenne's easygoing manner began to dissolve.

"Just trying to keep it friendly here, Segan," he said, "for Caroline's sake."

With the barrel of his Colt, Cheyenne gestured them both toward the wagon, where Royal Tarpis stood inspecting the rags.

"Never mind keeping it friendly either," Segan said, getting more and more jealous, threatened by the way Cheyenne and Caroline looked at each other. "We don't need your friendship—don't want nothing to do with you."

Cheyenne gazed at Caroline as he directed the two of them toward the wagon.

"Is that how you feel too, Caroline?" he asked in a lowered voice, giving her a guarded look that her husband didn't see.

Caroline almost blushed, Segan walking along in front of her, Cheyenne near her side and sidling even closer.

"Why, no, George—I mean, *Cheyenne*," she said, catching and correcting herself. "Segan is just an excitable boy—*man*, that is," she added quickly, knowing Segan could hear her.

Tarpis turned and pitched two burnt torches to the ground at their feet as the three stopped beside the wagon. Behind Cheyenne and the Udalls, Red Gantry and Dock Latin walked along, staring curiously—Gantry holding a wadded bandana to the bleeding cut beneath his swelling eye.

"It looks like we've got ourselves a couple of real live arsonists here, Cheyenne," said Tarpis, staring hard at Segan as he set the tin of coal oil on the ground at the brawny man's feet.

"That's a damn lie!" Segan shouted at Tarpis. "And you, *sir*, are a damned liar!"

"A liar, huh?" said Tarpis. He reached back calmly and picked up his rifle from where he'd leaned it against the wagon. Turning back to Segan, he said to Cheyenne, "Can I smack him around some, maybe knock out a couple of his teeth?"

"No, Roy, keep your head," Cheyenne said, knowing Tarpis wasn't joking.

He stooped and picked up the tin of coal oil and shook it a little, then set it down, judging it to be half-full. When he stood up he turned back to Segan and Caroline Udall and shook his head as if in resolve.

"*Segan*," he said in a low, even tone, "it looks like you've been a *naughty* boy. Maybe you're the one needs a good switching."

Segan blurted out, "I'd like to see you try—"

"Let me explain," Caroline said quickly, cutting him off. "Segan didn't mean anything bad by it. He just gets so upset and excited, he has to do something—"

Now Segan cut *her* off.

"Shut up, Caroline!" he said. "This is none of their damned business!"

"Leave her alone, Segan," Cheyenne warned. "Open your mouth again, I'll turn Roy and his rifle butt lose on you." He turned to Caroline and said quietly, "Go on, Caroline. Say whatever you feel like saying. He won't bother you."

Segan stared at him with a look of white-hot anger in his dark eyes. But he kept his mouth shut, seeing the eager expression on Royal Tarpis' face, his hand clenched around his rifle stock, just waiting to bust his head.

Caroline said hesitantly, "My—my husband and I have had some difficulty getting our lives together off to a good start." She paused and looked embarrassed. "I'm afraid we haven't even consummated our marriage as yet."

A dead silence set in. The gunmen all looked at each other, stunned expressions on their stony faces.

Segan hung his head in shame.

After a moment, Cheyenne cleared his throat and

looked Caroline up and down—a middle-aged woman standing covered by a wool blanket. Underneath, her naked body etched with countless small but painful burning switch marks.

He said in a gentle tone, letting his words trail, "You mean you haven't . . . ?"

"No, not yet," Caroline admitted. "We've tried—that's what we were doing when you come upon us—but so far, no, we haven't."

Segan sighed in pain, hearing his wife tell perfect strangers about their problem.

"And this causes him to set fires?" Cheyenne asked, making certain he understood.

Caroline only nodded.

"Jesus . . . ," said Cheyenne.

"I know," Caroline whispered, on the verge of tears.

Cheyenne looked off in the direction of the distant smoke. On the rock lands below, he saw elk running along the chasm, fleeing the oncoming devastation. He thought about the large number of species he'd seen over the past few days—most of them dead by now, he reckoned.

"All this beautiful woodlands," he said. "The lives of all these animals . . ." He shook his head, pondering the magnitude of the destruction.

But when he looked around and saw the glaring faces of his men, he quickly pulled himself together.

"*What?*" he said defensively. "It is a *good-looking* woodlands. No sense in wasting all that wood." He shrugged. "All those critters dying? Hell, that's just wasting food, far as I'm concerned."

The men just stared at him.

He looked back along the trail for a second to avoid their eyes, knowing how weak it looked to them, their leader giving a damn one way or the other about trees, or animals. Then he looked back at Caroline.

"Did he start any new fire back along this trail the past day or two?"

"Yes, he did start one," Caroline said, looking ashamed. "He started it a few miles back on this side of the rock lands. Then we rode up in a wide circle above it on our way here, just to see how it was doing."

"And how was it doing?" Cheyenne asked.

"It—it was just terrible when we saw it," Caroline said haltingly. "Probably the worst one yet. The winds caught it and speeded it up, blowing it east. But we hurried on up here, knowing when the wind changes, it'll head this way. It'll kill everything in its path."

"Really, now?" said Cheyenne. He gave the men a dark smile, then looked at the crestfallen Segan and said, "So, then, *Segan*. Anything on this trail behind us is either cooked dead by now or damn soon will be?"

Segan stared at him sullenly before finally replying begrudgingly, "Yeah, you could say that. So what? It's just trees and dumb critters. Who cares?"

"Hear that, fellows?" said Cheyenne. "Anybody who followed us up here is either cooked dead or soon will be." He turned back to Segan Udall and said, "We got off to the wrong start, you and me. But from now on I think we're going to get along just fine." As he talked to Segan, his eyes met Caroline's, the two of them saying something to each other that no one else could hear.

"Don't count on nobody being on our back trail,

Cheyenne," Red Gantry said in warning, the bandana against his cut and swollen cheek.

"I am counting on it, Red," Cheyenne replied confidently. "Who in their right mind is going to track us through a wildfire?"

Chapter 6

In the middle of the night, the Ranger raised his dozing head to the sound of the horses chuffing and whinnying where he and Gilley had hitched them to a rope strung between two pine trees. When he looked over in the moonlight, he saw them stepping back and forth nervously, high-hoofed, sawing their heads against their hitched reins.

A few feet away, beside a low campfire, Gilley awakened suddenly and sat up on the ground.

"What's got them spooked, Ranger?" she asked in a whisper.

"I don't know," said Sam, rising to his feet, his Winchester rifle in hand, "but we better find out."

They both hurried to the three restless horses and got them settled, drawing them by their reins, talking to them, rubbing their muzzles until the animals calmed down a little. But only a little, Sam noted, still seeing the wild, fearful look in the dark eyes of his rust-colored barb.

"There's something nearby," he said, examining the

moonlit woodlands beyond the circling glow of fire-light.

"What, do you suppose?" Gilley asked warily, looking all around with him.

"The way this land is stirred up by the fires, it could be anything," Sam said.

No sooner had he spoken than they both turned toward the sound of breaking brush and the shrill cry of a frightened panther cub. Instinctively, Sam threw the Winchester to his shoulder, just in time to see a young cougar spill from a broken edge on the hillside surrounding the camp and tumble into the campfire's glow.

"Oh, look," Gilley said, "it's only a kitten! Look how young it is."

Sam only lowered the rifle a little, still looking all around the broken hillside.

"Yes, it's young," he said, "too young to be out of its den on its own. Keep the horses settled," he added, stepping forward. "I've got a feeling it's not alone."

As if on cue, a loud roar came from the hillside as the mother cat with the missing half of an ear stepped into sight and crouched low onto her paws. She snarled over bared fangs.

"Oh no," said Gilley. "Look, she's hurt."

"I see," Sam said. "Stay back, watch the horses. Let her get her cub and go."

"How do you know that's all she wants?" Gilley asked, already drawing tighter on the sets of reins holding the horses to the length of rope hitch.

"We've met before," Sam said, his rifle up and ready, his eyes locked on the big cat and her feisty but fright-ened cub.

"You have?" Gilley said.

"Yes," said Sam. "I hate to say it, but last time I saw her she had two cubs with her."

"Maybe the other one is in the woods," Gilley offered.

"Maybe," Sam said, but he doubted it—owing to all the turmoil and disturbance on the tortured woodlands floor.

The mother cat sidestepped over, reached down and picked the small cub up firmly yet gently between her sharp teeth. The cub hung writhing and kicking in its mother's grip.

"Isn't there something we can do to help?" Gilley whispered, noting all the dried blood on the mother cat's shoulder, down her front leg from the severed ear. "She's bleeding terribly."

The horses settled a little on their reins, Gilley holding them firmly, her confidence assuring them there was nothing to be afraid of.

"We can stay back and leave her alone," Sam said. "She knows what she's doing. The blood is old. She had it on her when I saw her at the water hole."

Almost before the Ranger had finished speaking, the big cat turned in a flash of tail and hindquarter and bounded straight up in one powerful leap, vanishing back onto the treed hillside.

"And that's that," Sam said with a breath of relief. The last thing he wanted to do was kill an animal whose only purpose was to protect its cub—its last remaining cub at that, he reminded himself.

Gilley felt the horses settle almost immediately.

"Thank goodness that's over with," she said. She

patted the nose of one of the horses as it blew and chuffed and calmed itself down. "These fellows were getting hard to handle, knowing they were on somebody's menu."

"They knew the mama cat wasn't out hunting them for food," Sam said, "else you would have had a much harder time holding them." He let the rifle hang in his hand and turned and patted the barb's muzzle.

"How do they know that?" Gilley asked.

"I don't know," said Sam, "but they know the difference." He turned and looked off farther along the trail they had traveled throughout the day.

"What is it, Ranger?" Gilley asked, sensing something was troubling him.

"Something about the cat and her cub," Sam said. "When I came across her and her two cubs, they were heading the same direction as we are, to get farther away from the fire." He considered it, then said, "She would have gotten her cubs in a safe lair somewhere quick as she could."

"So?" Gilley said, trying to understand.

Sam looked at her; there was no hiding the concerned look in his eyes.

"So, what happened to her other cub?" he asked. "And why is this one back out on the move with her?"

Gilley only stared at him; she didn't get it for a moment. Then it came to her. She whispered under her breath, "Oh my God, the fire has moved in front of us?"

"I'm afraid so," Sam said, attempting to minimize the grimness of the situation as much as possible until he saw how she was going to react.

"How can we be sure?" she asked.

Sam gestured with his eyes toward the sky above the trail lying north of them.

"There it is," he said.

She gasped, looking up, seeing the ominous black cloud looming above the purple sky, an orange glow flashing on and off, flickering deep inside it.

"Holy Mother of God," Gilley whispered in terror and awe. She turned and stared at Sam, her eyes widened, the campfire light flickering in them. "When—when did you see it?" she asked, as if it made any difference.

"Only a moment ago," he replied. He attempted a smile. "But don't worry, there's lots of trails and game paths on and off these hillsides."

She gave him a critical look.

"And the fire knows which trails to cover and which ones not to?" she asked.

"Sorry," Sam said. "I didn't want to make it sound worse than it is."

"All right, then," Gilley said. "How bad is it, *honestly*?"

"It's bad, *honestly*," Sam said. He turned and walked back to the campfire.

"Okay, I've got that," Gilley said, hurrying alongside him. "What about turning back?"

"Can't do it," Sam said, staring down into the low flames of the campfire.

"Catching Cheyenne and his gang means so much that you'd risk your life . . . *my* life too?"

"That's not it," Sam said quietly. He nodded toward their back trail. "For all we know the fire back there has crossed the rock land by now. If it has, we get there with this fire dogging us from behind, we're all out of places to run to."

"I—I don't believe you," she said haltingly. "I think you just don't want to give up the chase. How can you risk my life like this? You don't even know if I'm guilty of anything, except delivering horses to the wrong man. It's not fair. I should have some say in it."

"Fair?" Sam said. "How's this for fair? You're free to go, if that's what suits you."

"You mean it?" she said, staring at him intently.

"Get the two horses and go," he said. He let out a breath and said, "I don't know if I'm taking the right direction or not. But you're right, I've got no right to take you this way—I might be wrong."

She stood staring at him, weighing her chances alone against her chance with him leading the way.

"Why do you think our best chance is going on toward the trading post?"

"The wind is down," Sam said. "It's been down all night. If it stays down 'til morning, we should get through. The trail runs up along the higher ridges for a ways. Then it runs down and levels off the rest of the way to Bagley's. With no wind, the fire will stay above the trail."

Gilley thought about it and said, "So, the wind stays down, you take the trail right around the edge of the fire?"

"That's right," Sam said. "At least that's how I'm going to play it."

"What if the wind comes back before dawn?" she asked.

"Then I expect I'll be dead," Sam replied. "But that's

the hand, either way. This is how I'm playing it." He nodded toward the horses. "Notice they still haven't settled all the way down? Their noses are pointed north. They're smelling fire."

"But you're still not sure this is the best thing?" she asked.

"No," Sam said. He rubbed the campfire out with the sole of his boot and turned toward the horses. "That's why you're free to go."

She stood watching him walk away in the shadowy purple darkness.

"Damn it!" she cursed to herself. "I get in trouble every damn time I follow a man—every time I listen to one—every time I even look in one's direction!" Then she shook her head and hurried along toward the horses.

Carlos Bagley stared out from the rear door of his log and stone trading post along the trail winding south-west across the badlands hill country. Five days ago he'd told himself the wildfires were not going to get close enough for him to worry about. But now he wasn't so sure, judging by the smoke drifting high up on the wind across the rock chasm. He'd seen his share of wildfire in the past ten years he'd owned his business here on the untamed frontier.

But nothing like this. . . .

This hateful, unruly fire didn't appear to follow any rhyme or reason in the way it moved. Fire was sup-posed to ride the wind, but not this one. *Huh-uh.* These fires—because it was *more than one* now, he reminded himself—seemed to have a mind and will all their own. It was almost eerie. Even in mixed wind, wild-fires did as the elements demanded of them. Yet this one appeared to disregard the wind. Its offshoots popped up whenever, wherever it suited them. These fires not only traveled the wind; they traveled cross-wind, and in some cases, it appeared, even *against the wind?*

That made no sense, he chastised himself. Yet he wasn't going to say it wasn't true, not from what he'd seen these past few days.

He'd always been able to rely on the wide, barren chasm of rock and sand to keep the wildfires con-tained. This time it wouldn't surprise him a bit if the fire managed to find its way across the wide buffer and come knocking on his door. For a silent moment he stood staring blindly, picturing in his wandering mind a large flame walking up in the night, making a fiery fist and rapping insistently on his door.

That was some picture all right.

Blinking, bringing himself back into focus, he saw Cheyenne and his men ride into sight. Two rode in front of an open wagon; two rode behind. Their horses moved at an easy pace along the trail that would run a mile past him, then switchback up and head right to his trading post.

A wagon? Bagley thought to himself, eyeing the pro-cession closely until they rode out of sight behind a wall of land-stuck boulders.

"Here they come, Dewey," he called back over his shoulder inside the darkening building.

"Cheyenne and his gang?" Dewey Fritz called out

in reply from behind a bar—a series of long, thick planks laid between beer barrels. Across the bar from him, two dusty horseback travelers gave each other a look and sipped their whiskey. Their rifles lay up on the plank bar top near their gun hands.

"None other," said Bagley. "How much goat's left?"

"Half or more," said Dewey. "These men chewed a good hole in it. But there's enough still for four more hungry souls. Plenty of beans to boot," he added.

Bagley chuffed to himself.

"I wouldn't accuse Cheyenne and his men of having *souls*, unless they managed to steal one somewhere." As soon as he said it, he caught himself and realized he should have kept his mouth shut with strangers standing at the bar.

One of the two drinkers turned to Bagley and looked him up and down.

"Did you say the Cheyenne Kid?" he asked in a quiet voice.

Bagley just looked at him and the other man, eyeing their rifles atop the bar.

"Who are you two fellows?" he asked, shooting a glance at Dewey Fritz. The bartender caught the subtle signal and reached below the bar for a double-barreled shotgun. He cocked both hammers.

"Easy, mister," said the first drinker, hearing the shotgun cock, noting the change in the air. "I'm Lou Elkins. This is Tanner Riggs." He jerked a thumb toward the other man. Then, instead of placing his hand back down close to his rifle, he rested it on the walnut grip of a holstered Colt.

"Bounty hunters, are yas?" Bagley asked warily.

"No," said Elkins. "But we are looking for the Cheyenne Kid and his men."

"That sounds a lot like bounty men or lawmen of some kind to me," Carlos Bagley pressed.

"If we were bounty men, or lawmen of *any kind*, why would I ask you politely if that's Cheyenne and his gang?" the man said, still calm and quiet. "Why wouldn't I have already jerked iron and put a bullet in this fool's head before he could swing that scattergun out of hiding." He turned a cold stare to Dewey Fritz and added, "I can still do it, far as that goes."

"You sure as hell could, *Lou Elkins!*" said Bagley, a change coming over him as he suddenly recognized both men's names from his days on the wild frontier. "I expect you or *Tanner Riggs*, either one, could." He emphasized their names, hoping Dewey would also recognize them—both men carrying a wide and bloody reputation with a gun. "But I would sure consider it a *kindness* if you don't do it. Ol' Dewey here means no harm. He's only doing his job. 'Sides, I just scrubbed down these walls less than a month ago."

"In that case, I'm going to suggest that you tell *Ol' Dewey* here to raise his hands up into sight and stick his fingers in his ears," said Elkins.

"I can do that, sure enough," Bagley said, eager to please now that he knew these two weren't just ordinary saddle tramps passing by his establishment. He looked at Dewey and said, "You heard him, *Dewey*. Get your hands up where they can see them. These are good men—friends of Cheyenne and his men, I'll wager?" He looked to Elkins with his question.

Elkins only stared at him.

Without another word on the matter, Dewey raised both hands and shoved a thick index finger into either ear.

Tanner Riggs let out a short laugh, seeing the large, slick-headed man staring straight ahead with a blank look on his pale, doughy face.

"Jesus, Dewey," said Bagley, a little embarrassed, "he didn't mean it, about sticking your fingers in your ears."

Elkins gave Riggs a bemused look; they both grinned.

"How the hell was I supposed to know?" Dewey said, taking his fingers down and wiping them on his bartender's apron.

Bagley shook his head in disgust.

"Go get some food ready for Cheyenne and his men, Dewey," he said to the big bartender. "Try to keep your dirty fingers out of it."

Dewey walked away grumbling under his breath.

"You'll have to excuse my hired help, fellows," Bagley said to the two gunmen. "All I get to choose from is rubes and lunatics up here."

The two looked at him stonily and sipped their whiskey. Outside, the four riders drew closer.

"Now that I know you're not bounty hunters," Bagley said, "I'll let you both in on something." He continued in an almost secretive tone. "I've got some real fine clean tents for rent out there. Your price, two bits a night. They've got cots in them—neither of you has to sleep on the ground."

"Our price, huh?" said Elkins.

"Yep," Bagley said with a wide grin. "Anybody else, it would be four bits each."

"Real clean, huh?" said Tanner Riggs.

"*Fairly* clean," Bagley said, his smile fading. "I'll guarantee there's no lice—not enough to worry about anyway."

Elkins ignored his words and gestured out the window toward the smoke in the distance.

"How long's the fire been burning?" he asked.

"It comes and goes, but off and on, it's been burning nearly a month, I'd calculate," Bagley said. "It was staying farther north along the higher ridgelines. But now it's getting a little too close to suit me." He gestured a hand around the shelves of goods and supplies. "I've got a big investment here."

"Investment . . . ," Elkins said flatly.

The two gunmen looked all around in distaste.

"If the fire took this place to the ground, it'd be doing you a favor," said Riggs.

Bagley looked offended.

"That's a matter of opinion," he said, trying to keep the growing anger out of his voice.

"Yeah, like everything else," said Riggs. He threw back his drink and set his shot glass down on the plank bar top as Cheyenne, his men and the couple in the wagon reined their horses up to the hitch rail out front.

Chapter 7

———◆———

The wind lay still along the jagged hillsides and ridges like some large sleeping animal as the Ranger and the women rode upward on the winding trail. Yet, as morning grew closer, even as sunlight began to wreath the eastern horizon, Sam felt the first gust of dry, heated wind sweep through the fire above them as if it had been seeking them out.

"The winds come up quicker than I expected," he said, looking up the hillside flanking them.

"You said it would lie down until daylight," Gilley said, a hint of panic in her tone.

"I didn't say it *would*," Sam corrected her in a steady voice. "I said *if* it stays down 'til morning, we should make it through." He nudged his barb forward, leading the extra horse beside him. "We've made it most of the way. There's no turning back now."

"I'm sorry," she replied, keeping her fear in check, "of course that is what you said." Gilley settled herself, taking some comfort in the calmness of the Ranger's voice. But she also read the seriousness in his tone, no matter how he tried to hide it.

She nudged her horse forward reluctantly, the two of them looking all along the burning hillsides running above them. Orange flames revealed themselves through the looming, charcoal-colored smoke. Even without the winds pressing the fire down toward the trail, underbrush had spread the flames over the ground like a gray, fiery blanket. Ahead of them, they both saw how dangerously close the fire had reached down toward their trail and was moving closer still.

"It's getting so hot, Ranger," Gilley said. "My horse is burning up."

Sam saw her press a hand to her horse's withers.

"Two more miles, we'll be out from under it," Sam said, realizing he was raising his voice to be heard above the roar of the encroaching fire. As he spoke, he reached for his canteen and shook it a little to remind himself it was full. He drew his barb and the spare horse back a step and rode beside Gilley between her and the intense heat. "Here, take this, use it when you have to, some on yourself, some on the horse."

"What about you?" she asked.

"I have another canteen," Sam said.

They rode in silence for another ten minutes until they watched a ball of fire the size of a house spill off the hillside onto the trail twenty yards ahead. The large, fiery ball exploded in every direction in a spray of sparks, flames, burning brush and timber. The remainder of the mass bounced off the trail and lay strewn, flaming and glowing, down the hillside below them.

Farther down the cliff, Sam saw part of the fire flash

and turn suddenly black; gray smoke quickly rose in the purple darkness.

"There's water down there," he said, quickly glancing behind them, the fire now burning in the middle of their trail. "Get down off your horse," he said.

"What? *Why?*" Gilley asked, even as she followed his order.

"It's been burning long enough that trees are starting to fall. It'll soon be covering our trail," Sam said, stepping down beside her. "We've got to get farther below it."

"My God, how're we getting out of here?" Gilley asked, down from her saddle, her horse beginning to panic as she gripped its reins in both hands.

"There's water down there. We'll follow it down as far as we can."

"What about the horses?" she yelled above the increasing roar of the fire.

"We'll lead them as far as we can," Sam shouted in reply. "Follow me."

Gilley looked down at what appeared to be a hand-to-hand downward climb over boulder and brush relieved only here and there by a thin rocky path.

"We can't lead them down through there," she said. "They'll never make it."

"They've *got to make it,*" Sam said, leaving no room for debate on the matter. "They know what's happening here the same as we do. If your horse won't lead, turn him loose. He'll go where there's less heat."

"No," she said, shaking her head. "If I turn him loose he'll die!"

Sam just looked at her, but his eyes said it all.

"Let's go," he said firmly, "else I'll turn him loose right here and carry you over my shoulder."

"All right, I'm coming," she said quickly, jerking on the frightened horse's reins. "I'm right behind you."

She followed the Ranger closely in the grainy predawn darkness as he stepped over the edge of the trail onto the steep, rocky hillside, leading his barb and the spare horse behind him. She was surprised at how the animals had not balked or hesitated to walk over into the dark nothingness that lay beneath them. Was it the firm direction she and the Ranger had taken, or their animal instincts telling them to get away from the fire?

She didn't know. But she did notice that the scorching heat immediately lessened the moment they had left the trail and put the hillside between themselves and the raging fire closing down on them.

As the roar of the fire grew distant above them, Gilley calmed herself and picked her footing, using the spare horse walking in front of her as a guide. All right, this was going to work, she keep repeating to herself, hearing the click of iron-lined hoof make its way over and around the narrow, treacherous path.

But when they had climbed down far enough that she could make out the black, glittering outline of water winding though the valley floor beneath them, the Ranger and the two horses in front of her stopped suddenly.

"Stay where you are," the Ranger called back to her with urgency. Then he whispered quietly to the restless horses to calm them, "Whoa, now, easy, now. . . ."

Gilley heard the barb chuff and nicker under its breath. She listened to the sound of both horses' hooves as they back-stepped under the Ranger's command. She had to back up herself and force her horse to follow suit to make room for the two animals.

"What's wrong, Ranger?" she asked.

"The path breaks off right here," Sam said to her over his shoulder.

Gilley looked behind her, along the path they had walked down. At the upper edge, she could see the orange flickering glow where the fire had crept down closer to the trail. In the short time since they'd left, the heat had turned the trail into a scorching furnace. Neither they nor the animals could survive on it for the two-mile run they would have had to take to get them out of danger—and that was provided no more of the trail ahead was covered with fallen, burning timber, she reminded herself.

"What do we do now?" she asked.

"It'll be tough going," Sam said, "but with a little luck we can climb down."

A silence followed. Above them the roar of fire had grown in volume and intensity as it moved farther down toward the trail.

"What about the horses?" Gilley asked.

"We have to leave them," Sam said in a tight voice. "They'll either stand it out here or find themselves a way down." He paused, then said, "Drop your saddle, get yourself ready."

Even as the Ranger spoke, Gilley heard him loosen his saddle from the barb's back. Without hesitation, she turned and loosened the saddle from her horse's back and set it on the ground at her feet. Then she dropped the bridle from the horse's mouth.

"What else should I do?" she asked.

Another slight pause.

"If you're religious, you might say a prayer," Sam said.

"*Jesus . . .* ," Gilley said.

"That's a good place to start," Sam said, holding the saddle next to his thigh.

"What if I'm *not religious*?" Gilley said, summoning up her courage.

"It's a good time to take it up," Sam said.

Gilley eyed the Ranger's saddle, Winchester, rifle boot and canteen all bundled in his hands. But she was paying closer attention to the saddlebags full of money that he had taken loose and draped over his shoulder.

She watched him swing the saddle back with both hands and hurl it out over a bottomless, black hole. They listened intently for what seemed like a long time before hearing the saddle strike one boulder, then another, then come to a loud, sudden stop.

"How—how far, Ranger?" Gilley asked, watching him drop the bit from the barb's mouth and pitch the bridle away.

"I don't know," Sam said, keeping his voice calm, "a hundred feet, maybe two."

Gilley shook her head, knowing he was only guessing, only playing it down to keep from spooking her. Well, she had news for him, she thought. She was past the *spooking* stage. The fire had scared her once she'd come to realize the danger of it. But she hadn't fallen apart. Besides, she had stood face-to-face with dangerous men—men with their knifes, their guns, their callous, cold-blooded killing. She could do this, she told herself. After all she'd been through, no downhill climb was going to weaken her knees.

"However far it is, I'm ready, Ranger," she said with determination. "It won't get any shorter, us waiting here."

"That's what I say," the Ranger replied. He took her hand and led her around the horses. He put her in front of him for a moment while he turned to the barb and slapped its rump, not hard enough to put it into a run, yet with enough force to give it permission to turn the other two horses and free them up to leave.

"See you at the water," he said to the freed horses, knowing his words were only wishful thinking. Then he turned, stepped around Gilley and reached a hand back to her as he stepped over the edge of the trail. "How's your climbing?" he asked, guiding her along behind him.

"It'll do," she said, as if it mattered now.

Nearly a full hour later, having picked their way step by step trough the gray hour of morning, the Ranger and Gilley stood on a narrow rock shelf and looked up toward the trail. Billowing smoke rolled out over the rocky edge. From within the smoke, tongues of flame streaked out as if peeping down, searching for them.

"My God, it crossed the trail?" Gilley said in disbelief, catching her breath after the last few yards spent climbing downward across a stretch of almost sheer rock wall.

"It looks like it," Sam replied.

"Then we would never have made it had we not climbed down here?" she asked.

"Hard to say," Sam replied. "It depends on how much burning timber started falling down the hillside—how much of the trail it would have blocked on us. That caught me by surprise."

"You did good," she said, leaning back against the rock wall beside him. She had turned loose of his hand when they'd stepped over on the ledge, but now she took it again. She held it to her bosom with both hands for a moment. "*Real good*, Sam, getting us down out from there."

Not Ranger, but "Sam" now, he noted to himself.

"We're not *out of there* yet," Sam replied. "We're about halfway down, I make it."

He gave the slightest tug of his hand, just enough so that she let go of it, allowing him to adjust the saddle-bags on his shoulder.

"Yes," she said, gazing down with him, "but it looks like it's getting a little easier."

Below them the water showed more clearly now that the day's early sunlight had begun spilling into the lower valleys. In spite of the smoke shrouding much of the morning sky, daylight had given them a better view of the steep and treacherous path they'd made for themselves as they'd moved along, a foot at a time, often inch by inch in the preceding darkness.

As they leaned forward a little and examined the path ahead, they heard the distant crash of brush and rocks tumbling down the hillside, amid it the sound of horses screaming out in terror.

"Oh no, the horses!" Gilley grabbed the Ranger and buried her face against his chest.

Sam winced at the sound and held her tightly to him until a silence moved in beneath the roar of the fire. When he turned her loose, he gazed into her tear-filled eyes and brushed a strand of hair from her cheek.

"We did what we had to," he said, as if he was still trying to convince himself it was the truth. "There was no other way."

"I know we did," she said, sharing the guilt of responsibility with him. She took a deep breath, collected herself and stepped back from him, wiping her face on her shirtsleeve. "I'm ready when you are."

They moved on.

An hour later at the bottom of the hillside, the Ranger left Gilley standing on a shoulder of a high-cut bank of rock and dirt, above the shallow-running stream. Scooting down, he turned and reached up to her.

"Thank goodness that's over with," she said, reaching for his forearms, letting him lower her, both of his hands on her waist, standing her on the edge of the stream.

"It's not over yet," Sam said, looking all around for his saddle and gear, estimating it could be lying anywhere within a twenty-five-yard stretch of the streambed, or even somewhere in the stream itself.

"I know we've got a ways to go," Gilley said, stepping out into the stream, "but for right now I want to pretend I'm at home somewhere." She turned and let herself fall backward into the stream. She dished water into her hat and poured it down onto her face, drinking some of it.

"Rest yourself," Sam said over his shoulder to her as he searched the stream bank along both sides. "I'll be right back. We'll get going downstream. I've got a feeling this isn't going to be the end of the wildfires."

She sat up as she saw the Ranger walking off along the streambed, searching for his gear among the rocks and boulders on the hillside.

"You're looking for your saddle?" she called out. Without hearing an answer from him, she stood up in the water. "Wait up, I'll help."

But Sam had already spotted the butt of his Winchester sticking up among some dry, wild grass amid a clump of rock.

He made his way toward it, but stopped suddenly when he heard the sound of hooves racing in his direction along the edge of the water. No sooner had he heard the hoofs than Gilley stopped in her tracks and shouted, "Sam, look out!"

The Ranger spun toward the racing sound of hooves, his Colt streaking up from his holster, cocked and aimed. But then he relaxed and lowered the barrel of his gun, seeing the rust-colored barb splashing along midstream, winding down almost to a halt at the sight of the Ranger standing facing him.

"Well, look who's here," the Ranger said aloud to himself as the barb settled into a walk the last few feet and stopped. Gilley stood watching as the Ranger stepped closer and rubbed the horse's muzzle. Then she moved along through the rocks to where the Winchester stood in the silvery morning light.

Sam let the hammer down on his big Colt and shoved it into his holster. He looked the barb over good, seeing cuts and scratches on the big horse's sides, rump and all four legs. The horse blew out a breath, shook itself and stuck its muzzle down into the stream. Sam rubbed its withers as it drew water. While the animal drank, he gazed up along the steep hillside. The fire still raged, the sound of it still audible from over two hundred feet below.

He gazed back along the hillside and saw a distant stretch where its steepness lessened by a large body of boulders and earth. The horses could have made it down there, he told himself. They would have slipped and scooted and maybe even tumbled, as it appeared the barb had done. But it hadn't been hopeless.

"I think the others made it down too," he called out over his shoulder. "Let's hope so anyway."

"Yes, let's hope so," he heard Gilley reply, her voice sounding closer than she'd been before.

He turned and saw her facing him on the water's edge, the Winchester in both her hands, cocked, the barrel pointed in his direction. His first instinct was to grab the Colt. But something told him not to—not yet anyway.

"I see you brought my rifle to me," he said quietly. As he spoke he saw that the rifle's butt stock had broken off in its long fall.

"Yes, I did," Gilley said. She reached down, and when she did Sam spotted his saddle lying in wild grass at her feet. "I brought your saddle too," she said.

Sam only nodded and stared in silence as she bent and stood back up holding the butt stock to the Winchester in her right hand, letting the rifle barrel slump in her left hand, pointing down away from him.

"The stock is broke," she said, holding it out for him to see.

"Too bad," Sam said, turning from the drinking horse and walking over to her. "But I suppose it had to break, a hard fall like that." He reached out, first taking the broken stock, then the rifle itself. He uncocked it, eyeing her closely as he did so.

She saw a questioning look in his eyes.

"I know," she said, as if reading his thoughts, "but I didn't, did I?"

The Ranger let out a breath and nodded. The look in his eyes changed slightly.

"Obliged," he said, lowering the rifle hammer. "I can replace the stock."

"The saddle is pretty battered up too," she said. "The horn's gone—feels like the cantle's broken."

"It doesn't matter," said Sam. "I'm not saddling him. We're not riding him unless we get in a spot and have to."

"Do you think we'll run into more fire between here and the trading post?" she asked, eyeing the saddle-bags on his shoulder almost with regret, then looking away, as if knowing she'd had her chance and didn't take it.

"I don't know," said Sam. "Let's push on, see what the day has in store for us." He offered her his hand. She took it and stepped off the bank into the cool, running stream.

PART 2

Chapter 8

Having seen the woman on the wagon seat next to the young man, Bagley spit in the palms of both hands and ran them back along the unruly gray wings of hair mantling his otherwise bald head. As soon as Cheyenne, his men and the wagon had stopped out in front of the trading post, Bagley stood on the edge of the weathered-plank porch and smiled down at them, the wagon having pulled in parallel to the long hitch rail.

"Welcome, one and all," he'd called out, ready to descend the porch steps and assist the woman down from the wagon seat. But a look from Cheyenne had stopped him in his tracks.

Bagley fell silent for a moment. He wiped his palms on his trousers and watched as Cheyenne swung down from his saddle, pitched his saddlebags over his shoulder and walked around to the woman's side.

Bagley eyed Cheyenne's saddlebags.

"I've got roasted goat, red beans and hoe cake ready and waiting for yas," he continued. "All the whiskey you can hold—tea for the lady too." He continued to stare at the woman, waiting for an introduction from Cheyenne.

"Obliged," said Cheyenne as the other three horsemen stepped down from their horses and spun their reins on a long, wooden hitch rail. "These are the Udalls, Segan and Caroline," he added, gesturing toward the couple on the wagon seat.

"Mister . . . ma'am," Bagley said, giving the two a nod. Then he looked back at Cheyenne and shot him a curious look, regarding the couple and their wagon traveling with the gang.

"I'll explain later," Cheyenne said. He extended a hand up and helped Caroline to the ground.

Segan stared, seething at the sight of his wife's hand in Cheyenne's. He started to turn and step down from the wagon, but Cheyenne stopped him with a raised hand.

"Not so fast, Segan," he said. He sniffed toward the front wagon wheels. "You've got a dry axle somewhere. I can smell it. You better drive this rig around back, give your hubs a good greasing."

Segan looked suspiciously at his wife and Cheyenne standing side by side. He tried to speak, saying, "They don't need greasing. I greased them all four less than a week—"

"It's all right, Segan," Caroline said, cutting her husband off. She noted Cheyenne's hand resting on the butt of his holstered Colt.

But Segan disregarded Cheyenne's gun hand; he stared at Caroline for reassurance.

"Please, Segan, I'll be fine," she said. "Go grease your hubs. I thought I smelled them getting hot earlier."

"Yeah, Segan," Gantry put in, "go grease your wheels." He gave a dark chuckle and stared at Segan, seeing the young man struggle to keep his rage under control. Segan turned and snatched up the wagon reins.

As the wagon rolled away from the hitch rail, Lou Elkins and Tanner Riggs stepped out of the trading post and looked down at Cheyenne and his men.

"Howdy, Cheyenne," said Elkins. Tanner Riggs touched his hat brim and gave a nod.

"Howdy, Lou . . . howdy, Tanner," Cheyenne said. "Glad you both showed up." He turned a cold stare to Bagley.

"Oh, I meant to tell you," Bagley said, "they showed up earlier. I told them you'd be coming."

"I'm glad you *decided* to tell me," Cheyenne said in a dry tone. He turned to Elkins and Riggs and gestured a hand back and forth between them and his three men. "I expect everybody here knows one another?"

The men exchanged nods and greetings.

"All of you go inside and pull some cork," Cheyenne said. "Bottles are all on me. Hell, rooms, food, everything's on me." He patted the saddlebags hanging over his shoulder. "I'll be right back."

"All right!" said Dock Latin. He and Gantry Tarpis bounded up the steps, following Riggs and Elkins back inside, all of them drawn there by the powerful lure of whiskey.

"Gantry," Cheyenne called out, stopping Red Gantry before he made his way through the open door, "get your bottle and come see me. I've got something that needs doing. Bring a rope," he added in afterthought.

"Bring a rope . . . ?" said Gantry curiously.

"Yep, you heard me," said Cheyenne.

Gantry just stared at him for a moment, then said, "Yeah, sure, I'll be right along—and I'll bring a rope."

"Red don't like taking orders, does he?" Bagley whispered as Gantry walked inside.

Cheyenne didn't reply. He turned back to Bagley and said, "We'll need some tents for the night, one for the Udalls, two for all the men and one for myself."

Bagley scratched the stubble on his chin and squinted in contemplation.

"That's four tents," he said. "You only told me to have three ready."

"I know that's what I said," said Cheyenne, staring at him. "But now I want *four* tents. Do you understand?"

"Sure, I've got four tents," said Bagley, "but only three of them have been smoked out and cleaned, if that's all right for yas."

"Give the one that's not been smoked out to the men," said Cheyenne.

"I'll do that," Bagley said. He lowered his voice and said just between the two of them, "Who are these folks and what are they doing with you?" He darted his eyes toward Caroline Udall, who stood behind Cheyenne.

"These two are newlyweds," said Cheyenne. "This woman was a widow. I knew her and her first husband. They once saved my life. We happened upon her and her new husband coming across the high trail." His voice lowered even more. "You won't believe what they were doing out there."

"Oh?" Bagley leaned and looked around him at

Caroline, then looked back in his eyes. "Are you going to tell me?"

"Yes," said Cheyenne. "Just as soon as I escort her to their tent and see to it she gets settled in." He gave Bagley a look and said, "Does that drunken Ute still live out back—still help out with wagon repairs?"

"Little Foot?" said Bagley. "Yeah, he's here, unless he's got drunk and wandered away again. He can't go too far without walking in a circle and coming right back. What do you want him to do for you?"

"I want him to help Segan grease his axles. Tell him not to get it done in any hurry. We don't want a shoddy job, do we?"

"No, sir-*ree*, we don't," said Bagley.

"Good." Cheyenne smiled. "Now go take care of that while I accompany the lady to her tent. Tell Little Foot when he's through with the wagon, I've got some more work for him." He paused before saying, "Does he know this country pretty well?"

"Better than anybody I know," said Bagley.

"He knows all of the main trails running north of here?" Cheyenne asked.

"There's only three, but yeah, he knows them, and all the game paths leading to them," said Bagley. "You want him for a scout, a *trail guide*?"

"Yeah, sort of," said Cheyenne.

Inside the trading post, Lou Elkins stepped away from the bar long enough to look out the window and see Cheyenne and Caroline Udall turn and walk toward a row of sun-bleached canvas tents. As he stepped back over to the bar, he shook his head.

"I hope Cheyenne ain't up to his old weakness," he said to anyone who cared to listen.

Behind the bar, Dewey Fritz set up shot glasses and unopened bottles of whiskey in front of each of them.

"Oh . . . ?" said Dock Latin. "And what *weakness* might that be?"

"Women," Elkins said bluntly. He jerked the cork from a bottle, passed the bottle back and forth under his nose, breathing deep, then filled his shot glass.

Latin and Tarpis just stared until he threw back the shot glass, emptying it into his mouth.

"All right, Lou," said Latin, "are you saying any more on the matter, or just leave us standing here?"

Elkins and Riggs both looked at them.

"Then you don't know?" said Elkins.

"Damn it, Lou, know what?" said Latin. "You've known him longer than we have. Tell us what you're getting at here, else keep your mouth shut."

"Cheyenne is a hell of a man," said Elkins. "But just between us four, he can't leave the womenfolk alone."

"So what?" said Latin. "That just makes him as red-blooded as the rest of us." He threw back his own shot glass in a gulp.

"Yep, but the problem is he's got to have every one of them. And he gets too tangled up with them, doesn't know when to cut one loose."

"We just saw him *cut one loose*," Dock Latin said. "It didn't seem to bother him any."

Elkins shrugged and said, "Maybe he's over it. I shouldn't have said anything."

"Yeah, maybe you shouldn't have," said Tarpis in an unfriendly tone of voice. "We haven't been riding with him long, but so far he's done a good job running things." He pulled the cork from his bottle of rye with his teeth and blew it away, staring at Elkins all the while.

"I'm just saying he plays too much with the women-folk," Elkins said almost under his breath. "He brings them in too close. Mixes them in with business—which to me is never a good idea. Sometimes I think he doesn't know he's doing it until it's done."

Tarpis and Latin looked at each other, thinking about Gilley Maclaine. Cheyenne could have set up horses with anybody. Why the young woman?

"Yeah, you're right," Latin said to Elkins, "women and business don't mix. Not in this robbing business anyways."

Inside the dusty canvas tent, Cheyenne and Caroline looked around at a battered chest of drawers, a ladder-back chair, a shaving mirror hanging on a tent pole, a wide cot covered with a lumpy but thin feather mat-tress.

"It'll do nicely," Caroline said over her shoulder, Cheyenne standing right behind her.

He placed a hand on her shoulder and felt her shiver slightly at his touch.

"You deserve better than any of this, Caroline," he said softly, raising his hand a little, seeing the thin switch mark on her exposed shoulder.

"Oh, no, George—I mean *Cheyenne*—this is fine, really."

"Turn around, look at me, Caroline," he said close to her ear, so close she could feel his warm breath on the skin below her ear.

"Oh dear . . . ," she murmured to herself, his voice sounding warm, compelling, moving over the skin of her throat like honey. She turned around, her head lowered, eyes closed.

"No, look at me," he persisted, raising her chin gently with his fingertips until she opened her eyes and looked into his. "What are you doing with a man like this *Segan Udall?*" he asked, just saying Segan's name seeming to sour his stomach a little.

She shook her head without answering, closed her eyes and tried to turn away.

"Don't look away, Caroline," Cheyenne said, drawing her face back to his. "He switches you like you're some unruly child. What else does he do to you?"

"That's all," Caroline said, looking ashamed. "And that's just until we get things settled between us."

"And consummate your marriage," Cheyenne said, finishing the explanation for her.

"Yes, just until then," she said.

Cheyenne shook his head as if in disbelief. He reminded himself that it was none of his business, but that didn't stop him from prying further. He looked at her closely and wondered just for a moment why he always seemed to find peculiar women. Peculiar women in peculiar circumstances, he told himself. He needed to give it some more thought when he had some time. For now . . .

"He's not a man, Caroline," he said almost as if he couldn't stop himself. He held her close to him.

"He's young, I have to admit," Caroline said, "but he's starting to understand—"

"He's not the kind of man you *need*, Caroline," he

said, cutting her off. "What's next, if switching you doesn't do any good? What will you allow him to do then to make himself full? Will you let him slap you around? Is that what you want? Do you *need* a man who treats you that way?"

"No, no, please," she said, almost swooning as she shook her head slowly, her eyes closed.

"There's women who like that sort of treatment," Cheyenne said, watching her reaction to his words as he spoke softly, persistently. "Do you need him to play rough with you? Slap your bare bottom until it's red and stinging in pain? Maybe use a belt? A paddle?" He observed the flushed look come over her face as he spoke.

"Oh God, no, Cheyenne!" she said, almost sobbing. "I'm not that kind of woman, really, I'm not."

But he'd seen that he reached something in her—the look on her face revealed as much.

"Than what kind of woman are you—?"

She grabbed him and pressed his mouth to hers, hard, almost before he'd gotten his words out.

Whoa . . . ! Cheyenne stood stunned for a second, taken aback by her sudden abandonment. But he caught up quickly; he returned her kiss, hard and deep.

"Oh God, what am I doing?" Caroline said in a breathless whisper, moving across the dirt floor, off her feet now, clinging to Cheyenne, his face buried in her bosom, guiding her toward the cot.

But Cheyenne stopped suddenly when Gantry called out from the other side of the tent fly.

"Cheyenne, are you in there?" he said.

"Jesus . . . !" The two separated enough for Caroline

to straighten her clothes and fluff her hair. Cheyenne wiped away his tortured face and collected himself.

"Yes, come on in, Red," he called out, seeing the tent fly already being pulled back, the top of Gantry's battered hat preceding him into the tent.

Gantry stood up inside the tent, trying to hide the knowing look on his face. He held out a coiled rope in his left hand. In his right he carried a bottle of rye whiskey.

"I brung the rope like you asked," he said. "What is it you want me to do?"

"Obliged," said Cheyenne, stepping forward, taking the rope from him.

Caroline eyed the rope closely, raising a hand as if checking to make certain her dress was properly buttoned.

"I want to send you on a little ride, making sure everybody is off our trail, and keep them off it until the rest of us are safe out of the territory. Are you up to that?"

Gantry gave him a haughty but puzzled look.

"I think I can handle it well enough," he said with a touch of sarcasm. "I thought we were in good shape already, though."

"It never hurts to make sure," Cheyenne said. "Now listen close. I want you to go to the wagon shed and tell Segan to stop greasing his axles long enough to get over here. Tell him I want to talk to him. Him and the Ute guide are going with you, in the wagon."

"That drunken Injun, Little—*whatever*?" Gantry asked, sounding prickly.

"Little Foot's his name. He knows this country like

the back of his hand," said Cheyenne, embellishing what Bagley had told him.

"He's a damn drunk and a dope eater," said Gantry, always ready to take issue. "One foot's small as a goat's hoof! He can't walk a mile without making a full circle."

"Go get Segan," said Cheyenne, dismissing him. "Bring him here and be ready for anything I tell him."

"Back your play, in other words," said Gantry.

"Is that all right by you?" Cheyenne asked.

"Damn right it's all right," said Gantry. "Far as I care, I'll gut that young boyo like a Christmas goose, after what he done to me." He looked at Caroline. "Begging your pardon, ma'am," he added humbly, "for talking ill about your husband."

Cheyenne stared at him until he backed up, stooped and left through the tent fly.

"My goodness, that was close," said Caroline, fanning herself with her hands. "Not that I can say I minded one bit." She gave Cheyenne a coy smile. "Although I guess you could say I've been a *naughty girl*?"

Cheyenne just looked at her.

"Want me to kill Segan for you?" he asked flatly.

"Why, no! Good heavens no!" exclaimed Caroline. She noted his eyes staying fixed on hers. "I mean, I don't love him, but I don't want him dead." She paused. "I mean . . . *not really*, that is."

Cheyenne continued staring in silence. "I've got something I want him to do for me," he said. "But after that, *say the word*."

She paused, clutching the neck of her dress in contemplation. "I have to admit, I've thought about it."

Cheyenne smiled a little and uncoiled a length of the rope in his hands.

"I understand," he said. "Now I want to ask *you* to do a little something for me."

"Oh . . . ?" Caroline eyed the rope again, curiously. "And what might that be?"

Cheyenne stared up at her from under his tilted brow.

"Does it matter what it is?" he asked, testing her. "Would you do anything for me, whatever I asked?"

"What is it?" she pressed timidly.

"Oh, nothing really," Cheyenne said. "If you let a man switch you all over, what I'm asking should be an easy thing for you to do." He stared at her and repeated firmly, "Would you do anything for me, whatever I asked?"

"Yes," she said in a lowered tone, her voice turning hushed and submissive. "Anything you asked of me, I'll do it. That's how I feel right now, Cheyenne—anything at all."

"Good," he said. "Come over here, turn around."

Chapter 9

Inside the wagon barn, Little Foot stood leaning against a barn post, holding a large bucket of black axle grease. He watched as Segan Udall raised the rear of the wagon on a steel wagon jack. Bagley had told him to take his time, see to it this young, board-faced white man didn't get his wheels greased too quickly. So that was what he intended to do, he reminded himself. He didn't understand why Bagley wanted him to take his time, but it didn't matter in the least. White men had peculiar ways.

As he stood thinking about it, he spotted another white man, this one carrying a big pistol in his hand. He walked in through the open front doors and straight toward the unsuspecting Udall.

Uh-oh. . . .

Little Foot backed away a step without warning the young white man. Behind Udall, Red Gantry stopped, his large Colt hanging down his side, his thumb over the hammer. Starring down at Udall's back, he cocked the Colt deliberately loud, wanting the big young man to hear it.

"I hope you give me some guff over this, Segan," he said as Segan turned to face him. Still stooping beside the wagon jack, he looked up at Red Gantry as the battered gunman continued. "Because there is nothing would suit me better than to paint your brains all over the wall."

Little Foot kept himself from smiling, thinking how much he would enjoy seeing something like that—one white man killing another, his brains splattered all over the wall. He stood and watched in rapt silence.

"What do you want?" Segan asked Gantry, dumbfounded.

"On your feet," Gantry demanded. He wagged his gun barrel, bringing Segan up from the floor. "Cheyenne wants to talk to you, *right now*."

"But he sent me to get my wagon—"

"That's just the *guff* I was hoping for," Gantry said cutting him short, leveling the Colt toward his chest.

"Wait! I'm coming!" said Segan, standing, his hands chest high in a show of submission.

Gantry looked disappointed, but wagged him toward the barn door.

"All right, get going," he growled. "Make one false move, I'll kill you. I haven't forgot what you done to me." His free hand touched the puffiness around the cut under his eye. His eye had turned the color of fruit gone bad.

Little Foot had moved farther to the side for a better view of the two as they walked out the door. But Gantry swung the Colt toward him quickly.

"What are you looking at, *cripple*?" Gantry growled, seeing Little Foot stagger on his withered foot, caught off guard, trying to regain his balance.

"Don't shoot," Little Foot said, hopping like a man stepping on tacks, both arms up, the bucket of grease in his right hand. His next move, he would swing the bucket around full strength and break Gantry's head open like a hollow gourd. *Swear to God!* he thought. He felt his blood begin to race. It felt good.

But Gantry lowered the tip of his gun barrel, knowing Cheyenne wouldn't take it well, him killing the Indian right after Cheyenne telling him Little Foot would be his trail guide.

Trail guide, ha!

All right, he decided, settling himself, he needed to go along with Cheyenne's plans. But it didn't hurt to let both these two plugs know he was the one who'd be running things.

"Don't worry, *lo*," said Gantry with a nasty grin. "I wouldn't waste a good bullet on you." He nodded at the wagon sitting on the jack. "Get this wagon up and ready to roll. My boss has work for you."

"Work . . . ?" Little Foot just stared at Gantry, letting go of the idea of crushing his skull for the moment. He allowed the bucket of grease to slump in his hand.

"That's right, *work*," said Gantry, following Segan out the barn door. "You know what work is, don't you? *Do-em* work, *make-um* money, *buy-em* more firewater? You do want to get more firewater, don't you?"

This son of a bitch. . . . Little Foot stared at him blankly. He gritted his teeth and watched in silence as the two walked away, Gantry giving him a dark laugh back over his shoulder.

Little Foot turned, set the grease on the ground beside the wagon and took up where Segan had left off.

On the way to the tent, Gantry keeping his Colt in hand, lowered, yet ready to raise it to the center of Segan's broad back and fire it at any second.

"Good thing you came along with me peaceful-like, *Segan*," he said, feeling his battered, mending face throb a little in its healing process. "One piece of guff out of you and—"

"I know," said Segan, cutting him off without looking around at him. "You would have painted my brains all over the ceiling."

Gantry fumed, his thumb itching on the lowered hammer of the Colt.

"Now you're going to back-talk me?" he said.

"No," Segan said stiffly, "I'm just repeating what you said in the barn."

"Yeah?" Gantry stared at the back of the young man's head beneath a wide slouch hat. "It just happens I never said nothing about the *ceiling*. I said the *wall*," Gantry corrected him. "What have you got to say about that?"

Segan walked on with determination.

"I'm not afraid of you, mister," he said over his shoulder. "I'm not afraid of any of you bummers. I'm only going along with everything because I don't want my wife molested." He paused before saying, "Kill me if that's what you all want to do—just leave my wife alone."

"You're just one crazy, naive, empty-headed rube, ain't you, Segan?" Gantry said, smiling to himself as they walked on to the tent.

"What's that supposed to mean?" Segan asked suspiciously.

"Nothing, Segan," said Gantry, thinking of the look that had been on Cheyenne's and Caroline's faces when he had walked into the tent earlier. "Not *one* damn thing." He paused for a moment as they stopped out in front of the tent. With his gun still leveled at Segan's back, Gantry found that he couldn't keep his venom from spewing out. "I will tell you this much. If ever I get another chance, I will hang your wife's undergarments on a tree limb and ride her like she's a—"

Gantry stopped short.

Segan spun around so fast Gantry didn't even get the chance to pull the Colt's trigger before the young man's powerful forearm knocked the gun from his hand. Gantry could only try to duck away from Segan's large powerful fist as it shot out at his jaw. But he wasn't quick enough. The punch connected, sending him flying backward off his feet, feeling the world explode inside his head. He floundered on a thin line of consciousness as the ground seemed to reach up and slam into his back.

Segan Udall was upon him, his big right fist punching hard and fast, like a carpenter nailing down roof shingles until, at length, a hard sidelong swipe from Cheyenne's long pistol barrel came out of nowhere and sent Segan tumbling over into the dirt, where he settled, knocked out cold.

Twenty minutes later, inside the Udalls' tent, Red Gantry stood with his bloody, bruised face more battered and swollen than before. He had managed to drag himself to his feet and stagger into the tent, then wipe his throbbing face with a wet cloth Cheyenne had tossed to him.

"He—he jumped me . . . when I was unexpecting it," he said, his brain struggling to clear itself from the hard pounding he'd taken.

"I saw the whole thing," Cheyenne said in a clipped tone, not inviting any more to be said on the matter. "Wake him up," he added, nodding at Segan, who sat slumped and unconscious, tied down to a ladder-back chair. Pressed against Cheyenne's chest, Caroline stood watching, seeing a thin line of blood run down and drip from the side of her husband's head.

"With pleasure," Red Gantry mumbled through numb, split lips. He drew back a half-filled bucket of water and slung it into Segan's face.

Segan jerked his bowed head up, spitting and spluttering until he opened his bleary eyes. Batting his eyes several times against the water running down into them, he managed to focus up at Red Gantry, then at Caroline, then finally at Cheyenne standing against her back, his left arm around her, holding a rope that was coiled around her neck. In his right hand he held his long revolver resting on her shoulder, pointed at her head.

"Turn loose of my wife, you son of a bitch!" he shouted, already struggling against the rope wound around him, binding him to the chair.

"Red . . . ?" said Cheyenne, giving Gantry a nod.

Gantry tossed the bucket aside and jerked up a rifle leaning against a tent pole. He slammed his boot down on the edge of the chair between Segan's legs, pinning man and chair in place. He cocked the rifle and held it an inch from Segan's face, ready to fire.

"Turn her *loose*?" Cheyenne said in a serious tone, the length of rope around Caroline's neck, down her bosom, wrapped in his hand. "Make one more demand, Segan, I'll put a bullet through her head. Then I'll turn her loose, if you don't do what I tell you."

Segan settled himself long enough to look into Cheyenne's eyes and decide that the outlaw leader meant what he said.

"Don't hurt her, mister, please," Segan said, his powerful chest and arms going limp, giving up all resistance. He paid no attention to the rifle pointed at his own head, only to the pistol resting on Caroline's shoulder, like some shiny snake ready to strike her.

"That's more like it," Cheyenne said, seeing the difference come over the young man. He let his revolver slump on Caroline's shoulder but still kept it in place.

"What do you want me to do?" Segan asked.

"Now we're getting somewhere," said Cheyenne. He gave Gantry a nod. The battered gunman stepped back with his rifle still pointed, as if at any second the powerful young man would rise, break the chair and rope as if it were kindling and string and hurl himself onto them.

"Caroline? Are you all right?" Segan asked.

Before Caroline could answer, Cheyenne gave a sharp jerk on the rope around her neck.

"Huh-uh, Segan," Cheyenne said. "Nobody talks unless I say they can talk. Don't make me say it again."

"I'm sorry, mister. Don't hurt her," Segan said. "It won't happen again."

"Good, then we're all going to get along," said Cheyenne in a no-nonsense manner. He paused and then said, "Here's the deal, Segan. I'm sending you and Gantry here out to set fires across the three main trails leading up out of the territory."

Segan stared at Caroline, then at Cheyenne. "I don't know the trails well enough—"

"Don't worry about that," said Cheyenne, cutting him off. "I'm sending Little Foot with you. He knows this country like the back of his hand."

"I'll do whatever you tell me, but Caroline must go with me. I won't go otherwise," he said firmly.

"All right, this ain't going to work," said Cheyenne. He cocked the revolver. "Sorry, Caroline."

"No! No! Hold it, please! Wait!" said Segan, rising, chair and all, then stopping as Gantry stepped in with the rifle and shoved him back down. "I'll go!" he cried out. "I'll go."

Cheyenne lowered the revolver enough to speak to Caroline, who stood shivering against him.

"I get the idea your husband doesn't believe I'll kill you, Caroline. Anything you want to tell him?"

"Segan, he'll kill me. I know this man, and I know what he'll do. You've got to listen to him and do what he says if you want to keep me alive. Do you understand?"

"I understand," Segan said, recognizing the desperation and terror in his wife's voice. He collected himself and said to Cheyenne, "Whatever you want from me, I'll do it. I'll burn this whole territory down if you tell me to. Only . . ." He stalled before saying, "Mister, please don't force yourself on my wife. That's all I ask."

"I don't want you to burn the *whole territory* down, just the pinelands along my back trail," said Cheyenne. He stared at Segan straight-faced. "Do that and you have my word I will not *force myself* on your wife while you're gone."

Segan appeared a little relieved. Gantry let his rifle down slightly and said to Cheyenne, "You best mention to him that I'm in charge. He doesn't do to suit me, I'll come right back here and tell you. Whatever happens to his wife after that is his own damned fault."

"Did you hear all that, Segan?" said Cheyenne.

"I heard it," Segan said. He looked at Caroline and said, "Don't be afraid. I need you to be strong for us. I'll be coming back for you."

"Yeah, yeah, write her a letter," Gantry said mockingly. Stepping around behind him, he tilted Segan's chair back and dragged the tied man out of the tent.

As soon as Segan was out of sight, Caroline let out a sigh.

"I don't like being a deceitful person," she said remorsefully. "I feel bad about doing this."

"Don't worry, you'll get over that," Cheyenne said. He turned her to him by the rope around her neck and kissed her. She returned his kiss. He started to remove the loop of rope, but she stopped him and pulled her lips away from his long enough to whisper, "You can leave it there, I don't mind."

"What about the gun?" he said, still resting the long barrel on her shoulder.

"That too—I don't mind," she whispered urgently.

Chapter 10

At dawn, Dock Latin sat on an empty nail keg out in front of the large tent Cheyenne had reserved for all of his men. An odor of wood smoke and brimstone permeated the air, wafting in on a morning breeze coming off the hill range. Dock sat smoking a thin cigar, pitching cards down onto the ground in a game of solitaire. Behind him the ragged tent seemed to rise and fall with a loud chorus of snoring.

After a while, Latin looked at the tent in disgust, gathered his cards and walked toward the front porch of the trading post. Before climbing the steps to the porch, he turned and saw the wagon roll into sight, coming from the weathered barn. Red Gantry rode beside the rig on his horse.

"What the hell happened to your face, Red?" Latin asked as the wagon rolled up closer to trading post.

"Not a damn thing, Dock," Gantry said in a brittle tone of voice. "What happened to yours?"

Dock let it go. He shrugged and looked at the small, thin Indian beside Segan Udall on the wagon seat.

"Where you headed off to this morning?" Latin asked.

"Any questions you've got, Dock," said Gantry, "I'll oblige you to take them straight to Cheyenne." He looked Dock up and down as his horse stepped past him. "I expect you were too drunk last night to hear what Cheyenne said."

Dock walked alongside his horse. Looking up at him, he scratched his head up under his hat brim.

"I guess I was," he said, remaining amiable. "What *did* he say?"

Gantry jerked his horse to a halt while the wagon rolled on and looked down at him crossly.

"He told everybody that me and this crippled Ute and the *arsonist* there are headed out to make sure nobody is able to get on our trail and stay there very long."

"Yeah?" said Dock, looking curious. "And how is it you're going to do that?"

"How do you think?" said Gantry, nodding toward the wagon where the tin of coal oil, torches and other fire starting paraphernalia lay in the wagon bed.

"Jesus," said Dock. "You're going to start more fire?"

Gantry looked at him, annoyed.

"Tell me something, Dock," he said. "When you saw me coming just now, did I look like I might want to stop and answer whatever damn-fool question you might come up with?"

"Keep riding, Red," Latin said, his tone of voice turning cold and testy. "No damn wonder to me your face looks like a busted washboard."

Gantry gigged his horse and caught up with the

wagon. He looked at Little Foot, then at Segan Udall, his hand going to the rifle across his lap.

"I'm telling you both right now," he said, "I don't want no damn trouble out of either damn one of yas."

Little Foot looked at Segan Udall, then settled back on the hard wooden seat and stared straight ahead.

Inside another rental tent, three tents down from all the loud snoring, Cheyenne sat straight up, wide-eyed, on the pallet of blankets he and Caroline had made up on the dirt floor after the cot gave way under the strain of their intense passion. He shook his head and batted his eyes to get his senses cleared and working.

Damn it, he thought to himself, why hadn't he checked sooner?

He stood up naked and picked up the set of saddlebags lying within arm's reach next to his gun and gun belt. *Come on, come on! Be there,* he demanded as he loosened the straps holding the thick leather bags shut. He felt the bags as he worked the straps in a hurry. They appeared right, just about the way he remembered them, he thought. He was worrying over nothing, he told himself, letting out a sigh of relief.

But then he upended the saddlebags and felt his heart sink and hit bottom as he watched Gilley Maclaine's undergarments and dirty clothes tumble from the bags onto the pallet.

"Holy God! *No!*" he cried aloud, clamping his hands on either side of his suddenly aching head. He fell straight down onto the pallet as if his legs had given out on him.

"What is it?" Caroline asked, awaking to the sound

of his voice. She rubbed her eyes, turned onto her side and propped herself up onto an elbow. Cheyenne sat staring in disbelief at the clothes and undergarments.

"Nothing . . . ," Cheyenne said idly, trying to get a grip on his situation.

"You kept your word to Segan," Caroline said dreamily. "You didn't *force yourself* on me." She reached a hand over onto his bare shoulder. He sat in silence.

"I'm going to hold you to your word not to *force yourself* on me *every night* while Segan is out starting fire for you." She lay back on the pallet, folded her arms back under her head. "I can't tell you how many times I've wondered how this would be . . . the two of us, alone, all the time in the world—"

"I've got to go," Cheyenne said abruptly, almost before she'd finished talking. He hastily stuffed the dirty clothes and undergarments back into the saddle-bags without her seeing them.

"Oh . . . ?" Caroline raised herself up onto both elbows and gave him a puzzled look. "Is everything all right?"

"Yes, everything's fine, Caroline," he said, reaching a hand over and stroking it down her cheek. "Perfect, in fact."

"Yes, wasn't it, though?" Caroline said, taking his hand and holding it to her lips.

Cheyenne smiled and kept cool about his findings. He wasn't about to let her know what was bothering him. He had to keep this a secret. He wasn't about to let his men know that Gilley Maclaine had gutted him of all his money. *Jesus!* How could he not have checked the saddlebags before riding away, leaving her there on that burning hillside?

"All right, I've got to get my men gathered up," he said, pulling his hand gently away from her.

"Right now?" Caroline purred.

"Yes, I'm afraid so," said Cheyenne, thinking about how much money he was going to owe Bagley for all the food, drink and tents. *Damn!* It struck him that he had less than three dollars in his pocket.

Caroline lay watching curiously as he stood up, dressed and turned to the door.

"I am going with you, aren't I?" she asked as he pulled his boots on and slung his gun belt up over his shoulder.

"You bet you are," he said. "Get dressed and ready. We'll be heading out of here in an hour."

"What are we going to do about Segan?" she asked, throwing the blanket aside and standing up naked in front of him. A length of rope still hung from her neck.

"Don't worry, Red Gantry's keeping an eye on him. They'll catch up with us," Cheyenne said, getting ready in a hurry now, hoping he could bypass Bagley altogether and get out of town without anyone knowing what had happened to his money. It was all about saving face, he told himself. Being the new gang leader, he had to show these men he was nobody's fool.

"That's not what I meant," Caroline said. She stared at him. "I meant is your offer still open?"

Cheyenne stopped and looked her up and down.

"What offer is that?" he asked.

"Your offer to kill him for me," she said in a calm,

steady voice. As she spoke she tossed the rope around behind her and hooked her arms on his neck. In reflex his arms wrapped around her. She drew herself against him, the rope dangling down her bare warm back. "You did say you *would*, after he was finished doing what you wanted."

"Yeah, sure, I'll kill him for you, Caroline, first chance we get," Cheyenne said offhandedly. He felt the heat of her through his clothes. He smiled, looking down into her eyes. "Anything else I can do for you this morning?" His hand found the rope hanging behind her and jerked down sharply on it, just enough to cause her to gasp in surprise.

He saw the excitement shine in her eyes. She clutched him to her, running her fingertips up and down his back. She grazed her hand over the gun belt hanging from his shoulder, enjoying the feel of the leather, the hard brassy feel of bullets standing in a row—the cold edge of the gun butt pressed to her soft flesh.

"Yes, there is," she whispered in a breathless voice, "now that you mention it."

Jesus, Cheyenne thought, how had he ever let this woman get past him before, back when she was Caroline Darby, when she and her late husband, Herbert, had nursed him back to health? He knew he'd been weak and wounded back then, *but damn!* He must've also been out of his mind. Well . . . he wasn't weak and wounded now, he told himself. He wrapped the length of rope around his hand and pulled her down to the pallet with him. Whatever else he had to do could wait awhile, he thought. What was another few minutes? Not everything had to be all about business.

Inside the trading post, Dock Latin rested his hand on the edge of the plank bar and watched as Dewey Fritz refilled a mug with hot, fresh coffee and slid it back in front of him. Steam wafted. Without being asked, Dewey reached around on a shelf behind him, took a black cigar from a tall leather cup and laid it on the bar beside Dock's coffee.

"Obliged, barkeep," Dock said, eyeing Dewey as he picked up the cigar and stuck it between his teeth.

As if out of nowhere, a match appeared in Dewey's thick hand. He dragged it along the underside of the bar top, struck it and held it out to the tip of Dock's expectant cigar.

"Obliged again," said Dock. He puffed the cigar to life, then blew out a thin stream of smoke. He sipped coffee from the mug and let out a breath of satisfaction.

"Where's your boss this morning?" he asked the large bartender, making conversation.

"He's out back of here, been watching the fire since before daylight," said Dewey, giving a nod of his bald head toward the rear of the building.

"More fire?" Dock asked, curiously.

"Nope," said Dewey, "it's the same fire, just closer, is all. Wind changed again in the night. It crept closer down the hillsides toward us whilst we slept."

"Damn wildfires," Dock grumbled under his breath. He picked up his mug of coffee, made his way to the rear door, swung it open and stepped out onto the back porch. As soon as he walked outside, he smelled the burnt air and saw a thin gray haziness that hadn't been present only twenty minutes earlier. How did something this big and noticeable manage to sneak up all of a sudden? he pondered to himself. The roar of the fire still clung faintly to the distant horizon. Yet Latin knew it would grow louder as he stood with his morning coffee.

A hot breeze swept down a steep hillside behind the trading post. Higher up, at a distance of less than a thousand yards, he could not only see where the preceding gray smoke turned black; he could make out tall orange flames in the belly of the brown-black smoke. Twenty yards from the back porch, Bagley stood with his shoulders slumped, staring up at the wide inferno. He held a shotgun loosely at his side, as if given to the delusion that powder and shot might halt such a relentless beast.

"What say you, Bagley?" Dock called out, first taking his cigar from his lips. "Is it going to blow past?"

Bagley turned and gave him a grim stare and shook his head slowly. He walked back to the porch and looked up at the gunman.

"After all these years of missing these fires, this one slipped right in and got me," he said. "I expect you fellows will have to get yourself a new stopover on your way to the gulch."

Dock gave him a pointed look.

"How do you know about the gulch?" he asked.

"Hell, I've always known about it," said Bagley. "I just don't mention it. Keeping a closed lip is among a merchant's most important services on this frontier."

Dock only nodded and sipped his coffee.

"What'll you do if it burns you out? Rebuild?" he asked.

"No," said Bagley. "I'm getting too long in the tooth for starting over. I'll take my beating, gather up what I can, go somewhere and lick my wounds." He looked past Dock Latin and inside the open rear door. "Where's Cheyenne? It's getting to be late morning."

"About now, I'd guess he's rousting everybody up, getting them ready to ride on out of here."

"You'd be guessing right, Dock," Cheyenne's voice called out from inside the building behind him. Dock turned, seeing Cheyenne walk toward him across the plank floor. As Cheyenne stepped out onto the porch, he looked up at the fire raging in the distance.

"Something to see, ain't it?" Dock commented.

"Yes, it is," Cheyenne replied. Then he said, "I just woke everybody up. They're getting ready to ride. Are you all set?"

"I'm good," said Latin. "I'll just go get my horse."

As he turned and walked back inside, Bagley walked around to the edge of the porch and climbed the three steps.

"Riding out, are you?" he said as he walked over to Cheyenne.

"Yep," Cheyenne said, already knowing where this was headed.

"Then I'll need you to settle accounts with me," Bagley said, leaning the shotgun against the porch railing. He took a piece of paper from his shirt pocket and unfolded it. "I wrote down what you and your men have spent here, yesterday, last night."

"Yeah, well . . . ," said Cheyenne, turning as he spoke and closing the rear door, "I suppose we ought to talk about that." He turned back facing Bagley. "I'll be paying you my next time through here, like we've done before."

Bagley held the paper in his hand and said, "Except this ain't like before. I was just telling Dock, this fire is going to gut me. I'm taking what I can and calling it a game." He wagged the paper a little and said, "So I'll take what's owed me today and wish you and your men the best."

Cheyenne said in a firmer tone, "Let's not ruin a good relationship, Bagley. I'm going to clear the account the next time I see you. Something come up."

"Something *come up* . . . ?" Bagley looked all around, his hands spread in bewilderment. *What the hell could've come up?*

"Why are you crowding me on this?" Cheyenne asked, his whole demeanor turning bristly, his hand going to the butt of his Colt and resting there.

"I just told you, I need my money *now*," Bagley persisted. He didn't reach for the shotgun, but he rested his right hand on the porch railing where he'd leaned it.

"Not now, *next time*," Cheyenne said heatedly. "Trust me."

"Trust *you*?" said Bagley. "Do I look like a fool? You're an *outlaw*, an outlaw gang leader. Pay me." He drummed his stubby fingers on the porch railing. Cheyenne took note of the shotgun standing near.

Inside the building, Royal Tarpis had just stepped down from his horse as Dock Latin walked out the front door. The rest of the men sat their horses, looking up at Latin with grim hangover leers.

"Well, we're all here, damn it," Tarpis said. "Where's Cheyenne?"

"He's coming," said Dock. He saw Caroline Udall sitting atop a horse back behind the men.

"I don't know why the big hurry," said Tarpis. "We ought to get breakfast—some coffee." He thumbed toward Caroline. "The lady is probably hungry."

"At least let's take a wake-up bottle with us," said Tanner Riggs. "It just makes sense."

Before Dock Latin could reply, a blast of gunfire resounded through the building from the back porch and echoed off along the rocky hills.

"What the hell . . . !" said Dock, running to the rear door, his Colt coming up from his holster, cocked and ready. The rest of the men scrambled from their saddles and followed Royal Tarpis through the trading post. Dewey Fritz's first response was to drop to the floor behind the bar. But then he rose warily, saw the gunmen crossing the floor and bounded along behind them.

"Damn, Cheyenne! You've shot Bagley," Latin shouted, slinging the rear door open and staring out at Bagley, who stood holding on to the rail with one hand, his other hand clutching his bloody stomach.

"Straight through . . . my guts," Bagley said in a strained voice.

Cheyenne stood with his Colt smoking in his hand.

"You tried to shotgun me, you son of a bitch," Cheyenne lied, reaching a boot out and kicking the shotgun away from the railing.

"Like hell—" Bagley groaned.

"Shut up," Cheyenne said, cutting him short. "I'll shoot you again."

"Easy, boss," Dock Latin said to Cheyenne, his Colt out and cocked, but lowered now that he saw what was going on. "He's a goner anyway."

The men looked at each other.

"Not to sound cold and callous," said Riggs, "but any reason why we can't pull a cork and wipe some rye worms out of our eyes?"

"Take what suits you," Cheyenne said. To Bagley he said, "Teach you to jerk a shotgun on me." He reached his boot out and gave the wounded man a kick. Bagley stumbled backward, fell and rolled down the steps with a tortured grunt, then lay silent and limp on the ground as Cheyenne slipped his gun back into its holster.

"You heard the boss, fellows, *load up!*" Riggs said with a laugh of delight.

"Hell yes," said Lou Elkins, looking back at the bar, then at Dewey Fritz, who stood staring wide-eyed in fear. "You going to service us, barkeep, or do you want the same as Bagley got?" He eased his Colt up from his holster halfway and gave Dewey a good look at it.

"I'm on my way," said Dewey, turning quickly, hurrying back behind the bar.

"Looks like drinks are on the house," Elkins said with a wide, cruel grin.

Chapter 11

Following the thin stream, the rust-colored barb behind them, Sam and Gilley Maclaine walked through the aftermath of fire that had swept the area two days earlier. Smoke still curled from long, blackened pines lying stretched out on the charred ground. The three of them heard the crash of the big timbers falling to the earth here and there on the hillsides. The impact jarred the scorched and rocky ground beneath their feet. The barb sidled up to the Ranger each time another tree fell. The Ranger patted the horse's muzzle, comforting it as they traveled on.

In the afternoon they had reached a water hole farther down the trail below the same stream they'd followed until it had disappeared underground. They had traveled throughout the day, in and out of thick pockets of smoke, while higher up along the hillsides both in front and behind them, the wildfire continued to rage.

For the past two miles, the wind had lifted the smoke and moved it away to the northeast, allowing them to lower their bandanas from their mouths and breathe easier. Yet more thick black pockets stood low on the hillsides, covering the trail lying ahead of them.

Enjoy it while it lasts, Sam told himself, taking a long, clear breath and letting it out slowly.

At the water's edge Gilley flopped down, submerging her face into the coolness of it as she drank her fill. Sam walked the barb into the wide water hole and sank his canteen in the clear water. He dipped water into his sombrero and poured it all along the horse's back and neck, washing away the black soot but knowing it would soon return.

Gilley raised her head, gasped and slung her wet hair back and forth. She wiped her hands over her face, watched the Ranger for a moment in silence and smiled to herself.

"I can't decide if you always care this much for horses or if you're keeping this one fit thinking he might be our ticket out of here."

"Horses under man's care always seem to fare less than they deserve," Sam said, patting the barb's wet side, inspecting a small cut there. "Of the three of us, he's the only one who asked for none of this." He picked up the full canteen, capping it.

"I didn't *ask* to be here in a fire, Sam," Gilley objected. "Did you?"

"We both did, in a manner of speaking, ma'am," Sam said, hanging the canteen strap over his shoulder. "Our paths have pushed us both in this direction. The fire was here, no matter. Our prior actions chose to lead us right to it."

"That sounds a little crazy to me, Ranger," Gilley said.

"I can see where it would." Sam smiled a little.

"Are you talking down to me?" Gilley asked, cocking her head to the side.

"No, ma'am," he said. "I'm not talking *down* to you, just *directly*."

She watched him pour a sombrero full of water onto his own head. He swabbed his hair back, placed the sombrero atop his head and led the barb toward her.

Ma'am, always ma'am . . . , she thought.

Looking up at him from the water's edge, she said, "Tell me something, Sam Burrack, when are you going to start calling me Gilley?"

"Right now, *Gilley*," he said, reaching a wet hand down to her, helping her to her feet.

"Well, I don't believe it," she said, feigning shock. She stood up close to him and looked into his eyes. Her wet shirt clung to her bosom; the top button had come undone as she drank.

Sam saw the roundness of her exposed flesh and looked away.

"Fix your clothes, Gilley," he said quietly.

"Oh. . . ." She reached up and buttoned the shirt. "Aren't you just the gentleman?" she said playfully.

Sam didn't reply.

"You know, we don't have to be strangers, you and me. We can be close. Just because we met under—"

"No, we can't," Sam said, interrupting her.

"Why not?" she asked quietly.

"Back to those paths of ours and where they've led

us," Sam said. "I'm a lawman . . ." He let his words trail.

"And I'm an *outlaw*?" she asked.

After a pause of consideration, Sam said, "You put yourself with outlaws—outlaws that I'm hunting."

"I can't see what that's got to do with anything," she said.

"That's too bad," Sam said sincerely.

"And what if you weren't hunting these men?" she asked without pause.

"There is no *what if I weren't*," Sam said, "because *I am*."

She stepped back and put a hand on her hip.

"Is there any harm in speculating?" she asked.

Sam had started to turn, but he stopped and looked at her, taking in a deep breath.

"Yes, there is," he said firmly, gazing into her eyes. "You're a beautiful woman, Gilley. We don't have to say . . . we both know how things would be under other circumstances. But there are no other circumstances, and there never will be. I'm not going to go past that point." He turned and led the barb away, back into the water hole.

She stared after him.

"You're right," she said in a huff. "What was I thinking—*a lawman*?" She gave a short, contrived laugh. "You're *hardly* my type anyway."

The Ranger didn't respond.

"I don't get along well with the self-righteous, high-minded, *father* type. You and your *our prior actions, our paths led us here*." She took a step into the cool water. "What is all that malarkey anyway—something you say to starry-eyed town girls at some church social, under some stupid apple tree?"

Sam stopped and stared straight ahead, hearing her at the edge behind him, her voice filling with tears.

"Well, I don't need that kind of man," she cried out. "I don't need another *father*. I don't need you, *Ranger Sam Burrack!* I don't need anybody!"

She saw him turn and stand facing her, a look on his face that she could not read. In the distance, thick smoke filled with thrashing orange flames erupted and spilled down the hillside, a landside of fire.

"*No . . . No, Sam . . . ,*" she whispered to herself.

The Ranger watched her run out into the shallow water and splash toward him with abandon. Keeping the reins to the horse in hand, he caught her as she threw herself into his arms, sobbing.

"I didn't mean it, Sam! I didn't mean any of it," she said, her tears wet against his chest as she pressed her face there.

"I know, Gilley," the Ranger whispered, his arms around her, holding her in a way he had held few women in his life. "I understand . . . I was being hard on you—it was wrong."

"Hold me, Sam. That's all I want. Just hold me. I'm scared," she said into his chest. "This fire, what it's doing to everything around us. The way it comes and goes, but never really leaves. I can't take any more of it. It's like being stalked by something evil."

"It's going to be all right, Gilley," Sam whispered into her cheek, his arms pressing her to him. "I've got you. You're going to be all right. We all three are, you'll see."

"Even the horse?" Gilley asked, childlike, needing his reassurance. She held her eyes closed as if hoping when she opened them again, the terrible beast would be gone, the world would be back to itself.

"That's right, even the horse," Sam said.

Even as he spoke, he lifted his eyes toward the smoke and flames and toward the black, churning heavens. As he looked up he instinctively drew her tighter against him, feeling the heat of her through his clothes, the wetness of her tears on his chest through his shirt. He closed his eyes and saw himself lift her into his arms and carry her out of the water. He saw himself tasting her mouth so clearly that he had to open his eyes and remind himself it was not real, only passion playing itself out. The fire was getting to him too, he decided, cautioning himself.

They stood in the water hole until the water she had stirred up settled around them. At length, when Sam realized her fear had subsided, he whispered in her ear, "We've got to go on, Gilley."

She nodded slightly against his chest.

"I know, Sam," she whispered. "Give me a minute."

A minute . . . Sam nodded; he closed his eyes tight for a moment and tried to clear his mind of the two of them in each other's arms. He had to focus on the job at hand, yet he found it difficult to turn her loose.

Finally he did manage to hold her at arm's length. He looked at her closely and said almost in a whisper, "Are you ready to get back in the fire?"

Absently she shook her head *no*. She looked out across the last stretch of trail to Bagley's Trading Post. But then she took a breath and looked into Sam's eyes.

"Ready when you are," she said.

When the Ranger turned to walk away toward the trail, Gilley stepped in beside him and pulled his free arm up around her shoulders. She looped her arm around his waist as he led the barb. He looked at her. Behind him, even the barb forced itself closer to his side.

"Couldn't we just walk like this for a ways?" Gilley asked quietly, looking up into his eyes. Sam glanced ahead at a dark, broiling world filled with smoke and fire with a thin ribbon of trail winding through its middle. He took strength in the horse and the woman relying on him.

"I can't see why not," he replied, drawing her closer beside him as they walked on.

From atop a ridge overlooking the smoky trail, Red Gantry looked down a battered telescope at the Ranger and the woman trudging along, their faces half covered by bandanas, the horse walking behind them with a soot-blackened shirt wrapped and tucked around its muzzle. Through a wafting black veil, he recognized the Ranger by his pearl gray sombrero, the soot-smudged badge on his chest; Gilley he recognized by her clothes. He remembered the last time he'd seen her—when he and the other two men had left Cheyenne behind to kill her.

Cheyenne, you lying dog! Red thought to himself. "I warned you and warned you!" he caught himself saying aloud. "Now she's riding with the damned law, bringing a Ranger straight to us!"

He closed the telescope and gigged his horse up a

six-foot path to where the wagon sat on a thin trail. Cheyenne might have made the mistake of not killing the woman, but damned if he would.

At the wagon, he jerked his horse to a halt and looked at the Indian sitting comfortably relaxed on the hard, wooden seat. In the wagon bed, Segan Udall sat making more torches, winding strips of cloth around the end of long, straight tree limbs and dousing them with coal oil.

"Are you sure this is the last trail we need to torch?" he asked Little Foot.

Little Foot just stared at him coldly without an answer. They had set fire to woods and brush surrounding two of the three main trails leading up toward the trading post. This was the third. Anyone with three or more fingers to count on would know it, he thought.

"Do *not* make me ask you again, cripple," Gantry warned, his hand resting on the rifle lying across his lap.

"Yes," Little Foot said grudgingly. "There are three main trails. We have torched two. This is the third." As he spoke, he held up two fingers, then three to illustrate.

"Keep up your belligerent nature with me, you little goat-footed turd," Gantry threatened, "and you'll never see Bagley's Trading Post again."

He swung around in his saddle and said to Segan Udall with contempt, "You, *arsonist*, have you made up enough torches for us to work our way down this hillside, make a circle and come right back up to this trail?"

Segan stopped dousing the new torches with coal oil and gave him a curious look.

"Yes, but are you sure you want to do that?" he said.

In the wagon seat Little Foot listened and just shook his head.

"Hell yes, I'm sure," said Gantry. "There's a couple of folks I want to trap down there—cook to a cinder."

"Whoa," said Segan, "I start fires. I don't set out to kill people."

"Yeah? There's where we're different, you and me," Gantry said with a clever grin. "I set out to kill people, not to start fires." He nodded toward the fresh torches and said to Segan and Little Foot, "Gather them up, both of you, and climb down from the wagon. We're working out way down on foot and back."

Little Foot and Segan looked at each other. Then Little Foot turned to Gantry.

"When he asked if you're sure," he said, "he was talking about the wind." As he spoke he looked down the hillside to the right, seeing large stands of dried wild grass sway on the wind among the rock and scattered woodlands.

"To hell with the wind," said Gantry. "Get your crippled ass back there, grab up the torches and let's get to work. These folks will be rounding up this trail toward us within an hour. I want them to run into a wall of fire." He stepped down from his saddle, walked his horse to the rear of the wagon and hitched it there. "We'll walk down a ways, light these torches and heave them as far as we can, just like before—let Mother Nature take things from there."

Gathering several torches under his arm, Segan

stepped down from the wagon bed with long matches standing in his shirt pocket. He took several matches and stuck them in Little Foot's shirt pocket as the Indian lowered himself from the wagon and wobbled for a second until he gained his balance. They both moved back and waited beside the wagon for Gantry.

"I don't like doing this anymore, Indian," Segan said under his breath, "not when it comes to killing *people*."

"Me neither. I was only supposed to show you two to these trails," Little Foot said. "I don't like starting fires and killing *anything*."

"Oh?" Segan looked Little Foot up and down and asked, "Why are you here, then?"

"For whiskey money," Little Foot said without hesitation. "Why are you?" He gave Segan a knowing look.

"You know why I'm here," he said, "to keep harm from coming to my wife."

"Your wife . . . ," said Little Foot, giving him a strange look.

"That's right," Segan said. "What about her?"

Gantry heard them as he walked from the rear of the wagon.

"If you think your wife didn't open her knees for the Cheyenne Kid before you were even out of sight, you're as stupid as you look, *arsonist*," he said with a dark chuckle.

Segan stood staring for moment in stunned outrage as Gantry reached into the wagon bed and picked up a couple of torches and the tin of coal oil. He struggled to keep his head, yet his fists had already started opening and closing at his sides.

He said through clenched teeth, "He gave me his word—"

"That he wouldn't force himself on her, you damned rube," Gantry laughed, finishing his words for him. "I haven't seen a woman that Cheyenne has had to force himself on. Women draw to him like flies to sugar." He laughed again. "She just might be *forcing her*self onto him, over and over and over—"

"Stop it! Take it back, you son of a bitch!" Segan blurted out, moving a step toward Gantry.

"Come on, *arsonist*," said Gantry, his Colt streaking up from his holster, cocked, aimed at Segan's belly. "You caught me by surprise last time. I'm ready for you this time! Make your move. I'll put a bullet—"

Segan's big hand swatted the Colt straight down from Gantry's hand and knocked the gunman backward with a long but fast roundhouse punch to his jaw. The Colt exploded on the hard ground and sent a bullet slicing through the tin of coal oil.

Little Foot stood staring as the two men fell to the ground, the wagon horses turning nervous at the sound of the gunshot. Beside the wagon, coal oil poured freely from its tin and spread on the ground and back under the wagon.

Uh-oh! This is going bad, Little Foot told himself. He limped in, grabbed the Colt and stepped back with it in his hand.

"Both of you, *stop!*" Little Foot shouted, raising the Colt and firing a shot straight up in the air.

On the ground, the two men separated quickly and rose to their feet, staring at the Colt in Little Foot's hand.

"Don't shoot, I've stopped!" said Segan, moving toward the armed Indian.

"I'm not!" Gantry shouted, wanting revenge. He snatched a torch up from the ground, ran up behind Segan and began beating him on his head and shoulders with it. The blows came so hard and fast that all Segan could do was roll away and curl up, covering his head with his forearms.

Little Foot fired the Colt in warning once more. This time Gantry turned to him and gave him a hard stare.

"It's over, cripple," he said. He held his hand out toward Little Foot. "Give me my gun."

"Don't . . . do it," Segan warned in a strained voice.

But Little Foot stood watching intently as Gantry walked toward him with a murderous look in his eyes. "You'll give me my damn gun if you know what's good for you."

"Wait," said Little Foot, letting out a tight breath. He let the hammer down on the Colt, turned it backward in his hand and pitched it butt-first to Gantry.

Gantry caught it and looked at it in surprise with a thin smile, as if he'd not really expected the Indian to give it up.

"Well, well, much obliged, cripple," he said. Then he cocked the Colt and fired. The bullet caused Little Foot to stagger backward.

On the ground, Segan lowered his face to the dirt and shook his head as the shot resounded out and echoed along the hillsides.

Chapter 12

Red Gantry stood facing Little Foot, who swayed in place, both hands holding his right side just above his hip. Blood ran down from his side and down his leg, seeping through his thin trousers and spreading atop his calf-high moccasin. Beside Gantry the wagon horses were spooked, nickering as he held the one nearest him with his free hand.

"Here's how it all played down, cripple," he said to Little Foot. "I tried my damnedest to get along with the two of yas, but you're both too hardheaded. You were half-drunk to begin with, talking weird, about scalping and that kind of stuff."

Little Foot just stared.

Gantry gave him an evil grin and wagged his Colt toward where Segan still lay on the ground, half-conscious from his beating with a torch handle. "This one, all he talked about was getting back with the others and killing Cheyenne." He shrugged. "I couldn't reason with him—had to kill him."

"You . . . won't get away with this . . . Gantry," Little

Foot said in a strained voice. "The Great Spirit . . . will see to it you—"

"Hold that thought," Gantry said, cutting him off, "while I go put a bullet or two in ol' *arsonist's* head for him. I'll take care of you next thing, I promise."

"You murdering bastard . . . you snake," Little Foot growled through his pain.

"Huh-uh, it's too late to try sweet-talking me," said Gantry. He chuckled. "Just wait right there."

But Little Foot wasn't about to stand waiting help-less, doing nothing to save himself. As soon as Gantry turned and stepped away from the horses, back along-side the wagon, and onto the dark wide circle of coal oil, the wounded Indian jerked a match from his shirt pocket. He struck it down his leather suspenders, pitched it underhanded and jumped back as flames leaped waist high, engulfing Red Gantry.

The burning outlaw let out a long, terrible scream. The tin of coal oil ignited where the potent fuel spewed from the bullet hole. The force and pressure of the burning coal oil propelled the tin container eight feet into the air, shooting out a long tail of liquid fire. Gantry—in his mindless panic—caught it on its way down and clutched it tight against his chest.

"*My God!*" Segan shouted, wincing hard at the sight of Gantry running off down the hillside, flames streak-ing out behind him.

But Little Foot didn't wince; he didn't so much as blink. He watched stonily as Gantry bounded, ran and rolled, sizzling and screaming. At the same time the team of horses took off in the other direction, the reins to Gantry's horse spinning free from the rear of the wagon. The wagon speeded away, flames licking and waving behind it. Gantry's frightened horse ran in a wild circle and came right back to Little Foot and Segan.

Segan lay staring in horror. In a shaky voice he said, "They say when a person's on fire you should knock him down and roll him in the dirt."

"Yeah?" said Little Foot. "Next time we'll know." He stared down at a black, greasy rise of smoke where Gantry had finally fallen among the rocks. Every few yards away, another patch of brush stood aflame in Gantry's wake. In the other direction, a hundred yards off, the wagon horses stood freed of the burning wagon.

"We're through here," Little Foot said, stepping wide of the burning circle of coal oil, over to where Segan lay in the dirt. He reached a hand down and helped Segan to his feet.

"What about the two riders he saw down there?" Segan asked.

"What about them?" asked Little Foot. "They heard the gunshot. They see the smoke, the fire. They've got no choice but to get through it."

"Then what about us?" said Segan, not seeming to know what to do.

"I don't know about you," said Little Foot. "I'm taking the horse and getting out of here. I'm wounded."

Segan looked at Gantry's horse and said, "We could double up."

"Huh-uh," said Little Foot. "Don't even think about it. Get one of the wagon horses if you don't want to walk." He turned and limped away toward Gantry's horse without looking back.

"I'm going after my wife, that's what!" Segan called out.

"Good for you," Little Foot said over his shoulder without looking back.

"If I get one of the wagon horses, can I ride with you a ways?"

"Suit yourself," said Little Foot. "But I won't wait for you. I feel my warrior blood rising." He pressed his hand to his wound and kept walking.

On the trail below, the Ranger and Gilley had heard the gunshot and the screams echo down the steep, sloping hills. Moments later, as they drew closer, they saw the sudden stream of fire rolling up from the burning brush among the rocks, followed by the rise of smoke. They stopped long enough to see the wind sweep the fire across their trail.

Watching, the Ranger felt Gilley's fingers go around his forearm and tighten there. "I—I don't think I can take any more of it," she said.

"Yes, you can," Sam said in a confident tone of voice. "The way the wind is blowing right now, we're going to space ourselves and weave right through it."

He turned his gaze toward her. They looked at each other's soot-streaked faces above the bandanas covering half their faces. Sam saw the fear in her eyes. He didn't want to lie to her.

"It's going to be hot, but we've got to keep moving. If we stop, it's got us." He took her hand in his and walked on, giving a jerk on the reins, pulling the frightened barb up on his other side.

"You've been through lots of these wildfires, then?" Gilley asked nervously.

The Ranger didn't answer.

"Sam, have you?" she persisted.

"No, Gilley," he said. "I've never been through anything like this in my life. But it doesn't matter, we've got no choice. We're getting through it."

Ahead of them the fire billowed and rose and twisted high and sidelong across their trail. Yet there was something in his voice, a strength and determination that sounded equal to that of the roaring flames.

"Keep hold of my hand," he said, giving a firm squeeze. "Stare down at the ground if you have to, but don't stop . . . don't turn loose no matter what."

They walked on, at times through what appeared to be a long, wide tunnel of orange, billowing flame. With her head bowed, she still caught sight of the flames licking above them, appearing and disappearing like angry fiery apparitions. Then, just when she knew beyond doubt that the fire would surely take her to the ground and devour her, it would dissipate as the wind died down, caught its breath and readied itself for another round.

"Gilley, are you with me?" she heard the Ranger ask her. She tried to answer, but she wasn't sure if the words came from her lips or only resounded inside her own head.

She felt the Ranger's arms raise her off the ground as the fire and wind fell away for a moment. Then she felt herself atop the horse, slumped on its neck, feeling it trudge forward beneath the blackened sky.

"It's moving away from us," she heard the Ranger say, or thought she heard him say.

"Thank God . . . ," she heard herself say as if from somewhere deep inside a terrible dream, and she allowed herself to fall away into unconsciousness with each rise and fall of the horse's hooves.

It was late afternoon when the Ranger led the barb up along the switchback stretch of trail leading to Bagley's Trading Post. Gilley Maclaine still lay collapsed on the barb's back. Traveling through the final two miles of thick pine smoke left a patina of black smudge covering her, the horse and the Ranger as they trudged the last few yards to the hitch rail and stopped and swayed in place for a moment. Sam pulled the bandana from across the bridge of his nose. His saddlebags hung over his shoulder covered with a thin layer of ash and black soot.

"Keep moving, stranger," said Dewey Fritz, who stood watching from a front window. "Take your pal and your worn-out cayuse with you, else I'll scatter-gun you where you stand."

Something in the man's voice sounded like a bluff. Sam didn't believe it. He looked all around at the silver-gray haze hanging like a thin veil over the trail and the land surrounding the trading post.

"Can't do it," he said in a hoarse and raspy tone. "I'm an Arizona Territory Ranger in pursuit of bank robbers. This woman is nearly done in. She needs water. I can pay for it—"

"Woman?" said Dewey, cutting him off. He strained

for a better look at the small figure slumped atop the barb, a bandana covering her face.

"Ranger Burrack . . . ," said another voice, this one belonging to the wounded Bagley. His voice sounded weak and pained. He lowered it and said to Fritz, "Let them in, Dewey. I've got . . . things the Ranger needs to hear."

"All right, come on in, then," Dewey said, stepping out onto the porch, a shotgun draped over his forearm, a bandana gathered beneath his fleshy chin. "I'm just doing my job here. Don't think harshly of me, Ranger."

Sam looked him up and down, too tired and smoked out to care.

"I heard Bagley's voice. Where is he?" he said, his voice still dry and raspy.

"He's inside," said Dewey, stepping down as Sam reached up and lowered Gilley to the ground. "Want me to carry her?" He sounded excited at the prospect.

Gilley managed to raise her head and look at the big bartender, then turn to the Ranger.

"I've got her," Sam said, putting a tired arm up around her and lowering her from the barb's back. He held her leaning against his side.

Dewey watched them closely as they staggered up the steps and into the trading post.

"Get them some water, Dewy," came Bagley's pained voice.

Inside the front door, Sam looked all around as Dewey hurried away behind the bar, picked up a large water gourd and came walking back with it.

"Back here, Ranger," said Bagley, sitting at a small

table in a shadowy corner. He watched the Ranger hold the mouth of the gourd to Gilley's parched lips and let her drink. "I'll tell you before you get here . . . I'm a mess. I've been shot bad."

"Who shot you, Bagley?" Sam asked, lowering the gourd and pouring a little of the cool water into his hand. He raised his cupped hand and swabbed the water around on Gilley's face. Then he walked back to where Bagley sat at a short table among stacks of wool blankets, beneath a row of pegs holding cooking utensils along the wall.

"Take a guess," Bagley said, looking up at him through pained, fading eyes. A big Remington revolver lay on the table near Bagley's bloody right hand. His left hand held a bath towel against his large bloody belly.

"The Cheyenne Kid," Sam said without hesitancy. He put Gilley down onto the stacks of blankets and helped her lean over onto her side while he talked to the badly wounded trading post owner.

Bagley gave a dark, strained chuckle.

"You kind of know us ol' boys, eh, Ranger?"

"Yep," Sam said. He raised the gourd to his lips and took a long drink, then filled his cupped hand and rubbed the water on his blackened face as he spoke.

"'Us ol' boys'?" Sam said, quoting him. "Are you saying you've been one of them?" He looked at Bagley's tortured face.

"Right up . . . 'til today," said Bagley, fighting a surge of pain racking through his stomach. "I know all you lawmen always thought it . . . never could prove it, though."

Sam surveyed all the blood—on the floor, on Bagley's chest and stomach, on the towel, the table.

"You figure you're dying?" he asked.

"What's your thinking on it?" Bagley said, lifting the bloody, wadded-up towel enough to give Sam a look behind it. "The son of a bitch shot me so close it caught my shirt afire." He coughed and held the towel back in place. "Bullet's hung somewhere in my damn hipbone—hurts like hell. Yeah, I figure I'm gone." He glanced at the Remington. If I ain't dead by dark . . . I'm taking it upon myself. I ain't sitting here and burning alive."

"Where's he and his gang headed?" Sam asked, focusing back on his purpose in being there.

"I knew you'd get around to that," Bagley said.

"He's no good, Bagley," Sam said with finality. "Tell me where he's headed."

Bagley grinned weakly and nodded.

"Hell, I know he's no good," he said. "I knew that long before he killed me. But the others haven't . . . wronged me in any way." He paused as searing pain rose from the bullet lodged deep in his hip. "But I expect you'll kill them too. I heard you like killing."

"You heard wrong," Sam said. "If they give themselves up, I'll take them in." He stared pointedly at the wounded man. "How many men you know want to give up their guns and go to prison?"

"I know . . . what you mean," Bagley said, his voice starting to sound even weaker, more labored.

"Tell me where they're headed," Sam persisted.

"Ah, hell," said Bagley, "they'll head where they

always head when somebody's hunting them—
Dutchman's Gulch."

"Blind Gully?" Sam said.

"Yeah, some also call it that," said Bagley. "Some
call it Dutchman's Gulch. You'll pick their tracks up
out front." He raised the blood-soaked towel from his
belly and wrung it between his thick hands. Blood
splattered heavily on the plank floor. "Ever seen that
much blood . . . from one human being?"

"It's a lot," Sam said. "How long ago did they leave?"

"This morning after sunup," Dewey Fritz said, speaking for his wounded boss. He stepped in and stood
beside the table. He reached down, took the bloody towel
and laid a fresh one in its place. "They argued over what
he owed for the drinking and the tents, and Cheyenne
shot him." He stared at the Ranger, then added, "He's
got a woman with him, you know."

"He does?" Sam said.

Gilley looked at the big bartender for confirmation.

"He does," said Dewey, nodding his bald head. "Her
husband was out there starting fires—crazy as a June
bug, that one. All because him and his woman haven't,
you know . . ."

Sam just stared at him.

Bagley gave a dark chuckle, gripping the fresh towel
to his stomach.

"Cheyenne has always had . . . a terrible weakness
for the womenfolk," he said haltingly as pain rippled
through his stomach and hip at the same time. "It's got
him in trouble . . . the last two gangs he rode with." He
gritted his teeth, stared at Gilley and asked, "Are you
the one he left out there to burn up?"

"That son of a bitch," Gilley said, in spite of her exhausted condition.

Sam watched her hang her head in shame.

"When are you leaving here, Bagley?" Sam asked the wounded merchant. "It looks like the fires are going to wipe you out this time around."

"I ain't leaving," said Bagley. "I'm dying anyway . . . why not here?"

"We'll take you with us," Sam said. "You can die somewhere else, away from the fire."

"Why would I do that?" Bagley asked. He patted a bloody hand on the big Remington. "This big banger will take me wherever I'm going."

"This is a bad way to die," Sam offered.

Bagley shrugged and said, "Once I'm dead . . . what does it matter how *bad* I died?"

"What about your bartender?" Sam asked.

"Dewey Fritz?" said Bagley. "He says he's staying too. He figures I'm dead. . . . This place doesn't burn, it's all his." He gave a weak laugh that ended in a cough. "Running a business . . . has always had its risks."

"We need a horse for the woman, some saddles if you've got any," Sam said.

"I have three horses," said Bagley. "Twenty dollars each, including saddles . . . thirty for the mare. Cash, of course . . . I'm past taking anything of a promissory nature."

"What can we do for you, Bagley?" Sam asked flatly, knowing there was no point in wasting his breath trying to get the man to leave.

Bagley didn't answer. He only shook his lowered head.

"Pay Fritz for that horse and rigging," he said in a pained voice.

Beyond the walls of the trading post, the deep roar of the fire echoed in off the rocky surrounding hillsides.

Sam reached into his saddlebags for a fold of cash he carried there. He counted out twenty dollars and dropped it on the bloody tabletop.

"I'll just pay you while I'm here," he said. He looked at Gilley and asked, "Are you able to ride?"

"I wish I could eat, get some rest, maybe drink some more water," she said.

"Can you do all that while we ride?" Sam asked.

She staggered to her tired feet and dusted the seat of her trousers.

"Yeah, sure, why not?" she said. "If it gets me farther from this blasted fire."

Chapter 13

In spite of his side wound, Little Foot rode hard, Segan right beside him, having caught up to the Indian on one of the wagon horses. The two had circled wide of the trading post and pushed their horses hard, farther up the trail, until the blackish smoke and the raging fire lay below them. From a high ledge, they stopped long enough to look down behind them, seeing the black-orange fire blow across an open stretch of wild grass between two stands of pine.

"I'm glad that's all behind me," Segan said with a sigh, looking back as far as his eyes could see at the devastation the wildfire—both his and nature's—had wielded on the wildlife and woodlands. "This being drought and fire season, I can't say how much was mine and how much wasn't." He paused, then said, "But I almost wish I hadn't done it at all."

The son of a bitch. . . . Little Foot just stared at him. He was sick of hearing about this man's wife and her first husband. He hadn't shut up about it since they'd out-ridden the fire.

"It's just that I went so wild-crazy, every time I thought of my Caroline being with another man, I had to hurt something. Else I would have exploded inside." He turned and stared at Little Foot. His eyes glistened with tears. "Have you ever had anything hurt that bad?"

Little Foot looked him up and down indignantly, offended that a white man should even ask him such a question. Then he jerked the horse around and rode it at a walk over away from the ridge to where a hillside of pine rose steeply from their trail.

"Wait," said Segan, "I meant no harm. I was considering everything I done, wondering if I should somehow make recompense for it."

Little Foot turned in his saddle and looked at him as he rode on.

"You think I would know?" he said.

"I was hoping you might offer some advice, I suppose," Segan said, riding beside him, both horses at a walk, cooling down.

Little Foot jerked his horse to a halt and stared at Segan, as if being put upon to even speak about such matters.

"Because this widow woman was once in the arms of her dead husband, your craziness has led her into the arms of yet another man?" he asked, sorting through it.

"I know how crazy it is," said Segan. "I know that right now she's with Cheyenne, doing God knows what. He gave me his word, but they're still doing it. I know they are!" He swallowed a knot in his throat and said, "I'm a blind, jealous fool, and there's nothing I can do to stop it."

Little Foot shook his head slowly.

"You should take a gun and shoot yourself in the head," he said flatly.

Segan looked at the butt of the big Colt standing above the edge of the Indian's trousers. Something grim and dark flashed across his mind for a moment, but he managed to shake it away.

"There's no cause for you to say something like that," he said, turning tight-lipped. He put his horse forward a few feet ahead of Little Foot.

But Little Foot saw the wagon horse jolt to a halt and rear up in terror so suddenly that Segan slid from the horse's bare back and hit the rocky ground, still managing to hold on to the long wagon reins he was using. No sooner had Segan fallen than Little Foot's horse also spooked at the sight of a thin, soot-smudged panther cub wobbling in the middle of the trail facing them.

Little Foot turned his horse sharply to the side and brought it to a halt sitting quarter-wise to the snarling cub. He patted the horse's withers, settling it.

"Shoot it, shoot it!" Segan shouted, seeing the cub snarl at him from twenty feet away.

Little Foot stared at the cub for a moment, then reached over, took the wagon horse's reins from Segan's hands and jerked the spooked animal back a step, getting it under control.

Seeing the ragged condition of the cub, Little Foot shook his head in sympathy for the small, frightened creature.

"Leave it be," he said. "It has lost its mother, to the fire, no doubt. It's mindless—doesn't know what it's doing."

"I see," Segan said, collecting himself, picking at the seat of his trousers. "It surprised me, is all," he added.

"Leave it alone. It will walk away pretty soon," Little Foot said.

"Pretty soon . . . ?" Segan said, a little embarrassed, needing to make up for having been so rattled by such a small animal. "We needn't wait all day while it makes up its mind."

"It is scared and lost," said Little Foot. "The fire has destroyed its lair."

"Watch this." Segan seemed not to hear him as he walked forward.

Oh . . . So you must fool with it. Little Foot watched blank-faced in silence; he crossed his wrists on his saddle horn. Patient.

Approaching the small cat, Segan stomped his big boots up and down on the ground to frighten the cub off the trail.

"Get out of here, pussy!" he growled, spreading his arms high and wide to shoo the little cat away.

The cub only cringed and crouched down in place as Segan stalked forward.

"Stubborn little pussy, huh?" he chuckled.

But his chuckle vanished as a sudden flash of tan-colored fur, of tail, claws and fangs streaked from out of nowhere, over the cub's cowering head and straight into Segan's open arms, taking him to the ground.

Segan screamed long and loud, his voice in strange duo with the snarl and growl of the big panther atop him, its back arched high, mauling, clawing, biting, slashing.

Well, he was wrong about the mother cat being dead,

Little Foot told himself. *So . . . ?* He shrugged mentally. *He didn't know.*

He watched in rapt fascination as the big cat rose on its hinds on Segan's stomach and slapped his head back and forth as if it were some child's ball in play.

Little Foot shook his head slowly as he raised the Colt from its holster, cocked it and took aim, hearing Segan screaming, pleading for help.

Yet, before squeezing the trigger, he noted that somehow Segan had managed to roll sidelong and wrestle himself atop the cat now, pinning it to the ground—a new twist of sorts, Little Foot thought.

He lowered the pistol a little for a second, staring at the snarling, screaming mass of man and cat. While Segan held the cat down, both hands clutching its throat, he turned his bloody face toward Little Foot in wide-eyed terror.

"Shoot iiiit! Please God! Shoot it!" he bellowed.

In a calm, level voice, Little Foot said, "I'm afraid I'll hit you."

Then in a flash, the cat's hind paws came up under Segan's belly, throwing him a high flip in the air.

Segan hit the ground on his knees; the cat backed into a crouch and got ready to pounce again.

"For God's sake, shoot iiiit!" he screamed again, tearfully.

Almost before he got the scream out of his lungs, the big Colt exploded, not once, but twice in Little Foot's hand.

The cat jumped three feet in the air, turned its ducked head toward Little Foot, then backed away toward its cub. Little Foot saw where half of the big cat's ear was missing; dried blood streaked its side and shoulder.

With the Colt still pointed straight up in the air, smoke curling from its barrel, Little Foot watched the big cat reach down, grab its cub by the scruff of its neck, jerk it up from the ground and leap out of sight up onto the treed hillside.

Little Foot watched Segan collapse forward from his knees onto the rocky ground. With the smoking Colt cocked, Little Foot waited a full minute or more before stepping down from his saddle and leading both horses forward. Segan lay facedown, bleeding, shivering, moaning into the earth. Most of his trousers and shirt were gone, slashed away. Blood circled under him and spread in every direction on the dirt.

"That was the cub's mother," Little Foot said, blank-faced.

"Hel—help me," Segan groaned. "Water . . ."

Little Foot looked all around again warily before letting the hammer down on the cocked Colt and sticking the big pistol back down into the waist of his trousers. He turned to his horse, took down a canteen and stooped down beside Segan, rolling him over onto his back.

As he uncapped the canteen and held Segan's bloody head up so he could take a drink, he didn't see the Ranger and Gilley ride into sight on the trail behind him, thirty yards away.

"You wouldn't shoot . . . ," Segan rasped, clutching the canteen in his bloody, mauled hands.

"I told you I was afraid I would shoot you," Little Foot said quietly. "Besides, you had no business mess-ing with the mother cat's little cub." He also held the canteen, helping Segan drink.

"Look at me," said Segan, his face a mass of dark blood, deep claw marks, puncture wounds. "I'm ruined. You should have took the shot."

"Maybe so. . . ." Little Foot thought about things for a moment, then said, "Do you want me to shoot you now?"

Segan gave it some thought.

But before either one could say any more on the matter, they both turned their eyes toward the sound of hooves and saw the Ranger and Gilley riding closer, moving at a gallop now that the Ranger had spotted a man on the ground.

Upon seeing the Ranger and the woman, Little Foot jerked a bandana from his hip pocket, wet it with water from the canteen and swiped it across Segan's raw, claw-torn face. He stood up and waved his arms back and forth as the two riders drew closer. When they were close enough for him to see the badge on the Ranger's chest, Little Foot dropped his arms to his side and stood waiting. The two stopped and looked down at him, at his bloodstained shirt and at the wounded man on the ground.

"We heard shooting," Sam said, swinging down from the barb, Gilley getting off her own horse beside him. "What happened to you two?"

"A cat got him a little while ago," Little Foot said, gesturing a hand toward Segan. "I was shot in my side by a man named Red Gantry. One of the men you're looking for."

Sam looked him up and down.

"How do you know who I'm looking for?" he asked, knowing Little Foot was the Indian who worked for Bagley at the trading post.

"Because the Cheyenne Kid and his men think you might be on their trail," said Little Foot. He looked at Gilley, then added, "He sent us out here to set fires on any trail you might be riding."

"Just as a safety measure?" Sam asked.

"Yes," said Little Foot. He pointed down at Segan. "Cheyenne got the idea from this one. He is the one who started the fires. Red Gantry was the one Cheyenne sent to make certain he did his job. But Gantry burned himself up."

Segan lay staring up at the Ranger. His face had started bleeding again.

"I did what I had to do to protect my wife," he said. "But I swear to God, I'll never burn nothing again as long as I live."

Sam looked around. Evening shadows had grown long across the hills.

"Don't talk right now," he said to Segan. "It's just going to make you bleed worse. Lie still. We'll make camp and get you bandaged up first. Then you can both tell me everything."

"Obliged . . . ," said Segan with a fading voice.

In the flickering glow of a campfire, Little Foot watched the Ranger and Gilley clean and dress Segan's countless wounds. As he observed them, he cut a corner of cloth off his own shirttail, pressed it to the wound in his side and left it stuck there in his blood. He told the

Ranger everything, about Segan being forced to ride out and start the fires while the Cheyenne Kid held Caroline Udall hostage.

Hearing the story, Sam looked down into Segan's eyes searching for confirmation.

"He—he gave me his word nothing would happen to my wife," he said as Gilley stayed busy bandaging cuts on Segan's face, arms, hands, stomach, legs, shoulders, back and head. "I've got to get to Caroline, Ranger," he said, hurting so bad he couldn't keep from shaking violently all over. "You ca-can't hold me here for anything. I ha-haven't broken any law."

Little Foot cut in, saying, "You have burned down the frontier, you fool!"

"There's no la-law against it," Segan replied sharply. "This is wilderness. It belongs to the government, but there's no law against starting a fire anywhere I want to start one." He stared up at the Ranger, shivering in pain, sweating feverishly. "Tell him, Ranger, tell him," he said.

"There's no law saying a man can't start a fire out here anywhere he sees fit," Sam said. "This is a free country."

"Then, I'm fr-free to go when the woman is finished with me?" he asked.

"You're out of your head, mister," Sam said. "You're not going anywhere until we get you treated proper. These rags and bandanas aren't going to keep you from bleeding to death for long." He turned to Little Foot and asked, "How far are we from Mandell Settlement?"

"Three hours at the most," said Little Foot, "if we

don't run into fires—" He glared down at Segan. "If some madman hasn't burned the settlement to the ground."

Sam stared at Gilley in the firelight. She glanced down at Segan's scarcely dressed wounds and shook her head slightly in appraisal of the bandages. There was no hiding the severity of his wounds.

"He needs treating quick," she said. "His belly is the worst. There's not much holding him together there."

Sam looked up at the clear purple sky, at a three-quarter moon standing overhead. He stood and took off his duster, then his shirt. He threw the shirt to Gilley.

"Tear it into wide strips," he said to her. "Bind him good and tight."

"We'll need more than this," Gilley said, already ripping the shirt apart.

"I'll get the shirt we tied around the horse's muzzle," Sam said. As he picked up his duster and put it back on, he looked down at Little Foot pointedly.

Little Foot shook his head.

"This is the only shirt I own, Ranger," he said. "Anyway, I don't know if this fool is worth it."

"We need your shirt," he said quietly. "I'll see to it you get a new one at the settlement."

Little Foot stood up, grudgingly unbuttoned his shirt and took it off. The cloth he had pressed to the wound on his side had already begun to dry in place.

"Every time I deal with a white man, I lose my shirt," he said in a stoic voice. He threw the shirt down beside Gilley and stared at the Ranger. "I'll just get our horses ready," he said.

"I'll help you," the Ranger replied.

"Don't you trust me, Ranger Burrack?" Little Foot asked as he limped along beside the Ranger. He sounded the least bit offended.

"Yes, I trust you," Sam said. "I trust you every bit as much as you trust me. Does that square us up?"

Little Foot smiled thinly to himself.

"Yes, we're squared up," he said. "But when I get my new shirt, I want a bottle of whiskey for my trouble."

"You've got it," Sam said.

Little Foot looked at Sam as they walked along.

"The woman rides a horse I've been feeding at Bagley's for the past month. Both of your saddles come from there."

"That's right," said Sam. "We lost two of our horses and both our saddles to the fire on our way there."

"Has the fire reached Bagley's?" he asked.

"It was getting close when we left there last night," Sam said.

"What about Bagley and Fritz the bartender?" he asked. "Did they leave?"

"No," Sam said. "The Cheyenne Kid shot Bagley in his guts. Bagley said he was staying there to die. He had a Remington ready on the table for when the fire got too close. I figured it was his choice."

Little Foot considered it.

"You did good, Ranger," said Little Foot. "It is a warrior's death."

"Bagley was no warrior," Sam said. "He was a merchant . . . and an outlaw as it turns out."

"A man does not have to live as a warrior in order to die like one," Little Foot said, limping along on his small, withered foot.

"I suppose that's true enough," Sam said. "A man does not have to be a warrior to have a warrior's heart."

"Yes, a warrior's heart." Little Foot nodded in agreement, limping beside him, his chest out, his chin up. "That son of a bitch Cheyenne," he said. "I should ride with you and take his scalp, as vengeance for shooting my friend Bagley."

"Don't push it, Little Foot," Sam said. "I'm not out for vengeance. I'm out to uphold the law."

Chapter 14

In the middle of the night, the Ranger and Gilley Maclaine rode into the frontier mining settlement of Mandell. During the moonlit ride, the Ranger had made sure to keep Little Foot and Segan Udall in front of him where he could fix an eye on them. Segan sat limp and wobbly in the saddle the entire trip. When they arrived at the settlement, Gilley jumped down from her horse and ran into a part-shack, part-tent saloon; it was the only structure in Mandell with a lamp still glowing at that hour of night.

"What the hell . . . ?" said a half-drunken bartender who stood behind a makeshift bar shaking a leather dice cup in his hand as Gilley entered suddenly and held the tent fly open wide. Two bleary-eyed miners turned and stared as the Ranger and Little Foot carried Segan through the open fly.

"Is there a doctor in the settlement?" Gilley asked the bartender.

"No," the bartender said, "our doctor quit us and went to Denver three months back." He stared past her at the sight of what appeared to be a blood-soaked mummy. The Ranger had helped Segan lie down on a battered faro table. "What happened to this poor soul?" the bartender asked. Segan's right arm fell off the edge of the table and swung back and forth like some bloody, ragged pendulum.

"A panther got him," Gilley said, a little out of breath. "He needs sewing up, bad."

The bartender gave a dark grin, still staring at the bloody, bandaged man on the gambling table.

"Hell, I can sew him up, far as that goes," he said. Seeing the badge on Sam's chest, he called out to him, "Always willing to help the law."

"Obliged for your offer," Sam said, "but who's been tending your miners since your doctor left?"

"That would be Madeline Moorham," the bartender said, pointing off into the darkness. "She's a nurse— lives in the last tent on the right nearest the mine trail. Be careful how you wake her. She sleeps heeled," he said, turning to Gilley, who had already walked toward the open fly.

"Do you serve Indians?" Little Foot asked, limping to the bar, bare-chested, wiping his palms on his trousers.

"No, we don't," said the bartender, "leastwise not wild blanket Indians."

The two miners stared drunkenly.

"He's not a blanket Indian," Sam said. "He's with me. He gave up his shirt for bandages."

The bartender looked at Sam and picked up a bottle from a shelf behind him. Turning to the two miners, he asked, "What say you, fellows? Give an Indian a drink?"

The two miners looked Little Foot up and down.

"I know him," said one. "He works for Bagley at the trading post."

"I don't know if that's a sound endorsement or not," said the bartender. He chuckled and poured a shot glass of rye, then slid it across the bar to Little Foot. As Little Foot drank, Sam walked out the tent fly to the horses. He looked off in the direction the bartender had pointed Gilley and saw her and another woman walking hurriedly back to the tent saloon. He took the saddlebags from behind his saddle and draped them over his shoulder.

Gilley eyed the saddlebags as she and the woman passed the Ranger and walked inside the tent.

Sam followed the two women inside the tent and stood to the side as the tall, broad-shouldered nurse set a leather bag on the table beside Segan and leaned over him for a better look.

"Good Lord Almighty! A mama-cat done all this?" she said to Gilley, shaking her head at the bloody mess stretched out before her. "What was he trying to do to her?"

"You might be getting too damn personal, Madeline," the bartender said with a dark, drunken chuckle.

"I need hot water, Russell, not jokes," the nurse said to him over her shoulder. She turned back to Segan and began loosening his bloody bandages and dropping them to the floor.

The two miners and Little Foot stood observing, drinking their whiskey.

"You want a shirt?" one miner asked Little Foot.

"No," said Little Foot, feeling the surge of warm

whiskey in his belly. "I might want to become a wild blanket Indian. I need no shirt."

"Suit yourself, then," said the miner. To the other miner he said, "Maybe I ought to go wake some of the boys up. They wouldn't want to miss this."

The other miner only nodded.

"You're Ranger Burrack, eh?" Madeline said over her shoulder to the Ranger.

"Yes, ma'am," Sam replied, watching her work.

"I'm Madeline Moorham," she said, "since none of these jakes have the good manners to introduce anybody." She peeled the bandages from Segan's face as she continued. "My hunch is you're on somebody's trail?"

"Your hunch is right," said Sam. "I'm after the Cheyenne Kid and his gang, for bank robbery."

Madeline nodded as she worked.

"The Kid and his men rode through here yesterday morning. They robbed the mine office and lit out." She shrugged. "They must've needed money awfully bad to rob the office in the middle of the month. Russell here should have told you."

"Obliged to you for informing me, ma'am," Sam said. He gave the bartender a cold stare.

"I'm sorry, Ranger," the bartender said. He gave a shrug. "I'm drunk. I plumb forgot."

Sam stared at him.

"This is Russell Gandelo," said Madeline Moorham, giving a nod toward the bartender. She continued. "Anyway, come daylight you'll have no trouble seeing their tracks leading away from town. I've seen these men ride through here before—the Kid too. But this is the first time they rode through here together. First time they done anything like this." She shook her head, staring at Segan's bloody chest. "Damn fire got everything and everybody going out of their heads."

Sam and Gilley looked at each other. Gilley gave him a guarded smile, knowing that Cheyenne needed to replace the money she'd stolen from him.

"How much money did they get?" Sam asked.

"Not enough to brag about," Madeline said, shaking her head. She wiped Segan's face with a wet cloth. "Forty-eight dollars, is what I heard. They should have come the first week of the month when everybody's getting paid."

Good to know. . . . The Ranger nodded to himself as she spoke.

Forty-eight dollars was a long way from what the outlaw leader needed to cover up for getting himself robbed. Sam thought about the nearest town with a bank in it.

Nawton, he decided. It would only be a short distance out of Cheyenne's way to Dutchman's Gulch. He gazed at Little Foot, who stood drinking at the bar. When he caught the Indian's eye, he nodded him toward the horses.

Little Foot cursed under his breath, feeling his wound throb with pain. He watched the Ranger stoop and slip away unnoticed through the tent fly while Gilley and Madeline Moorham tended to Segan. He hated to miss the good part, leaving just as the nurse began threading a long needle. But he threw back the last of his whiskey, set his glass on the bar and eased himself away, limping out of the tent behind the Ranger.

At the horses, Sam turned to Little Foot.

"How well do you know the trails from here to Nawton?" he asked.

"Better than anybody," Little Foot said, already feeling the whiskey warm in his chest. "Want me to take you there?" he asked.

"Yes," said Sam. "Somewhere along the trail to Dutchman's Gulch, Cheyenne and his gang are going to break away toward Nawton. Any idea where they might do that?"

Little Foot considered it for a moment.

"Yes, I know the trail they will take," he said. "We can be there by sunup if we do not run into fires."

"Good," said Sam. "Cheyenne is going to be thinking the fires killed off anybody tracking him. I'm hoping to catch him and his gang by surprise."

Little Foot gave him a questioning look and nodded toward the saloon tent.

"Yes, Gilley's going with us," Sam said. "I'm only leaving her here right now to help the nurse while we water and grain the horses."

In the town of Nawton, under the dark of night, Henry Dowers, the manager of the Nawton Bank and Trust Company, awoke to the sound of tapping on his bedroom window. He swung up onto the side of the bed, lit the lamp on his nightstand and trimmed it low. He pushed himself to his feet. On the other side of the feather bed, his wife, Marletta, a woman fifteen years younger than himself, stirred just long enough to pull her pillow closer to her head.

Henry looked at his sleeping wife and sighed to himself. He trudged to the half-open window in his long nightshirt. His sleepy brain tried to identify the source of the tapping. A pesky bird, no doubt, he thought.

But when he pulled back the thin curtain and looked out the window, instead of a bird, he saw the open bore of a rifle barrel pointed in his face, only a thin layer of wavy glass separating them. While he froze and stared wide-eyed, behind the rifle a bandana-masked face stared back at him. A hand reached in below the half-opened window, snatched the front of his nightshirt and jerked him forward.

"Don't move, Mr. Banker," said Dock Latin, the rifle in his other hand as he held the banker in place.

"Ple-please! Don't shoot," the banker said, his voice suddenly trembling. "What do you want here?"

"Stand real still and I'll tell you," Dock said, barely above a whisper.

From the big feather bed, Marletta called out, "Henry, what's going on?"

Dock Latin whispered, "Tell her nothing's going on. Tell her to go back to sleep."

"Nothing's going on, Marletta," the banker said, following orders. "Go back to sleep."

"Now stand real still for a minute," Dock whispered, opening the window farther, gun in hand, while he held on to the frightened man's nightshirt.

"Something's going on," Marletta said. "I hear you talking to someone."

"No, you're wrong, stay back!" Henry said, hearing the bed squeak as his wife stood up.

Behind him, he heard his wife gasp, almost scream before her voice cut off behind Cheyenne's gloved hand over her mouth.

"Got it," Cheyenne said toward the window as he picked up the big Starr pistol from atop the nightstand beside the bed.

Dock turned the banker loose, gave him a shove backward, climbed into the bedroom and stood with his gun aimed at Henry's chest. Behind Dock, Royal Tarpis climbed in and stepped to the side, also wearing a bandana pulled up over his nose, also pointing a gun at the banker. But the banker just stared at Cheyenne, the masked man who held Marletta against him, a gloved hand over her mouth, the Starr revolver to the side of her head.

"Oh God, don't hurt her, mister!" he pleaded.

"I'll kill her graveyard dead, banker," Cheyenne said, the woman shivering against him, "if you don't do like I say."

"Anything!" said the banker. "Anything you say!"

"I'm going to stay here with your wife, to make sure you don't get feisty while my pards here take you to the bank and have you empty the safe into a feed sack and bring it back here."

"But my wife!" Henry Dowers said, looking as if he might become ill any second. "How do I know you won't . . ." He let his words trail.

Cheyenne cocked his head slightly and said, "Oh, you want to argue with me?"

"For God's sake, don't argue, Henry," Marletta pleaded. "Do what he says!"

"Don't worry, *Henry*," Cheyenne said mockingly, "you have my word nothing's going to happen to her if you do like you're told."

"Let's go, Henry," Dock said, stepping behind him, "or would you prefer we call you Hank?"

The banker moved away across the bedroom and out the door.

Behind Marletta, Cheyenne waited until he heard the front door close. Standing behind her, he slid his gloved hand down the open top of her gown and cupped her warm breast.

"I told you I'd be coming to see you *soon*," he whispered in her ear, nuzzling her.

She continued to tremble out of control, but she closed her hands over his and offered the side of her neck to his lips.

"I should be furious, you bastard," she said. "This was dangerous. Someone could have gotten killed."

"*Shhh,*" he said, silencing her. "I remembered everything you told me—the gun beside the bed, everything."

"*Still,*" she said, "I wasn't expecting this."

"It's not going to take them long to empty the safe," Cheyenne whispered into her warm throat. "Do you want to spend our time *talking* . . . ?"

Outside, hidden in the shadows across the empty street, Lou Elkins and Tanner Riggs sat holding the horses for the other three gunmen.

Elkins had watched Riggs roll himself a cigarette and stick it between his lips.

"Don't try it," said Elkins firmly, as Riggs took out a match and started to strike it.

"I never seen a job where you can't take a damned smoke when you want to," Riggs grumbled. Still, he put the match away and held the cigarette between his fingers, looking at it. "Tell me something." He shook his head. "Why didn't you say something when you saw me going to all the trouble rolling it?"

"I never thought you'd be stupid enough to light it," Elkins said.

"Is that a fact?" Riggs stared at him, starting to bristle.

But before he could say anything, Elkins nodded toward the Dowerses' bedroom window and said, "Whoa, look at this."

The two watched Cheyenne's shadow on the wall in the flicker of the dim lamplight. They saw the woman's shadow move down out of sight; they saw Cheyenne pull his shirt off and toss it aside.

"Same ol' Cheyenne Kid, eh?" Elkins said with a dark chuckle. He shook his head. "I thought he might've changed, but I was wrong. He's still randy as a boar hog."

"Quiet," Riggs whispered. "Caroline might hear you."

"She's too far back to hear me," said Elkins, but he looked down the long dark alley anyway, knowing they'd left the woman at the far end, out of their way in case anything went wrong.

"I've got me a notion on why we're robbing this bank so soon after the last job," said Riggs, sticking his freshly rolled cigarette into his shirt pocket in disappointment.

"Yeah, tell it to me," said Elkins, keeping his eyes on the bedroom window.

"I'm thinking he lost his money to the little gal he had bringing them horses," Riggs said. "I think he lost it and didn't want to let it be known. I think that's why he shot ol' Bagley. He couldn't pay his account and didn't want to admit it."

"What makes a man this way?" Elkins said, puzzled. "Don't get me wrong. I like the tender sex as much as the next fellow, but *damn*. Cheyenne has got to nail down every damn woman he sees! It ain't natural."

"*Ain't natural*, meaning what?" Riggs asked.

"Meaning it *ain't natural*." Elkins shrugged. "Sometimes a man purports to love something so much you have to wonder if he loves it at all. Maybe he's just fooling himself—maybe he's fooling everybody else."

The two sat in silence for a second.

"Good God," Riggs said finally as some dark understanding seeped into his mind. "I ain't going to think on this matter. It's too damn crazy for me to grab hold of."

"I ain't either," said Elkins. "Forget I said anything." He took a deep breath and let it out slowly. "I'm just jealous it's not me over there."

"I *need* this cigarette," Riggs said sincerely. "I can't see the harm in it."

"Smoke the damn cigarette," Elkins said, exasperated. "What the hell do I know?" He tossed a gloved hand in the air in dismissal. "Come here to rob a bank in the middle of the damn night, the boss ends up stiff-legging the banker's wife." He shook his head in utter disgust and jerked his horse a few feet away.

"Jesus, Lou, look at yourself," Riggs said, taking the cigarette from his shirt pocket.

"There's not a thing wrong with me, Tanner," Elkins said, snapping around in his saddle toward him. He pecked a finger toward the bedroom window. "But that right there is not outlawing . . . not as *I* know it."

"Nor as I," Riggs said, agreeing with him. He lit the cigarette and blew out a thin stream of smoke. "But I've come to realize it does not pay to be *too rigid* in this changing world."

In the darkness behind them, Caroline Udall had stepped down from her horse and slipped forward on foot. She had heard everything, seen everything— Cheyenne's shadow, the flicker of lamplight in the bedroom. But she remained silent and swallowed a sick, bitter taste in the back of her mouth. She turned around as a match flared in the darkness. As the two gunmen continued talking, she slipped back to her waiting horse.

PART 3

Chapter 15

—◆—

During the thin silver hour before dawn, the Ranger, Gilley Maclaine and Little Foot eased their horses though a maze of rock and brush and stopped at the base of a rocky hillside that spilled onto the back alleys of Nawton. In silence, the Ranger looked back and forth for any signs of Cheyenne and his gang holding up on the outskirts of town. Seeing none, he nudged the barb forward at a slow walk. The three rode single file through connecting alleyways, staying close to the buildings, keeping out of sight.

"They are not here, Ranger," Little Foot whispered, riding up beside him. "I feel it in my warrior's blood."

Sam stopped the barb and let out a breath. In the night they had found hoofprints turning off the main trail and taking the smaller trail to Nawton. Yet here they were, Sam told himself.

Nothing . . .

"Something tells me you're right," he said to the Indian in a whisper.

Gilley nudged her horse up between them. Some-where in the near distance, a rooster crowed against a sliver of red sunlight on the horizon.

"What's this?" she said, looking down at the ground. She moved the horse back and looked closer, the Ranger and Little Foot following suit.

Sam stepped down from his saddle and examined several burnt stubs of cigarettes lying in the dirt.

"Somebody was smoking a lot here," he said, stand-ing with one of the stubs between his gloved fingers. He looked back down at the scattered hoofprints at his feet. Then he looked around the corner of the alley onto the empty street. "Why here . . . ?" he said to no one in particular. His eyes followed the hoofprints out of sight back along the alleyway.

Little Foot nodded at the dim lamplight in the win-dow across the street—the only light burning along the empty street.

"There is the reason," he said confidently.

Sam thought about it, unable to make any connec-tion between the lamplight, the cigarette stubs and Cheyenne's gang.

Still . . .

"Wait here," he whispered.

He started to hand Little Foot his reins, but seeing how Gilley looked at the saddlebags on the barb, then look away quickly, he changed his mind.

Leading his horse silently across the empty street, he stopped and stood beneath the half-open window. While he debated whether or not to spy on some inno-cent person in his sleep, he heard a scraping sound of wood on wood, followed by a muffled plea for help.

Without hesitation he stepped up, looked in over the window ledge and saw a man tied to a chair, lying tipped over on his side on the floor. Drawing his big Colt, the Ranger looked back and gave a wave, signaling Little Foot and Gilley to come to him. Then he shoved the window open and climbed inside.

On the floor, Henry Dowers stared up wide-eyed at the Ranger's big Colt. He began pleading against the cloth gag tied tightly around mouth. But as the Ranger pulled him and his wooden chair upright, he saw a glint of dim light on the Ranger's badge and almost swooned with relief.

"Thank goodness! Thank God! Thank heaven you're here!" he said the second Sam loosened the gag from around his head. He spit lint as he spoke while the Ranger loosened the rope that had been holding him to the chair.

"My wife, on the bed!" he said, springing up as soon as his ropes fell to the floor.

Marletta Dowers struggled against the ropes and gag when she saw the Ranger stepping toward the bed, her worried husband right beside him.

"Darling, are you all right?" Henry said as the Ranger untied her gag and pulled it from around her head.

"Yes, I believe so," she said with poise, also spitting lint from her lips as her husband untied her wrists from behind her back.

"My wife is a brave gal," Henry said, almost tearfully. "She never scares easily."

No sooner had he spoken than Marletta let out a bloodcurdling scream. Sitting straight up in the bed, she stared wide-eyed at the Indian lurking just inside her bedroom window.

Little Foot turned and started to limp back out the window, but Sam shouted, "Hold it, Little Foot." Then he said quickly to Marletta Dowers, "He's with me—my trail scout. I'm Ranger Samuel Burrack. I'm tracking a gang of bank robbers."

Little Foot stopped and stared at the three white faces.

Marletta looked at Little Foot dubiously as she composed herself. She stood up from the bed and tightened the sash of her robe around her waist in a huff.

"You've come to the right place, Ranger Burrack," said Dowers, wringing his hands. "But I'm afraid you're too late. They have been here and gone. My bank is cleaned out. Thank heavens there was little cash on hand. They only took a few hundred dollars."

"Robbed in the night . . ." Sam considered it.

"Yes, they stormed in, took my gun from beside my bed." He gestured a trembling hand toward the nightstand. "They forced me to the bank and robbed my safe—one of them held my wife hostage here," said Dowers. "I had to go along with them. What else could I do?"

Sam looked at Dowers and his wife, then at the nightstand where Dowers said he'd kept a gun.

"How did they know where you lived?" he asked the nervous banker.

"Oh my . . . ," Henry said. "I don't know, Ranger."

"Come, Henry," Marletta said, sounding a bit put out with her husband, "it is no great secret where we live. Anyone who wanted to know would be able to find out." She gave the Ranger a flat stare. "They should be easy enough to follow . . . especially with a *scout*," she added with a sarcastic twist to her words.

Outside, Marletta's screams had caused lights to glow in windows along the street. Townsmen and their wives who had already risen for the day came running from every direction.

"There's an Indian!" someone shouted.

"Get away from the window, Little Foot," Sam warned. Little Foot had already limped over a step.

"How long ago did the robbery take place?" Sam asked Henry Dowers.

"I—I don't really know," Henry said, still rattled by the night's events.

"An hour and a half," Marletta Dowers cut in, "two hours at the most, Ranger."

"Does Nawton have a new sheriff yet?" Sam asked, knowing the town had difficulty keeping a lawman for any length of time.

"No," said Dowers, "but we're a town that takes care of our own interests. If you're wanting to get on those scoundrels' trail, by all means, please do."

"Obliged, sir," Sam said, stepping over to the open window. "Come show yourself, tell your people who we are. We'll get in pursuit."

Dowers walked to the window and called out to a gathering crowd, "Folks, listen to me, the bank was robbed in the night. This man is Arizona Ranger Samuel Burrack. Let him and his scout pass through. He's on their trail."

Sam looked down and saw the barb and Little Foot's horse standing among the crowd. But he saw no sign of

Gilley Maclaine. Looking back at the barb, he noticed the saddlebags were missing from behind his saddle. Standing at Sam's side, Little Foot saw it too.

"She got away, Ranger," he said flatly.

"Yes, I see that," Sam said over his shoulder.

"What about a posse, Mr. Dowers?" a townsman called out to the open window.

Dowers looked at Sam.

"No posse," Sam called out to the crowd, "not under me. I'm heading out now. If you want to form a posse and send it out on your own, I can't stop you. But you'll want to be very careful we don't shoot each other riding the switchback trails."

The townsmen fell quiet considering the Ranger's words.

Then one called out to Dowers, "How much money did they get, Henry?"

"A few hundred is all, thank God," Dowers replied as Sam climbed down out of the window and stepped over to the barb, Little Foot limping down behind him.

The townsmen milled and looked at each other.

"Give the Ranger room to do his job, I say," a townsman called out.

"Yes," said another, "let's stay out of his way."

"Obliged," Sam said, touching his fingers to the brim of his sombrero while the townsmen stepped aside and made a path for him and Little Foot to ride away.

As soon as they'd ridden through the crowd and were following the street out of town, Sam leaned a little in his saddle and looked down at the single set of fresh hoofprints left by Gilley's horse.

"Are you going after the woman now?" Little Foot asked as they rode on past the edge of town and onto the trail.

"I'm going after Cheyenne and his gang," he said. "But I don't think we've seen the last of Gilley Maclaine."

They rode on.

In the morning sunlight as the two rounded a turn on the stony trail, Little Foot stopped his horse suddenly at the sight of Gilley seated on a rock alongside the trail. Her horse's reins dangled from her hand. Her horse stood resting beside her, chewing on a clump of dry wild grass. On the ground between her feet sat the saddlebags she'd taken from the Ranger's barb.

"Don't shoot, Sam," she said with a thin, wry smile.

"I should," Sam replied in an even tone.

She stood and dusted the seat of her trousers as the two rode closer.

Sam stopped his barb sideways to her and looked down at her face. Little Foot eased his horse forward behind the Ranger, but he stayed back a ways and watched the two as they spoke.

"All right, Sam, I knew I was wrong, doing it," Gilley said, avoiding the Ranger's eyes. She sighed, reached down and lifted the saddlebags up to him. "As soon as I did it, I felt guilty. I didn't even open them. That's the gospel truth. Go on and count it. It's all there, I swear."

The Ranger looked at the particular knot he'd twisted into the leather strap when he'd tied the flaps closed. She wasn't lying; the saddlebags hadn't been opened.

"Are you ready to ride, Gilley?" he asked, throwing the bags up over his shoulder for the time being.

Gilley looked surprised; so did Little Foot, sitting back listening.

"Why would I count it?" Sam asked. "You told me the money's all there."

"And . . . you *believe* me?" she said with a curious look.

"I believe you," Sam said. "Mount up. We've got a hard ride ahead if we're going to catch up to Cheyenne." He looked in her eyes now that she showed them to him. "You do still want to catch up to him, don't you?"

"You bet I do," Gilley said. She swung up into her saddle, turned her horse and faced the Ranger. "You have my word I'm not going to try anything like that again. Old habits are hard to shake, I guess."

"I wasn't going to ask you for your word, Gilley," Sam said quietly. "But I'm obliged you gave it."

"Why are you so trusting of me, Sam?" she asked as they turned their horses toward the trail together. Little Foot nudged his horse forward and rode alongside them.

"Somebody needs to," Sam said, "just to prove to you that you can be trusted."

The three rode on.

It was midmorning when Cheyenne and his men stopped at a wide stream to water and rest their horses. As the outlaw leader and Caroline Udall lay on a blanket, partly hidden by the low-hanging branches of a large mountain oak, the men—Riggs, Elkins, Tarpis and Latin—sat near the water's edge, passing around a bottle of rye whiskey Latin had been carrying in his saddlebags.

"Fellows," said Elkins, holding his share of the stolen bank money folded in his left hand, "this robbing business has gone to hell when a long rider can hold his whole take in one hand—folded at that."

Royal Tarpis took a drink from the bottle and passed it on to Tanner Riggs.

"I hate giving Gantry his cut," he said. "He's going to be suspicious of me holding out on him."

Riggs took a drink and passed the bottle on to Latin.

"Tell him to see the boss if he don't like it," Riggs said, wiping his shirt cuff across his lips. "That's what I'm thinking about doing myself."

"If I was you, I'd put that notion out of my head," Tarpis warned him.

"It's a bad idea," said Latin.

"Yeah? Why's that?" said Elkins.

"Just is," said Latin. He shook his head, dismissing the matter. "But speaking of Gantry, I wonder where he is." He gazed back along the horizon. "They could have burnt everything from here to Texas by now and still made it back."

"If you're just changing the subject, trying to take my mind off of this wad of short money," said Lou Elkins, "it's not going to work."

"No, it's not," said Riggs, standing, looking over at the two resting on the blanket, the woman only half-dressed. "I don't like risking my skin for a little dab of pocket change." Still staring at the Cheyenne Kid and the Udall woman, he reached a hand back and said, "Give me one more cut on the bottle, Dock."

Latin shrugged. He pulled the cork he'd just stuck down into the bottle.

"Tell him it's a bad idea, Dock," said Tarpis.

"If he don't know that by now, he's not smart enough to live anyway," Dock said. He took the bottle when Riggs had finished and held it back to him.

"So long, Tanner Riggs," Tarpis whispered to himself.

The men watched Riggs walk to the blanket with his hand poised beside the Colt holstered on his hip.

Cheyenne lay stretched out bedside Caroline, a wildflower sticking behind his ear. Seeing the gunman coming toward them, Caroline grabbed her blouse, hurriedly put it on and held it closed over her breasts.

"Cheyenne, I've got something to say to you," said Riggs, stopping a few feet back, seeing Cheyenne's gun belt lying at the edge of the blanket.

"Get it said, then," Cheyenne replied, already seeing gunplay coming by the look on Riggs' face—his demeanor. Yet he lay on his back propped on his elbows, looking up at Riggs.

"Get on your feet," Riggs said.

"I'm good right here," Cheyenne said firmly. Caroline stared, afraid to move a muscle or bat an eye. She lay with only inches between her and Cheyenne.

"Suit yourself, then," said Riggs. "I don't like working for chicken scratch," he said. "You're not running this gang right."

"Since when is making money working for chicken scratch?" Cheyenne said.

"When you set up a job half-assed, just to make up

for money some damn woman stole from you," Riggs said, bluntly, removing any question about where this was headed.

Cheyenne's face turned dark.

"Who thinks that?" he asked. The rest of the men sat staring intently.

"I think it," he said. "So does Lou," said Riggs.

"You're both crazy," Cheyenne said evenly.

"Yeah . . . ?" Riggs nodded toward Cheyenne's horse standing nearby, the saddlebags tied down behind its saddle. "You're going to show us the bank money," he said.

"I'm not showing you a damn thing," said Cheyenne. "Maybe I'll show everybody else while you're lying in the dirt."

"Or maybe you won't," Riggs said with determination.

"All right, then," said Cheyenne. He let out a breath. "Can I get on my feet now?"

"No," said Riggs, "you had your chance."

"You know I'm still sore and stiff some from this wound healing," Cheyenne said, nodding to his chest.

"Aw, that's too bad," Riggs said mockingly. "I'll tell everybody you were at a disadvantage, if they ask."

Cheyenne saw Riggs' gun hand streak up holding his big Colt, his thumb cocking it quickly.

Before reaching for his own Colt, Cheyenne gave Caroline a hard shove, rolling her out of the way. Riggs' first shot hit the blanket right between them. Caroline let out a shriek. Cheyenne rolled back the other way, his hand snatching his Colt from his holster.

Riggs swung his gun sideways toward Cheyenne, trying to get his next shot off to make up for the one that missed.

But Cheyenne rolled up onto his knees, quick as a snake, Colt in hand. He fanned three shots that exploded almost as one. Each shot hit Riggs dead-center; each shot punched him backward a step. Cheyenne waited, ready to fan the Colt again if Riggs' sagging gun came back up. It didn't.

Riggs sank to his knees and fell forward onto his face, dead.

At the water's edge, Dock Latin nodded slowly.

"See?" he said quietly to Elkins. "That's what makes it such a bad idea."

Chapter 16

───◆───

Cheyenne caught Caroline and held her tight, the two of them on their knees on the blanket. Caroline could feel Cheyenne's smoking Colt barrel hot against her back through her blouse. The three remaining gunmen still sat frozen at the edge of the stream.

"Are you all right, Caroline?" Cheyenne whispered into her ear, feeling her tremble against his chest.

"The bullet came so close," she said, also in a whisper. "It almost shot me."

Cheyenne heard not only terror in her voice, but also a shiver of dark ecstasy. She simultaneously clung to him in fear and moved against him achingly. She made no attempt at hiding how badly she wanted him after coming so close to death.

"Easy, Caroline . . . ," he said, holding her back inches from him, her open blouse hiding none of her. "I've got something to take care of." He stood up, his Colt still hanging in his hand.

Caroline watched him walk over to his horse, untie his saddlebags and heft them over his shoulder.

The men sat watching as he walked over and stopped a few feet from them. Dock Latin and Royal Tarpis looked cool but concerned. Lou Elkins looked unsettled and worried. Cheyenne took the saddlebags from his shoulder and pitched them on the ground near Elkins' feet.

"Open them," he said flatly.

"*Open them?*" Elkins stared in ignorance. "What are you talking about?" he said, denying any and all knowledge of whatever Tanner Riggs *might* have told him.

"Riggs said you and him thought we robbed the bank in Nawton because Gilley Maclaine stole my part of the bank money," said Cheyenne. "He told me to open the bags. I said *no*. But I let him know that once I killed him, I'd see if you wanted to take a look."

He stood poised, his big Colt hanging down his side, his thumb over the hammer.

"Whoa, now, Cheyenne," Elkins said. "I don't know what that fool was talking about. I don't care what's in them saddlebags or what ain't."

"It might be that everybody here is wondering," Cheyenne said coolly. "Open them on everybody's behalf."

"No," said Elkins, "I ain't going to." He nodded toward Riggs' body lying in the dirt. "Tanner was getting crazy as a June bug. He got all riled at me back in Nawton because he thought I didn't want him smoking." He offered a tight smile and glanced all around. "Can you imagine that? Like I give a damn whether or not he smokes?"

"Open them *now*," Cheyenne said, leaving no room for further discussion. "Settle anybody's doubts."

Elkins sat staring at the saddlebags for a moment, his right hand lying on his lap near his holstered Dance Brothers revolver. Finally he shrugged.

"All right," he said quietly, "if that's what it takes to oblige you." He leaned forward to picked up the saddlebags and open them. He let his gun hand ease back to the butt of his gun.

Cheyenne raised his Colt and shot him once, straight through his forehead, sending him flipping backward half into the running stream. Blood and brain matter splattered on Tarpis and Latin even as they ducked their heads away.

"Damn it to hell," Tarpis cursed, taking his hat off and slinging it free of gore. But then he looked at Cheyenne's stony face staring at him and Latin and froze.

"Who else wants to take himself a peep?" Cheyenne said in the same cool, even voice.

"Come on, Cheyenne," Latin said, "don't put us with those two. They came the other day bad-mouthing you. We put no store in it."

"That's a fact," said Tarpis. "I thought I would have to box that one's jaws before it was over."

"What were they saying?" Cheyenne asked.

"It was nothing," said Latin, "just everyday belly-aching, the way men will do—"

"What were they saying?" Cheyenne demanded, smoke still curling from the barrel of the Colt in his hand.

The two gunmen looked at each other with apprehension.

"He was remarking how you had some kind of

weakness for the ladies," Tarpis said, lowering his voice. He shot a glance over toward Caroline, who stood at the edge of the blanket adjusting her clothes and hair.

"Royal here saw fit to tell him to keep his mouth shut, in so many words," Latin cut in.

Cheyenne took a breath and looked back and forth between them.

"I do like the women," he admitted.

"Hell, of course you do," said Latin, with a devilish grin, "as do all us lusty ol' long riders."

"We'd be concerned about you if you didn't," said Tarpis. "It was none of their business, though, the way we both see it. Right, Dock?"

"Right as hard cider," Dock replied.

Cheyenne wagged his gun barrel down at the saddlebags on the ground.

"Then we're good with the saddlebags?" he asked. "Neither of you wants to take a look, make sure Gilley didn't take all my money?"

"Go on now, stop it," Latin said, dismissing the matter as nonsense.

"These two were sore-heads, you want to know the truth," Tarpis put in.

"All right," said Cheyenne, "let's hear no more on it." He realized that even with the money from the bank robbery last night in Nawton—the few hundred dollars—he was still short. Sooner or later it would show. He knew he had to build up his holdings pretty quick or still risk looking bad in everybody's eyes.

"We're short of men now," he said, looking all around. "And I was wanting to make a hit on Iron Hat."

"There's no bank left in Iron Hat," said Tarpis. "Remember? Last winter it fell in under the snow and nobody ever rebuilt it."

"I know there's no bank," said Cheyenne, "but there's a saloon and brothel there that makes more money than the owner knows what to do with."

"Are we going to wait until Red Gantry catches up to us?" Latin asked.

"No," said Cheyenne. "We'll take it ourselves, maybe pick up new men while we're there."

"Let Gantry find us if he can?" said Tarpis.

Cheyenne just looked at him for a moment.

"The fact is, Roy," he said, "I'm worried we're never going to see Gantry again."

"I feel that way myself," said Dock Latin. "All that fire back there, it'll be a wonder if anything makes it out alive."

Tarpis said to Cheyenne, "You do realize there's a big birdcage hanging in this saloon you're talking about, don't you?"

"A birdcage is only as bad as the birds in it," Cheyenne said. He looked Tarpis up and down. "You're starting to sound like Gantry," he said.

There was a warning in there, Latin thought, listening.

"Roy and I will take care of whoever's in the cage," he put in quickly. "You can count on that."

"Get ready to move out," Cheyenne said. "I'll go see to Caroline."

"How long is she staying with us?" Tarpis asked before Cheyenne could walk away.

Cheyenne stopped and looked back at him.

"Until I say it's time for her to leave," he said with finality. "Is that clear with you both?"

"Clear as can be," said Latin before Tarpis got a chance to reply for himself.

The two watched as Cheyenne walked away. When he was at the blanket with Caroline, Latin turned to Tarpis.

"Are you out of your mind?" he said. "He sent Gantry away with that woman's lunatic husband because he was questioning everything Cheyenne wanted done. You want to wind up like he did?"

Tarpis said, "I don't know, *how did* he wind up?"

"All right," said Latin dismissingly, "act the way it suits you. I'm here to make money."

"So am I," said Tarpis. "But I like to know a man doesn't have his head so far turned on a woman that he ain't paying attention to business."

"You saw how fast he put three into Tanner Riggs' chest," said Latin. "He's atop his game, you can bet your tobacco."

"I'll tell you something else," said Tarpis, staring over at Caroline Udall as he readied his horse. "There's no reason he can't share some of that woman with us, far as that goes. We are his pards after all."

"I didn't hear you say that, Roy," said Latin, "for both our sakes." He turned to his horse and readied it for the trail.

In the town of Iron Hat, a gunman turned saloon guard named Curly Bob Adcock stood in the afternoon light on the covered boardwalk of the Colonel's Sky-High Saloon and Sporting House. He twirled an ivory-handled Colt on his finger. Every fourth or fifth twirl, he stopped it with his thumb, flipped it and dropped it into his holster. Then he started the pattern all over again. Beside him another gunman, saloon guard, drunkard and pool hustler named Delbert "Handy" Pace watched idly as he smoked a thin black cigar.

"A man wants to stay good with a gun, he needs about an hour a day of this," said Adcock. "That's what the colonel doesn't seem to understand," he added. "Else he wouldn't object to me doing it inside the cage—he don't mind you *being drunk* in there. My practicing might save his life someday, his business too."

"So might my drinking," said Pace. He gave a whiskey-lit grin.

"I'm serious," said Adcock. The Colt spun in a fast blur of metal and ivory and stopped cold. "Have you ever seen anybody faster?" He flipped it and dropped it into his holster.

"Oh, I agree, you're fast," said Pace, having turned his gaze away from Adcock, along the street into town, seeing the four riders come into sight. "It ever comes to twirling a man to death, you're the huckleberry can do it, I've always said."

Adcock stared at him, catching the sarcasm.

"I don't like your drunken remarks, Handy," he said. "I was just saying why I practice so much. It makes me fast."

"I understand," said Pace, "and don't think your practice has gone unnoticed. "I say to myself most every day, '*Whooee*, Bob Adcock is fast. I bet it's because he practices so much.'"

Adcock's jaw tightened.

"Okay, how about you, Handy?" he said. "I've heard

you're fast. I never see you practice. How do you keep your edge on, by swilling rye day in day out?" He turned to face the thin, hard-boned gunman.

"You have found me out," Pace said.

Anger flared in Adcock's eyes. His hand opened and closed beside his holstered Colt.

"All right, I want to see how fast you are. I count to three, we both pull our fastest draw."

"Huh-uh," said Pace. "As drunk as I am, I might mistakenly kill you. I'd feel bad about it for hours."

"I'm not worried you'd kill me," said Adcock, getting angrier with the irritating gunman. "Now I'm starting to wonder if you're fast with anything other than your mouth. What do you say to that?"

Pace didn't answer. Instead, staring out over Adcock's shoulder, he recognized the Cheyenne Kid.

"Father, son and holy goats . . . ," he murmured under his breath.

"Holy goats . . . ?" Adcock gave him a confused, agitated look.

"What if I told you, the fastest, baddest, killingest, *thieving*est sumbitch I ever saw is riding atop your right shoulder this minute?" said Pace.

"What are you talking about, Handy?" Adcock said, agitated, brushing a hand over his right shoulder as if a scorpion might be perched there.

"It will take much more than a flick of the wrist to get rid of this one," Pace said with his grin. "You may have to show him how *blindingly fast* you are."

"Damn it, make sense, Handy," Adcock said, actually cocking his head, eyeing his right shoulder.

Pace took him by his forearm as if leading the blind and turned him toward the four approaching riders.

"There now, *Bob*, see them?" he said, patting Adcock on his back as if he were some dumb animal. "The man with the woman riding beside him is the Cheyenne Kid. Ever heard of him?"

"Jesus," said Adcock, "I've heard of him, sure enough." He glanced at the dilapidated, abandoned bank building, with its caved-in roof, across the street. "He wouldn't go anywhere unless it's to rob something. What do you suppose they're doing here?"

"Now, think about it, Bob," said Pace. "If you were him, what would you be coming here to rob?"

"Damn it, you're right, Handy," he said. "We better warn the colonel right away!" He started to turn back to the doors of the saloon, but Pace grabbed the tail of his short corduroy coat and stopped him.

"Slow down, Bob. We're not on duty right now. This is Virgil and Eddie's problem." He grinned. "The worse they do, the better it looks on us."

Adcock thought about it, turning back around, watching the four riders draw closer.

"Sometimes you make a little sense, Handy," he said, settling down, staring at the riders. "Let's not mention nothing about gun twirling or how fast we might be," he murmured. "Sometimes it's best not to say anything."

"I could not agree more, Bob," Pace said.

As Cheyenne and the other three stopped at a hitch rail, Delbert Pace stepped down and met them, smiling up first at Caroline, his cigar clamped between his teeth. Curly Bob Adcock stood awkwardly on the boardwalk, no longer interested in looking like a man fast with a gun.

"Want me to guess why you're here, Kid?" Pace asked, turning his eyes from Caroline to Cheyenne after giving Latin and Tarpis a scrutinizing glance.

"Do your best, Delbert," Cheyenne said, looking away from Pace, eyeing the busy saloon appraisingly, not putting much effort toward hiding his intentions.

Pace smiled. "Lucky you ran into me first," he said. "It happens that I used to work the birdcage in there—shotgun guard."

"No kidding?" said Cheyenne, still looking the place over. "How long ago was that?"

Pace gave a slight shrug and said, "Half an hour ago, give or take."

"So, you and this big fellow know the setup here?" said Cheyenne, giving a nod toward Adcock.

"Oh yes, we certainly do," said Pace.

What the hell is this? Adcock thought, watching. It sounded as if Handy was siding right up with these thieves. *Whoa!* He wanted no part of—

"Bob, come on down here," said Pace. "I want you meet the Cheyenne Kid—an old friend of mine." He looked at Cheyenne and said, "Can I call you an old friend?"

"Yeah, sure, why not?" said Cheyenne.

An old friend of his? Christ!

Adcock felt a numbness creep down his right arm and set into his gun hand like frostbite.

"So, Bob," said Cheyenne, "Handy talks like you

both know how many guns the colonel has guarding this place any time of night?"

Adcock stared dumbfounded at Pace.

Pace smiled and said, "Go on, Bob, it's all right. There's no law against talking things over among friends."

Curly Bob Adcock was pretty certain there *was* a law against it. But he wasn't going to mention it just now. Handy was only playing along with this outlaw, he tried to tell himself, maybe finding out what Cheyenne was up to without tipping his hand? Something like that? Hell, it had to be! If not, he was talking about *helping* them rob the place!

"Well . . . ," Adcock said hesitantly, everyone's cold eyes on him, making him feel as if he *had* to say something. "There's a birdcage with two armed guards in it—shotguns and rifles, not to mention their sidearms."

"Hell, Bob," Pace said with the wave of a hand, "he'd figure all that for himself over a drink at the bar. Tell him what else," he coaxed. "Tell him about the *other* guards, the ones spread out here and there."

Damn, what was Pace doing?

Adcock looked at Cheyenne and started to speak. But Cheyenne cut him off before he began.

"Why don't we climb down and walk around into the alley, out of sight? Maybe Bob doesn't want to talk about this right here on the colonel's front doorstep."

As the men and the woman climbed down from their saddles, Adcock stood in close to Pace and whispered in his ear, "Are we doing right, telling them what we know about the place?"

Pace gave him a look and said, "What do you mean *we*? You're the one's been telling him everything."

Adcock gave him a sick look as the three gunmen and Pace moved him along with him into the alleyway. The woman stood among the horses at the hitch rail, as if keeping watch on them.

"Do you know any gunmen who'll hold this town down for us while we make a getaway?" Cheyenne asked Pace inside the alley.

"Sure do," said Pace. "There's several here who'd jump at the chance to do some shooting for you." He smiled and patted Adcock's shoulder. "Bob here can set all that up for you."

Adcock stared at him, dumbstruck.

Chapter 17

———

Leading their horses in the long shadows of evening, the Ranger, Little Foot and Gilley Maclaine—her horse limping—stopped walking when they came upon the bodies of Tanner Riggs and Lou Elkins. The two outlaws lay where they had fallen: Riggs beneath the mountain oak, Elkins half in the running stream, his bullet-shattered head bobbing slightly.

"Looks like trouble amongst themselves," Sam said, eyeing the surrounding area. He moved upstream from the corpse and let his barb drink. Beside him, Little Foot dropped his horse's reins and let it drink as well.

Even though the water had long since quit running red with Elkins' blood, Little Foot stooped down, took the outlaw by his boots and dragged him a few feet out of the water. The outlaw's head fell limp to the side.

A few feet farther upstream, Gilley led her limping horse into the cool water and splashed water onto the animal's foreleg with her cupped hands.

"How's the horse's leg?" Sam called out to her.

Gilley looked back at him and shook her head.

"He's bruised bad," she said. "He'll be all right with some time off it. But he's not going to carry a rider for a while."

Sam thought about it. Beside him Little Foot shook his head, knowing how hard this terrain could be on a lame animal.

"I can't take her with me, and I can't leave her behind," Sam said. He looked at Little Foot. "Cheyenne didn't get what he needed from the bank in Nawton. What's his best shot at making a good-paying robbery?"

"Iron Hat," Little Foot said without having to think about it. He pointed north, into a line of tall, jagged peaks.

"Another bank?" Sam asked his trail scout.

"No," said Little Foot, "the bank in Iron Hat went out of business last winter. There is a saloon there that draws its people from every direction. It is called the Colonel's Sky-High Saloon and Sporting House."

"I've heard of it," Sam said. "It belongs to Colonel Steadly Moser?"

"Yes," said Little Foot. "He was a colonel in the army of the South, cousin to President Jefferson Davis himself."

"Known by his men as 'Ol' Bloody Sword,'" Sam added.

Little Foot nodded and said, "His saloon is the only business in Iron Hat worth robbing. If they did not go to Iron Hat, they took a lower trail leading northwest. But there is no place along that lower trail with the kind of money a man like Cheyenne would be interested in."

Sam gazed off along the trail, considering things.

"Will you stay back with Gilley, the two of you ride double, bring the lame horse forward easylike? I'll leave you sign of which trail I take following them."

"We will ride double and take it easy with the lame horse, as you say," Little Foot said. "But you do not have to leave me any *sign*. I am a trail scout," he said indignantly. "I track without you leaving me any *sign*."

"I know *you* can," Sam said diplomatically. "I was thinking about the woman."

"Don't worry, I'll show her which way you went," Little Foot said. "But it's better that you tell her what we're doing. I don't think she will listen to me."

While the barb drank, Sam walked to where Gilley led her horse back to the stream bank.

"I'm going to ride on by myself," he said. "I want you and Little Foot to follow. Where the trail forks three ways, I'll leave a sign which direction I went. I've got a feeling they'll head for Iron Hat. Little Foot says it's the nearest place Cheyenne can pick up some money."

Gilley smiled. "I really tied a big knot in his plans, stealing all his *stolen* money, didn't I?"

"Yes, you did," Sam said. "For what it's worth, Cheyenne was a fool to take you lightly." He paused, then said, "He was an even bigger fool, treating you the way he did."

Gilley looked a little embarrassed.

"You don't have to say that, Sam," she said, "but thanks all the same."

"I'm not just saying it, Gilley," Sam said. "I'm saying it because I mean it."

She smiled.

"You and Little Foot look after each other," Sam said. "I'll see you as soon as you catch up to me."

She watched him gather his reins, step up into his saddle, turn the barb to the trail and ride away.

In Iron Hat, Cheyenne and his men stood in an alley behind a freight office watching the two off-duty saloon guards, Pace and Adcock, walk toward them. As the four approached, Latin and Tarpis stood flanking Cheyenne. Caroline Udall was back a few yards holding the reins to their four horses. Beside Cheyenne, Dock Latin stared straight ahead.

"This fellow Pace talked like you and him are *good friends* from way back, Cheyenne," he said sidelong. "Any truth to it?"

"No, not a lick," Cheyenne said. "I met him a time or two, but we never made a job together, never had to drop a hammer side by side."

"So, he's just a weasel?" asked Tarpis, standing on Cheyenne's other side.

"He was a politician in Kansas, I heard," Cheyenne said. "Once he got thrown out of office for drinking so much he couldn't find his horse. There was nothing he was fit for except shooting pool, stealing, lying, double-crossing."

"All the traits of a public office holder," said Tarpis. "Can I shoot him when we're all finished up here?"

"Let's see how it goes," said Cheyenne. "He talked this Adcock fellow right into siding with us. He's pretty slick. I have to give him that."

Tarpis spit in contempt and wiped his hand across his lips.

"I always wanted to shot a politician, just to see if there's any blood in him," he said.

Cheyenne smiled to himself as the four men stopped a few feet back and stood looking at him.

"Cheyenne," said Delbert Pace, "this is Neil Corkins and Sandy Hollenbeck. Two good gunmen." To Corkins and Hollenbeck, he said proudly, "Fellows, this is the Cheyenne Kid, a very good friend of mine."

"This son of a bitch . . . ," Tarpis growled under his breath.

Bob Adcock stood staring rigidly, a man clearly knocked off center by the events unfolding around him.

"Howdy, Cheyenne," said Neil Corkins. "Handy tells us you're looking to add to your gang."

"I am," said Cheyenne, "but nobody walks in without proving himself."

"That's understandable," said Corkins. "I wouldn't have it any other way."

Hollenbeck just stared, his hand resting on his gun butt.

"What about you?" Cheyenne asked the silent gunman. "Does that sound fair to you?"

"Tell me who you want killed, they're dead," he said without the slightest change in his expression.

"I like that attitude," Cheyenne said. He gave a thin smile and spoke to both of them. "We're taking the Sky-High tonight. I need two good men in town here to keep everybody pinned down for a few hours. Kill whoever you need to, then ride like hell and meet up with us on the trail to Dutchman's Gulch."

"What's the pay look like?" Hollenbeck asked flatly.

"Leave here clean with nobody hanging on your

tail, you get an equal cut same as everybody else."
Cheyenne looked him up and down. "We treat our
men right," he added. "We're not the railroad."

Hollenbeck almost smiled, liking what he was hearing. He turned to Corkins.

"Damn it, Neil," he said. "I think I'm going to like
riding with the Cheyenne Kid."

A full share? Adcock perked up and started making
better sense of the situation. He'd seen the large sacks
of cash the colonel toted into his office of a night.

Delbert Pace saw the look on Adcock's face change
from shock to excitement and greed as Cheyenne
turned to him and said, "Same share for you, Adcock.
All you've got to do is spot the guards for us, and stick
with my *good friend* Handy."

"You got it, Cheyenne," Adcock heard himself say,
excited now that he realized how much this was worth
to him.

"See, Bob? Who looks out for you?" Pace said with a
sly grin. He slapped Adcock on his back.

"When are we doing this?" Corkins asked Cheyenne.

"Soon as the crowds starts tapering down tonight,"
said Cheyenne. "We want *all the money* that's taken in
tonight, not just part of it."

"There'll still be lots of guns there," said Hollenbeck. "This will not be a peaceful place we're robbing."

"Does that not suit you?" Cheyenne asked pointedly.

"Hell, that suits me fine," said Hollenbeck. "I'm just
speculating on how much hardware to carry." He
grinned. "I like guns that leave big holes."

"Shotguns," Cheyenne said. "When everybody shows
back up here, have a shotgun hanging in one hand. I

don't care what's hanging in the other, so long as it can kill a man with one shot."

The men all looked at each other and nodded in agreement.

"All of you stay in close with Tarpis and Latin here until the time comes," Cheyenne said. "You don't get out of their sight, even to go to the jake, until we're ready to make our move. They'll let you know when I give the word."

Near midnight the crowd at the Sky-High waned down to only a few passed-out miners, and a few more tittering at the bar ready to fall to the floor. In a corner musicians packed their guitars into coffin-shaped cases; fiddlers kneaded their aching necks with tingling, rosin-coated fingertips. A Jew's harp player dipped his small instrument in a whiskey glass, wiped it clean and put it in his shirt pocket. An angry squeeze box player cursed under his breath as he wiped beer and broken glass from his stylish Hartz Mountain accordion.

Above the horseshoe-shaped bar, in an iron cage hanging by rope and pulley, two shotgun guards, Virgil Stokes and Eddie Kindle, sat in wooden chairs, still alert, but a little less so now that the night had started winding down. They watched the musicians file out the rear door. Neither man paid any attention to Handy Pace and Bob Adcock, when they walked in separately ten minutes apart. Each man stopped and stood on the right beside two guards planted strategically at the bar.

In the cage, Virgil grinned at the sight of Pace wobbling at the bar below.

"Looks like Handy is enjoying his night off," he said, sitting sprawled, a hand slid half down behind his belt.

Eddie Kindle sucked a tooth in contempt and said, "He's drunk so much, I can't tell when he's sober."

"A man drinks so much for so long," Virgil offered, "he stays a little bit drunk, even when he thinks he's not."

"Well, that's good to know," said Eddie, bored. He fished a bag of tobacco from his shirt pocket and rolled himself a smoke.

Below, at the bar, Delbert Pace grinned drunkenly at the guard beside him.

"Anything up?" he asked.

Behind the bar a few feet away, Colonel Steadly Moser stood taking cash from an ornate iron register and stacking it into a folded-down feed sack atop the bar. Beside him stood his son, Steadly Junior, shotgun in hand.

The guard, Stanley Rait, eyed Pace up and down and said, "Go away, Handy, you drunken pig, afore I backhand you."

"Pardon the hell out of me, Stanley," said Pace. "I can't help that I'm a man who takes interest in his work, even when I'm not working."

"Nobody's supposed to know I'm a guard," Stanley said sidelong to him, watching the half-empty saloon as he spoke.

"Damn it, Stanley, am I jumping up on the bar and shouting here's a guard right here—pointing a finger down at you?"

"You're drunk enough you're apt to," Stanley said, looking away from him.

"I'm sorry you think so little of me," Handy said, turning to leave. "I'll go somewhere now and stick my head in a meat grinder if that'll make you happy."

"It would," said Stanley, not giving an inch.

Pace backed away and stood by the post where a long-handled crank held the cage ropes secured.

Stanley Rait stared across the bar at a busty young dove named Silvia—the colonel's favorite—standing pressed against a customer, a hand up under the back of his shirt, half of his left ear buried in her red-painted mouth. As Stanley watched, Silvia let the customer's ear flip out of her mouth. She stayed close and whispered into it.

Doves . . . , Stanley thought. He'd give anything to hear what was being said.

Across the bar, Silvia whispered in her husky voice, "All this ear sucking makes me feel naughty. Why don't we go upstairs, get ourselves comfortable?" She gave the customer's back a squeeze with her sharp nails, then dragged her hand out from under his shirt.

"I'd love to," the customer whispered in reply. "But I'm working tonight."

"Working?" she asked. "What are you doing that's so important you can't give me some sweet time?" She moved back a few inches, enough to look him in the eye.

"The fact is, I'm getting ready to rob this place," Cheyenne said, leaning closer, whispering it into her parted lips.

She gave him a look, judging his sincerity. *A game player*, she decided, seeing him give her a slight wink.

"Oh, really, are you!" she said, doing a good job feigning excitement. "Can I help? I love a good robbery!"

"It could get bloody," Cheyenne cautioned her, his voice still calm, gentle, easy sounding.

"I'll take my chances," she whispered huskily. "What part will I play?" Her long nail drew circles on his chest between two shirt buttons.

Cheyenne looked into her eyes. With a hand at the small of her back, he jerked her tight against him and held her there.

"You can be my hostage," he said in a voice filled with promise.

"I like it," she said, moving against him. "Go on. . . ."

He patted the Colt in his holster. Through the open door, Latin and Tarpis stepped inside unnoticed, shotguns held up under their long tan riding dusters. Cheyenne saw them split off in different directions.

"I'll spin you around like this—" He spun her, grabbed her from behind and pressed her back close against him.

"Oh, don't stop," she said, feeling his breath hot on her throat. She moved against him again.

"Then I'll draw this Colt, throw it up against the side of your head—" She felt the cold steel gun barrel press against her temple.

Wait a minute! What kind of game . . . ?

"And I'll say—" His voice went from a soft whisper to a shout. *"All right, nobody move. This is a robbery!"*

Silvia's mouth dropped open as she heard the Colt cock against her head. Suddenly she was standing facing the colonel, his son and the guards at the bar, all with guns pointed in her direction. Overhead, the cage creaked on its ropes as the two guards sprang to their feet, also pointing guns down toward her.

Silvia found her voice and said, "You son of a bitch. I should have known you're an outlaw. You taste just like one!"

"Take it easy," Cheyenne said. "You'll be all right. You're being robbed by the best."

Behind the bar, the colonel stood frozen in place while he looked around, assessing the situation. Less than ten feet from Stanley Rait, Royal Tarpis stood with his shotgun up and cocked toward his head.

On the other side of the bar, Dock Latin had his shotgun up, pointed at a man wearing a battered coachman's top hat. The man, Albert Shank, was only a few from his own shotgun. But the colonel saw what would happen if Shank made a grab for it. Overhead, the two guards in the cage had their guns up and ready.

"It's a bloodbath, either way it goes, Colonel," Cheyenne said quietly, seeing everything pressing on the colonel's mind. "I understand Silva and you are real close. You really want to see her insides all over the wall?"

"You're the Cheyenne Kid, aren't you?" the colonel said in a tight voice.

"If I was, would I say so?" Cheyenne replied. "Make up our mind, Colonel," he pressed. "It's only money."

The colonel raised his hands slow and easy.

"Men, *stand down*. We're being robbed," he said. "Everybody act right. Don't do nothing stupid." He stood staring evenly at Cheyenne. "The floor is all yours, sir," he said.

Chapter 18

———

Along the bar, the few remaining customers watched in drunken, detached silence, as if they were seeing someone else's bad dream unfolding before them. One of them, a grizzly teamster named Harman Pettibone, stood with his head bowed, eyes closed, smiling absentmindedly at the beer-soaked bar top.

"Has the music stopped?" he asked anyone nearby.

"Shut up, Pettibone. We're being robbed," a drunken miner hissed.

"The hell we are," said Pettibone, his hand fumbling for the battered Starr revolver stuck down in his waist behind his fringed, buckskin coat.

Another drunken miner shoved Pettibone's hand away from the big pistol.

"Stop it, fool. You'll get us all killed."

Pettibone shrugged and plopped his gun hand back atop the bar.

Cheyenne continued holding the dove from behind, his Colt aimed at her head. But he did feel a sense of relief when the colonel told all of his guards to stand down.

"Have your men up there unload their scatterguns and drop them out of the cage," he said to the colonel, gesturing toward the birdcage above them.

The colonel stared at Cheyenne coldly, even as he did what he was told.

"Careful with that woman, *Kid*," he cautioned Cheyenne. "Anything happens to her, there's no coming back for any of us."

"I hear you," Cheyenne said, keeping his forearm around Silvia.

That being said, the colonel gave a gesture up toward the birdcage.

"Men, unload them shotguns, drop them out to the floor," he said.

Latin kept his eyes and shotgun on Albert Shank, who was staring blankly at him from beneath his coachman's top hat. Across the horseshoe bar, Royal Tarpis held his sawed-off twelve-gauge on Stanley Rait. Delbert "Handy" Pace stood watching as if frozen in place, not letting the colonel or his guards know he had turned sides against them. Bob Adcock, having identified the guard at the bar for Dock Latin, managed to slip into the background between the drunken customers and the standoff.

Overhead, the two guards unloaded the shotguns, held them out between the cage bars and dropped them clattering to the plank floor.

Cheyenne breathed easier, but only a little easier.

"Now tell them to slip their sidearms, unload them and drop them," he said.

"You heard him, men. Skin 'em and drop 'em," the colonel said up to the birdcage.

The two guards looked at each other. They slowly raised their Colts from their holsters and began to unload them.

At the bar, the teamster Pettibone heard the shotguns land and jumped in surprise without opening his eyes.

"Has the music stopped?" he asked mindlessly.

"*Shhh!* Shut the hell up, Pettibone!" the nearby minor hissed again. "We're being robbed, damn it!"

"Music! Damn it to hell! *Play music!*" Pettibone shouted, his eyes still closed. He raised his broad hand and slapped it down hard on the bar top, resounding like the crack of a whip.

Hearing the loud sound shatter the tense silence, Latin jerked his head away from Albert Shank for a split second. But a split second was all Shank needed. His shotgun was not in reach, but a Remington came up from his holster, firing at Dock Latin from ten feet away.

"No! Wait!" the colonel pleaded loudly, no doubt in his mind that the Cheyenne Kid would kill Silvia.

But his plea went unheeded as Shank's bullet nipped the shoulder of Latin's coat and sent white bits of garment flying in the air.

Albert Shank was not so lucky. Even as he fired wildly again and ducked away from Latin's shotgun blast, iron pellets slammed his shoulder in a tight pattern, spun him and sent him flying backward head over heels.

Seeing the battle begin, the colonel's son swung his shotgun toward Royal Tarpis, just as Tarpis pulled the trigger, the blast of his shotgun lifting Stanley's big head from his shoulders, sending it flying away in a torrent of blood and brain matter.

"Junior, *no!*" the colonel shouted, still trying to halt the ensuing carnage.

Tarpis turned quickly away from Stanley Rait's headless corpse, ducked to the side and fired just as Junior Moser pulled the trigger. Junior's shot missed Tarpis; but Tarpis' shot hurled the colonel's son backward and flipped him over the bar. His shotgun flew from his hands. He crawled with one hand to the wall and fell back against it, leaving a trail of blood, alive but with a large hole pumping blood from his shoulder.

Overhead, the two guards had stopped unloading their revolvers and quickly started firing down into the melee. At the post beside the iron wheel, Handy Pace jerked a knife from his boot well, let out a war cry and slashed it through the cage ropes. The colonel dived out of the way as the cage crashed down upon the big horseshoe-shaped bar and split open at its door seams.

The two guards spilled out of the broken cage. Only half-conscious from the fall, they struggled to their feet and stood up in time to see Cheyenne, Dock Latin and Royal Tarpis still unscathed, still pointing guns at them.

"Let's try it again, Colonel," Cheyenne said flatly.

"Yes, please!" the colonel said, his hands up, splattered with blood from both Junior's shoulder wound and Stanley's head being blown away. "Let me help my son!"

"Do it. Hurry up," Cheyenne demanded. His hat had been shot away; a bullet graze left a bloody streak along the side of his head. The dove stood against him, wild-eyed in terror.

From either side of the horseshoe bar, Tarpis and Latin bounded over and began gathering the money with both hands. The two stunned guards from the cage stood watching, helpless.

As the colonel hurriedly climbed over the bar top to Junior, grabbing a white bar towel on his way, Cheyenne felt the dove trembling against his chest.

"Hey, sweetheart, are you all right?" he asked gently, his lips brushing against her ear.

Are you all right? she repeated to herself in disbelief.

"You've—got—some—nerve!" she said haltingly, shaking all over.

"It comes with the work," Cheyenne whispered. He kept from smiling to himself. "When we're through, I owe you dinner."

Silvia forced herself to calm down enough to speak without sounding shaken.

"You, owe me . . . more than that," she said.

Cheyenne liked her answer—he liked *her*, this tough young dove, already thinking how to make something out of all this.

He looked over at the colonel, who stooped beside Junior, stuffing the towel into his gaping shoulder wound.

Moving right along . . . , he told himself confidently.

As he watched his men load the money, keeping his Colt on the guards now instead of against Silvia's head, Cheyenne whispered into her ear, "You know you've got to come with us a ways—until we make sure the trail's is safe."

"Huh-uh, I don't think so," Silvia said defiantly, regaining her composure quickly now that the shooting had stopped.

See? That's what he liked . . . , he told himself, the way she handed it all back to him. He smiled a little.

"I wasn't *asking* you," he said. "I'm *telling* you." He gave a sharp little tug with his forearm, letting her know who was in charge. "You're going."

"All right, then, *cowboy*, it looks like I'm going with you," she said coldly.

The colonel, his wounded son, the wounded Albert Shank and the two guards from the cage, Virgil Stokes and Eddie Kindle, stood in a row along the bullet-scarred, bloodstained bar. Behind the bar, Royal Tarpis and Dock Latin finished stuffing money into the large feed sack, tied the top shut with a strip of rawhide and threw it over the bar. It landed at Cheyenne's and the dove's feet with a thud.

"I know what you're thinking, Colonel," Cheyenne said to Colonel Steadly Moser, making sure the saloon guards heard him. "You're thinking, 'I can't wait to get in a saddle and ride these sumbitches down for doing this.'" He gave him a thin smile and raised his voice a little, the dove still against his chest, but the Colt no longer at her head. "But that's a mistake—one that will get you killed."

"You've got what you came for. Why don't you go?" said the colonel. He gestured toward Steadly Junior. "My son needs medical attention bad."

Ignoring the colonel, Cheyenne passed back and forth in front of the men, Silvia moving along with him. "I have two men out there in the dark. They're sighted in on this place with rifles. Any of you trying to follow us will be cut down in the street." He looked back and forth, making sure they understood him. Then he shot a glance at Handy Pace, still standing by the wheel post.

Getting a nod from Cheyenne, Pace stepped forward, hefted the bag full of money onto his shoulder and turned toward the door, giving Virgil and Eddie a sly grin.

"By the way, fellows," he said to them, "you can work mine and Bob's shift tomorrow too."

The two guards glared at him, but they remained silent.

"Let's go, Bob," Pace said to Adcock.

Bob Adcock, who had been reluctant at first, then tempted by the lure of fast money, was now excited by his new prospects. He hadn't fired a shot, but he had been sure to make things appear as if he'd taken a more active role, stepping forward after the shooting stopped with his gun drawn, looking around as if searching for his next target.

"You got it, Handy," he said, his Colt still drawn and cocked. He gave Virgil and Eddie a smug look as he and Handy Pace filed past them and out the door.

Cheyenne turned to the colonel and said, "Silvia here is taking a little midnight ride with me. I see, hear or smell any of you on my trail, I'll leave her head hanging on a tree."

"For God's sake, Kid!" said the colonel. "You're leaving riflemen here to pin us down. Why do you need her?"

With Silvia still held tight against him, Cheyenne took a deep breath, smelling her hair.

"Why do I need her?" Cheyenne grinned. "Colonel, that's a damn stupid question."

"Don't you worry about me, Colonel," Silvia said as Cheyenne guided her with him toward the door. "I can handle this randy jackrabbit."

"There, see?" said Cheyenne. "She's a big girl. She'll be all right—so long as none of you come after us," he added, a grim, menacing look coming over his face.

Stepping out onto the boardwalk, Tarpis and Latin covering the men inside the saloon from the open front door, Cheyenne looked at the small gathering of townsfolk standing in the street, many of them in their robes and bedclothes.

"If there's a doctor here in Iron Hat," he called out to the townsfolk, "you need to send him to the saloon."

"I'm the doctor," a young, bald-headed man called out, stepping forward. "Shall I fetch my medical bag?"

"Sounds like a dandy idea, Doc," Cheyenne said, feeling satisfied now that the job was over and the take looked good. He watched the young man turn and run toward an office farther up the dirt street.

Among the horses standing at the corner of the alley running alongside the saloon, Caroline Udall looked down at the dove, Cheyenne's arm around her neck. Beside Caroline stood Pace and Adcock, Pace tying the money bag down behind Cheyenne's saddle.

"Why is *she* going with us?" Caroline asked Cheyenne in a prickly tone, looking the busty young dove up and down.

Silvia returned Caroline's harsh stare.

"She's part of the reason the colonel and his gunnies won't be dogging us," Cheyenne said.

"We don't have a horse for her," Caroline said.

Cheyenne walked to the hitch rail out in front of the saloon and picked out a strong-looking roan. He sat Silvia up in its saddle and led it to the corner of the alley.

"She does now," he said.

From the open saloon doors, Tarpis and Latin looked at each other, knowing there had been no mention of or plans made for taking a hostage.

"Always, with the women," Tarpis whispered to Latin under his breath, both of them shaking their heads.

As Cheyenne sat the dove atop her saddle, he looked across the street and up at the roofline. From a spot atop an apothecary shop, Neil Corkins waved a hand back and forth slowly. Cheyenne did the same, knowing that above him on the same side of the street, Sandy Hollenbeck was also in position with a rifle.

"Pards," Cheyenne said to Latin and Tarpis, "let's get out of this town before they start charging us rent."

From up the dirt street the young doctor came running in his nightshirt, his black leather medical bag in hand, a streamer of gauze sticking out of it, fluttering in his wake.

"Good for you, Doc! Go heal somebody," Cheyenne said, swinging up into his saddle as the serious young doctor bounded past him and into the saloon.

Latin and Tarpis looked at each other again as Cheyenne and Caroline turned their horses together onto the street, Cheyenne leading the young dove's horse by its reins, keeping it sidled up close to him.

"One of us is going to have to talk to him," Tarpis said to Latin under his breath, leaning over toward him as the band rode out of town at a strong gallop.

"That would be you, then," Latin replied. "I saw how well talking to him went for Riggs and Elkins."

They rode away into the night, leaving the town of Iron Hat fading into the darkness behind them.

Three miles along the high trail, Cheyenne brought the four gunmen to a halt and looked at them in the moonlight, the two women flanking him.

"Roy, Dock," he said to Tarpis and Latin, "now that we've all three had a chance to see these new men's work, what do you think about them joining us?"

Tarpis and Latin turned to Delbert Pace with a hard gaze. Pace had started lifting a bottle of rye from his saddlebags. He stopped cold and sat staring.

"I fear with this one around, we'll always have to worry if our whiskey's safe," Tarpis said.

"That's what I think too," Latin agreed.

A tense silence set in as Pace raised the bottle the rest of the way from his saddlebags, pulled the cork and took a long swig. He let out a whiskey hiss and passed the bottle to Latin, returning their stares.

"What about it, Delbert?" said Cheyenne. "Can they trust you around their whiskey?"

"If there's whiskey around, I'll drink it if I have to cut their throats in their sleep," Pace said matter-of-factly, his hand rested on the butt on his holstered Colt.

"You can't beat that for honesty," Latin said. He swigged the whiskey and passed the bottle to Tarpis.

"Any man won't kill for whiskey don't deserve to drink it," Tarpis said. He turned up a long drink, then wiped a hand over his mouth. "He's in, far as I care."

"That's Pace, then," said Cheyenne. "What about Bob here?"

Before anyone could answer, Pace's Colt streaked up, cocked and fired. Bob Adcock flew backward out of his saddle and hit the ground dead. The gunshot resounded out along the hilltops and valleys.

Cheyenne and the two other gunmen sat in silence for a moment.

"Well, there you have it," said Tarpis. "I couldn't have said it better myself."

They turned their horses as one and rode on.

Chapter 19

Atop the roof of the apothecary shop, Neil Corkins stood with a boot hiked up on the edge of the storefront's wooden facade, a Spencer rife in hand, the butt of it resting on his thigh. Beneath his wide hat brim, he wore a long tan riding duster with its collar upturned. He held a cigar in his mouth. When he heard footsteps on the roof behind him, he didn't even look around.

"What are you doing over here, Sandy?" he said. "You're supposed to be keeping watch over on the other end of town."

"I got tired of sitting there doing nothing," said Sandy Hollenbeck. "Nobody's coming into town from that direction this time of night. Tarpis said Cheyenne has gotten overcautious about somebody being on his trail."

Watching the saloon below, Corkins gave a short, dark chuckle under his breath.

"Looks like you got here just in time," he said over his shoulder.

Hollenbeck walked up beside him, stopped and

stared down toward the open door of the Sky-High Saloon.

"Yeah, why's that?" he asked.

"I've got one at the window looking back and forth along the street. I figure he's getting ready to step out onto the boardwalk any minute," Corkins said. He puffed on his cigar and kept his eyes on the open saloon doors.

"It could be that young doctor," said Hollenbeck. He rested his Winchester up over his shoulder, a little disappointed that they hadn't seen any action since Cheyenne and his gang left town.

"Yeah, I figure it's the doctor," said Corkins, "but this job has been dull as hell. I'm going to take a few shots at him just to keep myself from falling asleep up here."

"I know what you mean," said Hollenbeck. "It's been over two hours."

"These peckerwoods don't even know if we're still up here or not," said Corkins. "Seems like one of them would have to go to the jake by now." He stifled a yawn.

"I haven't been this bored since my grandpa's hanging," said Hollenbeck. He paused. They stood in silence staring down at the saloon doors. "Course I was only a child at the time, didn't realize there was betting could be made on how long he'd wiggle—"

"Here he comes!" Corkins said all of a sudden, cutting Hollenbeck's story short. "You push him forward. I'll keep holding him back."

The two gunmen raised their rifles to their shoulders. Below them at the saloon doors, the bald-headed young doctor stepped out onto the boardwalk and looked up at the two black silhouettes outlined against the purple night sky.

"I'm Dr. Weltz," he called up to the blackness, walking slowly along sideways, his arms spread wide, holding his leather bag out for the gunmen to see. "I've got to go pick up some more bandages and supplie—"

His words stopped beneath the sound of a rifle shot. The bullet thumped into the boardwalk an inch from his foot, causing him to jump farther away from the saloon doors. Another bullet hit near his foot, forcing him to jump again.

Holy Jesus!

"Don't shoot, I'm the doctor!" he shouted. He ran three steps, then stopped short as Hollenbeck joined the game and put a bullet in the thick boardwalk plank on his other side. The doctor shrieked and jumped back in the other direction, his black bag still in hand. Corkins put another bullet dangerously close to the doctor's foot. Dr. Weltz shrieked again.

Without facing Hollenbeck, Corkins jacked a fresh round into his rifle chamber and said, "What do you say, Sandy, ten dollars?"

"You're on," Hollenbeck replied, his rifle up, ready to fire as the terrified doctor stepped back in his direction. "First one hits his foot loses?"

Corkins nodded in agreement.

"Let's keep him dancing," he said.

"Go!" said Hollenbeck.

Bullets thumped rapidly into the boardwalk on either side of the young doctor, kicking up bits and slivers of wood. The doctor bounced back and forth on tiptoes, like some mindless marionette attempting to keep both feet off the ground. His black bag flapped up and down at the end of his outstretched arm.

Bullets pounded; splinters flew. Townsfolk stared in shock.

"*Whooee!* Look at him go!" Hollenbeck said sidelong to Corkins, keeping his voice down.

No sooner had Hollenbeck spoken than the doctor collapsed backward against the front of the saloon and his bag flew from his hand, landing a few feet away. Corkins lowered his Spencer rifle and puffed on his cigar.

"Damn, we've come to a draw," he said, sounding almost disappointed that neither of them had shot the doctor in the foot.

"I expect it's bound to happen," Hollenbeck said, lowering his Winchester, "two crack shots like us going head-to-head." He grinned and added, "I'll shoot him in the foot *for fun*, if you want me to, but the bet's off."

"Naw, forget it," said Corkins. "I'm losing interest. Shoot his bag instead," he said.

"*Ouch!*" said Hollenbeck, giving him a look, even as he levered a bullet into his Winchester.

"I mean his *doctor's* bag," said Corkins.

"Good thing you said something," Hollenbeck replied. He raised his rifle to his shoulder again.

On the boardwalk, Dr. Weltz took the lull in rifle fire as a chance to get back indoors. He scrambled toward the leather bag, stretching his arm out for it. But just as his fingertips touched it, the impact of a bullet from Hollenbeck's Winchester lifted it in the air and sent its contents flying in every direction.

"Hold your fire, *damn it!*" the colonel shouted out from inside the doors of the saloon.

"You were warned about trying to leave," Corkins shouted back to him.

"He's the doctor!" the colonel shouted. "He needs more medical supplies!"

Corkins chuckled and turned to Hollenbeck.

"Listen to this, Sandy," he said, grinning. He shouted down at the saloon, "Who's the doctor?"

"He is, damn it," said the colonel, "the man you're shooting at!"

Keeping himself from bursting out laughing, Corkins pressed his gloved knuckles to his mouth and got himself under control.

"Why didn't he just say so?" he called out.

"He did say so, *damn it to hell,*" said the colonel. "He said so several times!"

Hollenbeck stifled his laughter.

"Then he should have made it more clear," he shouted down to the saloon.

Corkins stood chuckling beside him.

But they both stopped laughing at the sound of a gun hammer cocking on the roof behind them. They turned around slowly, rifles in hand, and stared at the dark, shadowy outline of the Ranger. Moonlight glinted off the big raised Colt in his hand.

"Shame on you two, shooting at an unarmed doctor," he said, his face blackened out by the brim of his wide sombrero.

"Who the hell are you?" Corkins demanded.

"Arizona Territory Ranger Samuel Burrack," came the quiet voice from beneath the sombrero.

"Ah yeah. Well, I've heard of you, *Arizona Territory Ranger Samuel Burrack*," Corkins said mockingly. "I've got news for you, this ain't Arizona Territory."

"I didn't say it was," Sam replied coolly.

As Sam and Corkins spoke, Hollenbeck eased his right hand back along his rifle until his thumb lay over the hammer.

"Here's some more news for you," Corkins said. "You're not taking us in. You're not taking us *anywhere!*"

Hollenbeck cocked his Winchester. Corkins started to raise his Spencer rifle.

"I didn't say I was," Sam said in the same quiet voice. "That'll be up to you."

Corkins and Hollenbeck made their move as one, without hesitation.

But Sam saw it coming. The big Colt bucked in his hand. An orange-blue flame split the darkness. His first shot hit Corkins dead center and hurled him off the facade to the street below. Corkins' long duster flapped out around him like the broken wings of some great dying bird.

A shot from Hollenbeck's Winchester sliced through the air past Sam's cheek. But then the big Colt bucked again and Hollenbeck sailed off and down behind Corkins.

As the shot resounded, Sam stepped forward on the empty roof and looked down on the dirt. Ten yards away the townsfolk stared up at him, seeing the big Colt hanging in his hand, yet unable to make out the rise of smoke curling up its barrel and across the back of his hand.

In the gathering of townsfolk, an elderly woman crossed herself and stared upward.

From the doors of the saloon, the colonel had seen both bodies fall to the dirt as if cast out of heaven. He gazed up at the dark outline of the Ranger.

"Who's that up there?" he called out.

"Arizona Territory Ranger Samuel Burrack," Sam said for the second time in the past five minutes. "Tell your men to hold their fire, Colonel Moser. I'm coming down."

The Ranger turned and walked to the rear of the roof. He looked off to the southwest and saw an orange, fiery glow against the purple sky. *More wildfire coming,* he told himself. After he'd climbed down a wooden ladder Corkins had leaned against the building, he gathered his horse from where he'd left it hitched and walked out to the street, through grateful, onlooking townsfolk.

By the time he'd gotten to the salon, Dr. Weltz had gathered his bullet-struck medical bag and scattered supplies from the boardwalk and gone back to work bandaging Junior Moser, who lay limp atop a battered faro table.

When the Ranger walked in, Dr. Weltz gave him a quick nod of appreciation on his way to the bar, where the colonel stood surveying the mess the robbers left behind.

"We're grateful to you, Ranger," the colonel said, pouring them both a glass of whiskey. He slid Sam's drink in front of him.

"Obliged, but not tonight," Sam said. "I'm on the trail." He pushed the glass away with a finger. "Any of these bodies Cheyenne's men?"

"Not a damn one," the colonel said in disgust. "He also took a young dove of mine hostage named Silvia." He gritted his teeth. "I expect I know what he's got in mind for her."

"How long ago did all this happen?" Sam asked, seeing the tangled and twisted birdcage still lying atop the bar, the blood, the bullet holes, the bodies being carried out to the dark street.

"A couple of hours, three at the most," the colonel said. He threw back his shot glass of whiskey in one drink. "What brought you here anyway?"

"Tracking these same men," Sam said. "Luckily I didn't ride into their gun sights. I heard shooting, came on a back street and caught those two pinning you down."

"Yeah, the sons a' bitches," said the colonel, pouring himself another glass of rye. "Both of them are gunmen who've been living here among us for a while. Cheyenne must've talked them into keeping us holed up while he made his getaway." He shook his head. "Gunmen are not known for their powerful brains." As he spoke, by coincidence, two men carried Stanley Rait's headless corpse past them and on out the front door. The colonel shook his head.

"They're going to pay for this," he swore. "Soon as I see Junior is going to live, I'm in a saddle leading my men. We'll stretch their necks from a tree, or shoot them down where they stand. I don't care which. I want my money back, and I want the dove back too."

Seeing there would be no talking the colonel out of riding after Cheyenne and his gang, Sam said in an even tone, "You and your men be careful. I saw more wildfire coming—and watch your shooting. I'll be on the trail in front of you."

"You can wait and ride with us," the colonel invited. But Sam had already turned and started toward the door.

Cheyenne and his gang stopped at the rocky three-forks in the trail where they would turn north and ride on to Dutchman's Gulch. While they rested their horses, Cheyenne stepped down from his saddle and helped Silvia from hers. Caroline Udall stayed atop her horse, staring in silence. When Cheyenne came around to help her down, she took his hand. But once her feet touched ground, when he offered her a canteen of water, she only turned and walked away.

"I sense a lover's quarrel in the air," Silvia said quietly, taking the canteen, uncapping it and raising it to her lips.

"We're not what you call *lovers*," Cheyenne said. "At least not anymore."

"Oh?" said Silvia. "Does she know that?" She handed the uncapped canteen back to him.

"Not exactly," said Cheyenne. He paused and said, "It's sort of a complicated story."

"I bet it is," Silvia said knowingly. "I'd love to hear it."

"Not right now," Cheyenne said. He gave her a smile. "I'd rather talk about you."

"Huh-uh," Silvia said. "I'm your prisoner, remember? I'm not giving anything up."

"Don't be that way," Cheyenne said. "We can still be close—"

"Cheyenne! Somebody's coming," said Royal Tarpis, standing beside his horse, the closest man to the trail leading back toward Nawton.

"Who could that be?" Cheyenne said with a puzzled look. "We left everything ablaze behind us."

"Ever think it might not be somebody following *you*?" Silvia said smugly. "There are other people in this big world besides you, you know." She winked and turned away from him.

Damn it! He needed some time alone with this one to bring her around, he thought. But that would have to wait.

"Everybody take cover," he said to Tarpis and the other two gunmen, he himself starting to hear the soft clack of iron shoe against rocky ground. He stepped over closer to the trail and hid himself behind a tall rock. The others vanished behind tree and rock until the trail stood silent and empty.

Thirty yards back, from the direction of Nawton, Little Foot and Gilley Maclaine walked along leading their horses. Gilley's horse hadn't stopped limping, but it was doing better without the weight of a rider on its back. Still shirtless, Little Foot wore a thin, ragged blanket he had foraged from the livery barn in Mandell and wrapped around himself.

"I heard something," Little Foot said, stopping suddenly in the moonlight. He jerked his horse to a stop beside him. He paused for a moment in the silence of the night, listening intently. "Did you hear something?" he asked in a whisper.

"No," Gilley replied, also whispering.

"Well, I did," said Little Foot. "I heard it with these Ute ears of mine—ears that are as powerful as those of the wolf."

Gilley only stared.

Little Foot waited with a puzzled look on his face, not hearing another sound. He tugged the blanket around himself, the cloth still dried tightly to the wound on his side.

"All right," he said, "perhaps my ears are wrong, too much of the white man's whiskey." He tugged the horse's reins and started walking on. "Perhaps instead of hearing somebody, I smelled them. It's easy to mistake things with senses are as keen as mine."

"That must be it," Gilley whispered in reply, walking her limping horse.

A few minutes later as they reached three forks in the trail, Little Foot squatted to search the dark ground for the barb's hoofprints. But when he spotted the freshly made hoofprints leading back for the direction of Iron Hat, he stood up with his hand on his pistol and looked all around warily.

Dock Latin's voice called out from among the cover of rock above the trail, "Lift your shooter with two fingers, Injun, and let it fall."

Little Foot thought about drawing the Colt and blasting away. *Warrior-style,* he told himself. But as he looked up and around and saw the black silhouettes of the four gunmen rise as if ascending from the bowels of hell around him, he sighed heavily, lifted the Colt slowly and let it fall.

"Holy cats, Cheyenne, look who's here," said Dock Latin, recognizing Gilley standing with her hands chest high, facing him on the grainy, dark trail. "It's Gilley Maclaine."

"Gilley . . . ?" said Cheyenne, stepping into sight, walking toward her while Tarpis stepped over and picked up Little Foot's Colt from the dirt. "Jesus, Gilley, I thought you were dead," he added.

"Oh?" said Gilley. "What you mean is you thought *you* killed me, right?" she said.

"Well, yes," Cheyenne said. "We did have that little spat between us."

Just listening to the sound of his voice, Gilley could tell he hadn't told his men everything that had happened. He didn't sound upset about her stealing his money—didn't sound like it, but she knew he was, she told herself. She decided to keep quiet, see what gains she could make for herself and Little Foot by letting Cheyenne know she would keep her mouth shut.

"A *little spat* is putting it mildly," she said. "You tried to kill me. Then you tried to burn me alive. But none of that is why I'm here. I came because you *forgot* to pay me for those horses." There was sarcasm in her emphasis.

"Gilley." Cheyenne grinned, taking her by the arm. "You're making it sound worse than it was." He led her away from the others, shooting a nervous glance at both Caroline and Silvia. Caroline stared blankly. Silvia gave him a smug twist of a smile, judging him poorly, he thought.

Latin and Tarpis shot each other a look.

"What's going on here?" Delbert Pace asked, a fresh bottle he'd taken from his saddlebags hanging in his hand.

"Keep still, Handy," whispered Latin. "We'll tell you all about it later."

Chapter 20

─────

While the three gunmen, the Indian and the two women sat watching, Cheyenne turned Gilley by her arm and walked her away a few yards, out of listening distance. When he jerked her to a halt, he squeezed her arm tight.

"Where's *my damn* money?" he said, in a harsh, threatening tone.

Gilley didn't back an inch. She stared at him with a short vengeful grin and said, "Where's *my damn* undergarments?"

"Don't be funny with me, damn it . . . and do not think I won't kill you," Cheyenne threatened. The words came out of his mouth at a rapid pace.

"Kill me?" she said in disbelief. "Now, there's a surefire way to get your money back." She rounded her arm free from his grasp.

"I mean it, Gilley," said Cheyenne, calming down, softening a little. "You don't want to play with me on this."

Also calming down, Gilley looked him in the eye, reached up and brushed his hair from his forehead.

"I don't have it, Cheyenne," she said, "and that's the gospel truth. Ranger Burrack has it. He saved me from the fire, then took it from me."

"Burrack . . . ," said Cheyenne. "All right, where is he? I'll kill him and get it back."

"He's trailing you, Cheyenne," she said. "If you're smart you'll stay clear of him. I've been with him long enough to know that he is tough as a pine knot. He'll kill you graveyard dead."

"You've been *with* him?" Cheyenne asked, his voice taking on a different tone. "How do you mean?"

Gilley noted the change. She relaxed even more and decided to take advantage of it.

"I mean he saved me after you left me behind to burn up in the fire," she said. "I was more than just a little grateful. . . ."

"You and the Ranger . . . ?" He let his question trail.

Gilley didn't answer. Instead she left his mind free to conjure up whatever image it found within itself.

"Sam is a *real man*, Cheyenne," she said, "not some phony like men I've grown accustomed to finding. We went through *fire* together, him and I. When most men would have fallen apart and given up, he kept his guts together—kept me together too. There's nothing I wouldn't do for him. He's the kind of man any woman prays she'll someday find in her life, in her bed, in her—"

"All right, I get your point," Cheyenne said, cutting her off, sounding sour and envious. "He's a hell of a fine fellow, this *Ranger* of yours."

"You're right, he is a *fine man*," she said defiantly.

"Now where is he?" Cheyenne asked.

"I'm not telling you," Gilley said.

Cheyenne looked back through the grainy darkness along the winding trail toward Iron Hat.

"If he tracked us to Iron Hat, he took the trail we took going in." He grinned to himself. "But we took the steeper trail coming back."

"It doesn't matter what trail *he* took, or the trail *you* and your gang and all your *womenfolk* will take from here. Sam will catch you. When he does, you're all through," Gilley said.

"It should matter to you which trail me and my gang take, Gilley," Cheyenne said. "Because you and your crippled Indian pal are going with us."

"I'm not going anywhere with you, Cheyenne," Gilley said, taking a firm stand for herself. "Not unless you want your womenfolk to see you in a fistfight with a woman half your size. They might get a kick out of that."

"Oh, you're going with me to Dutchman's Gulch," Cheyenne said, "and you're doing it without a fistfight." He drew his Colt from his holster and hefted it in his right hand, making sure she saw clearly what he was about to do. "Unless you want to count how many bullets I can put in Little Foot's chest from here." He raised the Colt as if to take aim at the helpless Indian.

"Don't shoot him, Cheyenne," she said. "I'll go with you peacefully."

Cheyenne cocked the Colt as if he didn't hear her. He smiled to himself taking aim.

"I promise, Cheyenne!" she said with urgency. "I'll go along without a fight!"

"Huh-uh, not good enough, Gilley," he said. "You have to also promise you're going to keep your pretty little mouth shut about stealing the bank money from me."

"All right, I promise that too," Gilley said. "Now lower the gun or I'll start shouting it out about the money, right this minute."

Cheyenne chuckled as he lowered the Colt and let it hang from his side. He liked that about Gilley, he recalled to himself, the way she would bargain and deal with a man. He hated to admit it, but maybe he'd cut her loose a little too quick. He looked her up and down and stepped over closer to her.

"Whatever turned us so bitter against each other?" he asked. He reached out and brushed a strand of hair from her cheek.

"Well, let me think," she said, feigning contemplation on the matter. "Oh, now I remember. I think it was when I walked out the back door and overheard you telling your men you were going to kill me."

"All right, that was a rocky time for us," Cheyenne said. "But there was some good times too, huh?" he coaxed.

"Oh? You want me back, Cheyenne?" she asked.

"I can't say I wouldn't like things to be like they were between us," he said, still standing close to her, running his hand up and down her shoulder. "What about you?" he asked softly.

Gilley looked at the silhouettes of the two women a few yards away in the darkness.

"What would you do, Cheyenne," she asked, "fit me in between these other two women? You want to give each of us two days a week with you, and on the seventh day you can *rest*?"

Cheyenne stared into her eyes.

"Take me serious, Gilley," he said. "Some men need more than one woman. Some need more than two or three. We could all four get along—"

"You're a crazy bastard," she said, cutting him off, "and you make my skin crawl." She jerked her shoulder away from his hand. "If we're all through talking, I want to get back to the others. I don't like being alone with you."

"Go on, then," Cheyenne said. He gave her a slight shove back toward the others. "Remember what you promised. Either keep your mouth shut or I'll shut it for you—yours and your gimp-legged Indian. . . ."

At the horses, the men heard the two arguing on the way back.

Tarpis stepped forward leading his horse and Cheyenne's. He handed Cheyenne his horse's reins and said, "Boss, it looks like the whole damn world is burning down back toward Nawton."

Cheyenne looked south and saw a swell of brown-black smoke and streaking flames that had risen rapidly while he and Gilley had been standing aside talking.

"Damn!" he said. "That came up fast." He stared in disbelief, seeing the fire overtake the distant horizon on a wind blowing up from the southwest.

"Think this is blowback from sending Gantry and this woman's idiot husband starting fires?" Dock Latin asked.

"I don't know, let's ask the Indian," Cheyenne said.

"I want to hear what happened to Gantry and Segan anyway."

They turned to Little Foot, who stood with his hands still raised chest high, Tarpis' gun still loosely pointed at him.

"Of course it is from the fires that we started," Little Foot said. He eyed the bottle in Delbert Pace's hand. "Handy, can I have a drink, before my bones rattle off my skin?"

"I'd almost pay to see that," Pace chuckled. He pitched Little Foot the bottle.

The men watched as the Indian took a long swig and let out a deep hiss when he finished. Little Foot ran the back of his hand across his lips.

"Obliged, Handy," he said to Pace.

Pace reached a hand out for the bottle, but Little Foot didn't seem to see it. He held the open bottle clasped to his chest.

"Segan and Gantry started fires from the top of the hill line to the valley down there," he said to Cheyenne, pointing a finger from atop the black shadowy hills to the east to the dark valley as far west as they could see.

"Instead of burning out, it's coming this way," Cheyenne speculated.

"Did you think the fire would get tired and stop to rest?" Little Foot asked him pointedly. "In this dry weather it will rage until there is nothing left in its path to burn."

"What about Gantry? Where is he?" Cheyenne asked, getting away from the subject of the wildfire.

"Gantry tired to kill me and Segan," Little Foot said,

feeling the warm surge of whiskey. "I set him on fire—"

"You sumbitch," said Tarpis, "you burned ol' Red!" He cocked the pistol in his hand.

"He made the squealing sound a dying pig makes," Little Foot said.

"Why, you . . . !" Tarpis aimed his pistol at the grinning, whiskey-lit Indian.

"Lower your gun, Roy," said Cheyenne. "Can't you see he's lying? One drink and he turns into Geronimo."

Little Foot let out a sigh and stood staring at Cheyenne as Tarpis let the hammer down on his gun and lowered it.

"Answer me without all the warrior talk," Cheyenne said. "Gantry is dead, right?"

"Right," said Little Foot without elaborating.

"What about *crazy* Segan?" Cheyenne asked, seeing the question in Caroline's eyes.

Little Foot shrugged and looked back and forth between Caroline Udall and Cheyenne.

"He was eaten alive by a cat," he said. "I was standing no more than twenty feet from him. But I could not shoot or I would have killed him." When he finished his tale of Segan and the cat, he raised the bottle to his lips again and took another long swig.

"So you let a cat eat him instead?" said Cheyenne, skeptically, seeing the look of horror come onto Caroline's face. He jerked the bottle from Little Foot's hand and passed it back to Pace.

Gilley watched and listened in silence. She knew Segan was alive the last time they'd seen him. He'd been getting himself sewn back together in Mandell.

But she owed no explanations here. For two cents, she thought, she'd make a run to Little Foot's horse, jump into the saddle and race away from here—warn the Ranger where Cheyenne and his men were, and where they were headed from here. But that would be leaving the Indian in a bad spot, leaving him behind with only her lame horse to ride. . . .

"Okay," said Cheyenne, "I've heard enough. Everybody mount up. We're all headed to Dutchman's Gulch."

"I can't mount up," Gilley said. "My horse is lamed-up with a bruised foreleg."

"You'll ride him anyway," Cheyenne said firmly. "Or else you'll ride double with me, on my lap."

"You go to hell," Gilley snapped back at him. "I'm not ruining my horse." She planted her feet on the ground in her determination. "I'm not sitting on your *randy* lap, getting myself short-horned every step of the way."

Cheyenne's felt his face redden, grateful to have it hidden in the darkness.

"I'll ride with Little Foot, or one of the others," she said.

Cheyenne took a deep breath, wanting to put a bullet in her. But he knew how bad that would look to Silvia.

These damn women . . ., he thought. "All right, you and Little Foot mount up, if he can stand you."

"I'm taking my horse too," Gilley insisted.

"Jesus! Take your damn horse," Cheyenne said. "Let's get out of here, before this wildfire comes licking up our backs."

Tarpis, Latin and Pace swung up into their saddles.

"Fellows," Pace whispered to the other two, "this beats all I ever seen."

"Hey, Delbert, shut up," Tarpis whipped back to him. "This ain't Dock or me causing the problem, is it?"

"No, I see it's not," said Pace, corking the whiskey bottle and slipping it back behind him inside his saddlebags. "But I always say, we're only as good as the brand we ride for."

Tarpis and Latin looked at each other in the darkness as the three of them nudged their horses over to Little Foot and Gilley and half circled them.

"Both of you get mounted," Tarpis demanded, seeing Cheyenne step his horse over to Caroline and Silvia, as if he was leaving Gilley for them to reckon with.

When the two had mounted Little Foot's horse, Gilley leading her lame horse by its reins behind them, Latin sidled close to them.

"I always liked you, Gilley. But one false move out of you or this Injun, either one, I'll kill you both quicker than a cat'll kill a cricket."

"You won't have any trouble from us, Dock. You've got my word on it," Gilley said. "I want to stay alive long enough to see *Mr. Cheyenne Kid* get what's coming to him."

"Me too," Little Foot said with a thin whiskey smile, his ragged blanket tightened around him against the cool of the night air.

Where the two women sat atop their horses waiting, Silvia gave Cheyenne a wry smirk as he rode up to them.

"Trouble with the little woman?" she asked.

"She's not my *little woman*," Cheyenne said. Not wanting to devote all his attention to the dove and leave Caroline out, he turned to her and said, "I'm sorry you had to hear about Segan."

"I don't care about Segan being eaten by a cat," Caroline said stiffly, looking away from him. "I wanted you to kill him for me, *remember*? Or have you forgotten about us?"

"I haven't forgotten," Cheyenne said. He looked at Silvia and saw her smug grin. He'd have to deal with her later, he decided, when he had time to show her his better side—explain everything to her in a way she'd understand. "Both of you better stay close beside me," he said. "It's an all-night ride to Dutchman's Gulch. We'll need to stay clear of any wildfire on the way."

Chapter 21

The Ranger had ridden halfway back along the same fork of trail the gang had taken out of Iron Hat when he saw the fire and smoke moving sidelong on the wind less than fifty yards to his left. If this was the same orange fire glow he'd seen from atop the apothecary roof—and he was certain it was, given the strength of the winds tonight—this new outburst of wildfire was traveling faster and wider than it had done for the past week.

Seeing the fire already encroaching dangerously close to his trail, he looked back into the darkness toward town and wondered if the colonel would have the good sense to turn his posse back. He hoped so, he thought, nudging the barb along the dark, rocky trail. He'd already begun to catch the familiar smell of burnt pine and brush wafting in around him.

"We've gotten used to this," he murmured to the barb, keeping his reins taut as he patted the horse's neck to keep it calm. But when they had gone another twenty yards, the barb began sawing its head and shying away from the rocky cutbank on their left.

All right, it's not the fire, he told himself.

Stopping the horse, he stepped down from his saddle and hitched the reins around a spur of rock. He drew his Winchester from his saddle boot and checked the rifle as he stepped forward, his eyes scanning the darkness along the inside edge of the trail. When he saw the tan creature stretched out along the bottom of the cutbank, he stopped and raised his rifle to his shoulder, recalling what Segan Udall looked like after his brush with the mama panther. As he stood ready to fire, he heard the muffled whine of the young cub, its face buried against its mother's belly.

"You again," Sam whispered under his breath, recognizing the familiar streak of dark dried blood still on the dead mother cat's shoulder.

He remained frozen in place with his rifle for a moment until he realized the mother cat wasn't going to spring up onto her paws and fling herself at him. He heard not so much as a warning growl from the still, silent animal, only the soft whimpering of the cub.

Inching forward, his rifle ready to fire until he stood directly over the animal, he stared down at the cub. The weak, barely conscious animal nursed at its dead mother's breast.

"Oh no . . . ," Sam whispered in regret. To be on the safe side, he reached down and poked the rifle barrel into the mother cat's furry neck. She didn't move. Then he sighed to himself, lowered the Winchester's hammer and stood in silence a moment longer, hearing only the roaring voice of the distant fire and the soft whimper of the orphaned panther cub.

When he crouched down and looked closer at the mother cat, he saw a gaping, blood-crusted wound on her side. He saw the glazed look of death in her open eyes and he felt a compulsion to close them with his gloved hand. But he didn't. Instead he reached down and raised the cub by the nape of its neck and turned it in his gloved hand and looked at it—*a little female*. He looked off again in the direction of the fire, already feeling the drifting heat of it nearing him on the night wind. Then he looked back at the half-conscious cub pawing weakly in the air toward his face.

"What's to become of you, little gal?" Sam asked, as if the helpless cub might speak up for itself. He shook his head and cradled the thin, furry animal in his arms as he stared down at its dead mother. With his rifle leaned against his chest, he stroked the dead mother cat's fur. *You did all you could, ol' mama. I'll attest to that for you. . . .*

He stood up with the cub against his chest, the animal too weak and stunned from traveling through smoke and fire to resist him. He'd known since childhood that it was wrong at worst, and foolish at best, to interfere with the will of nature. Yet he couldn't walk away and leave this cub to die, not after having witnessed how hard its mother had struggled to protect it.

He stared back at the silvery gray smoke forming down the hillside toward him, advance warning of the darker smoke and flame soon to come. How much of this devastation had resulted from Segan Udall's mindless action—*man's hand*—and how much had come from the forces of nature—*drought, winds, lightning*—he did not know. But there is such a thing as humanity, he told himself, and humanity need not explain its actions to either nature or itself. He clutched the cub to his heart as he lowered the tip of the rifle barrel an inch from its mother's head.

"You're coming with me, little gal," he whispered to the cringing cub, "see where this life takes you."

Sam was certain the mother cat was dead, but for the cost of a bullet he would never question himself. The Winchester bucked in his hand; the cub stiffened at the sound, then burrowed itself against his chest, its head hidden behind the open lapel of his riding duster.

When he walked back to the barb, the horse chuffed and grumbled and stomped a hoof at the scent of the cat. But Sam settled the protesting animal, shoved his rifle back into the saddle boot, unhitched the reins and swung up on the horse's back.

"I'm not asking you to be best friends," he said to the barb, putting the horse forward, the cat tucked inside his riding duster resting exhausted on his crossed forearm.

He pulled his bandana up over his nose and rode on, feeling the scorching heat begin to press him on his left.

Descending the trail two miles farther along, Sam stopped again and looked ahead warily. He could tell by both the closeness and the intensity of the wind-driven smoke and flames that there would be no reaching the three-fork junction on horseback. The fire was moving down in front of him like some element on attack, bent on stopping him.

This time he left the Winchester in its boot as he swung down from his saddle. When the panther cub stirred and growled a little behind his duster, he rested a hand on it to settle the animal.

"I should have told you," he murmured, "it's not always easy traveling with me."

For the next few minutes while the roar of the fire overtook the night and the black-streaked smoke moved across the purple starlit sky, the Ranger led the barb along the outside edge of the trail until he found a thin, steep game path leading downward. It was not the best of paths, but it beat the one he and Gilley Maclaine had taken, he reminded himself. Leading the barb to the edge, he coaxed the horse onto the narrow, rocky decline in front of him and followed the sure-footed animal, holding on to its tail.

The farther the horse led him down the side of the steep hill, the less he felt the heat of the fire and the choking grip of the smoke—the less he heard the bellowing roar of the fire. *So far so good . . .* , he told himself, feeling the steepness of the path level a little. Yet no sooner had he thought it than he felt his boot heel slip off the edge and he righted himself just in time, gripping the cub close to his chest.

Do not take this night for granted, he cautioned himself.

Above him, a spewing fire made up of burning brush and timber cascaded out over the edge, showered down the hillside and appeared to rise in an explosion at the bottom. This time there was no water waiting down there to stop it, to turn it into blackness,

Sam told himself. This time the fire was free to ride the wind.

The sight of the fire caused the barb to halt suddenly and back-step against Sam's raised hand.

"Whoa, now, easy, boy . . . easy," the Ranger said, soothingly, forcing himself to keep a calm voice even as he felt the strength of the barb pushing back on him. He knew there would be no stopping the big barb if it refused to let him settle it. The horse would take him, the cub and itself off the hillside, the three of them plunging down into an endless blackness.

"That's a boy," he whispered, feeling the horse settle a little for a moment as he eased around it and side-stepped his way along the thin edge of rock until he stood in front of the horse and drew its attention to him instead of the falling fire. "I'll take it from here, give you a rest," he whispered, rubbing its muzzle.

The barb chuffed and settled and blew out a tense breath, smelling the scent of the panther inside the Ranger's duster, but learning to live with it. Sam eased back between the horse and the rocky hillside, loosened the reins from around the saddle horn and eased back in front of the barb.

"Don't worry," he said to both of his weary, frightened traveling companions, the horse behind him, the cub lying once again quietly in his crooked arm, "it'll get better."

With the barb's reins in hand, he walked on, the thin path growing a little wider, a little less steep beneath his feet.

When he led the horse off the path and onto the

lower fork of the trail a half hour later, he jerked his canteen from the saddle horn, found a knee-high rock and plopped down on it. He pulled off his sombrero and set it upside down on the ground between his boots. He took a swig of water, swished it around and spit it into the open hat. He shoved the barb's nose back firmly as the animal stuck it in toward the canteen and nickered under its breath.

"*Shhh*, don't wake the cat," he said as he poured more water into the sombrero and watched the barb lower its muzzle and drink.

Ahead of them the Ranger saw where the fire he'd watched spill from the hillside took hold on a short stretch of flat valley land. The wind would have it swept across the valley floor and headed up the hill-sides in only a matter of minutes. It was flanking the trails and hillsides in the same direction he would be taking toward Dutchman's Gulch.

More of the same the whole way? he asked himself. He sat staring at the smoke and flames for a moment. It made no difference, he decided, cradling the sleeping panther cub. There was nothing he could do about it. He capped the canteen with his free hand while the barb nipped and sniffed at the inside of his sombrero for more. The fire was there to be reckoned with—one more part of the job. He picked up the wet sombrero and put it on.

"Are you ready to go?" he asked the barb, as if the barb might answer. Inside his duster he felt the rattling purr of the panther cub on his chest and forearm. *I know you are, little gal,* he thought toward the cub, wondering how she would react when she awakened to this new world around her.

In the morning light, a gunman named big Dave Tierney starred out from atop a ledge overlooking Dutchman's Gulch. In the southeast he saw the greasy black smoke standing high above its silvery-gray counterpart rolling across the valley floor. Streaking orange flames leaped high inside the smoke. The gunman gripped his rifle tight in both hands.

"I hate fire worse than anything," he said to a thin, swarthy gunman named Earl Weedy, who stood beside him, staring out through a long naval telescope. "That's why I don't want to go to hell when I die," he added solemnly.

"Ha!" Earl Weedy chuffed as he continued staring out through the lens. "You don't believe in hell, Big Dave," he said. "Nobody does, not really."

"The hell I don't believe in hell," said Big Dave. "I might be a no-good sumbitch myself, but I come from decent, God-fearing folks. They believed in hell and they grew me up to believe in it too."

"Bull," said Weedy. "Do you think you're going to hell when you die, Big Dave? Tell the truth." He gave him an edgy grin behind the telescope.

"I am for sure," said Big Dave. "I can't say I'm happy about it either."

"See," said Weedy, "if you *truly* believed in hell and you truly believed you're going there, you'd be doing everything you could to keep yourself from it."

"What are you doing, turning preacher on me?" Big

Dave offered with an uneasy chuckle, looking out at
the bellowing smoke and flames.

"No," said Weedy, "I'm just saying the truth. Man
who knows a gun is pointed at him and doesn't get out
of its way is a fool, don't you think?"

"I'd say so," Big Dave agreed.

"Because you believe in that bullet. You know it's
real, you know without a doubt it'll kill you." He lowered the scope from his eye and stared at Tierney. "But
you see hell coming straight at you, you don't do nothing to get out of its way?" He shook his head. "I say you
must not *really* believe in it. At least not as much as you
believe in a bullet."

"Give me that," said Tierney, reaching for the telescope, staring at him with a troubled look on his face.

Weedy held the telescope out to him, but he tightened his grip, not giving it up right away as Tierney
tried to take it.

"*Repent! Repent*, Big Dave, least ye burn in *e-ternal*
hell!" he said in a harsh, mocking tone.

"You're crazy as hell," said Big Dave, jerking the
telescope free from him. "I *believe* that."

Weedy cackled to himself and turned his naked
eyes back out across the valley floor.

"Look down there, just this side of the rocks," he
said. "Tell me what you see."

Tierney searched over to the right spot and looked
at the riders coming out of the forward-most veil of the
silvery gray smoke.

"I'll be damned," Tierney said, "he's made it. I was
wondering if he would, these fires such as they are."
He paused and studied out through the lens for a

moment, then said, "Damn, he's bringing a string of womenfolk with him."

"That's what I always admired about Cheyenne," said Weedy. "He always seems to have plenty of women on hand."

"Jesus," said Tierney in surprise, "one of them is Silvia Darnell, Colonel Moser's own special dove."

"I don't understand this," said Weedy. "Silvia is known to have a head on her shoulders. I can't see her leaving the colonel for the likes of the Cheyenne Kid."

"Neither can I," said Tierney. "But I can't wait to hear why it's taken him and his men so long to get here." He lowered the telescope and looked out with his naked eyes at the riders who had turned into tiny black dots moving across the valley floor. "Let's go wake Papa Nulty, tell him there's company coming."

The two gunmen turned and half climbed, half slid down a large, land-stuck boulder to where they'd hitched their horses. In seconds they were mounted and gone. They pushed their horses hard, maneuvering the animals through a maze of rock-work and sparse timber down to a stone and split-pine shack hidden by a stand of thick, towering mountain pine.

As they crossed a short stretch of cleared ground and slid their horses down to a halt at a weathered pine hitch rail, a big, burly man with a full black beard stepped out onto the plank porch wearing his gun belt, boots and ragged, graying long johns. He tied his holster down to his thigh. He carried a small empty metal pail looped over one wrist.

"Papa, we were coming to wake you," said Weedy, springing from his saddle to the ground with the agility of a tree frog. "Cheyenne and his men are cross-ing the grass flats right now, headed here."

The thin gunman looked and sounded excited. Papa Nulty straightened from tying down his holster and stared at Weedy evenly as he adjusted his big Walker Colt, loosening it in his holster. He held the empty pail out and shook it.

"Neither one of you sons a' bitches brought any fresh water up."

Big Dave Tierney stepped down from his horse beside Weedy. The two gunmen looked at each other and followed the big, ambling gunman across the clear-ing to where a thirty-foot braided runoff stream slid into the yard and out again into the pines.

"I told Big Dave to bring some in, Papa," said Weedy, hurrying alongside the big bearded gunman.

"The hell you did," Big Dave said sorely.

"Anyway," Weedy said to Papa Nulty, "Cheyenne's bringing some women up with him."

"Damn it to hell," Nulty said, squatting on his haunches at the edge of the stream, sticking the pail down and catching it half-full of cold water. "Bad enough we got wildfire licking at our backs. Now we got women coming?" He bowed his big head and poured the cold water over it.

Weedy gave Big Dave a puzzled look, then turned back to Nulty.

"Papa, we thought you'd be glad to hear it," he said.

Papa Nulty wiped his face, squeezed his thick beard and blew water from his lips.

"Any time you've got women, you've got trouble," he said with knowing finality.

The two looked at each other again.

"Dang, Papa," said Big Dave, "I never really seen a woman start any trouble."

"I never said they *start* it," Papa corrected him. "They just *bring* it." He stuck the pail back into the stream and this time filled it. He stood up laboriously, the full pail in hand. "Any time a woman's around, men are going to fight over her." He paused, then added, "If they're any kind of *men* at all."

The two thought about it, following Papa Nulty back to the porch of the shack.

"How many women are there?" Nulty asked over his shoulder.

"Looked like three—three and one Indian," said Weedy.

"I'd take the Indian," Papa said absently, "if I were given a choice."

Weedy chuckled.

"No, Papa," said Big Dave, "the Indian's not a woman."

Papa stopped in his tracks and pointed a thick, threatening finger at Weedy. "You're supposed to make some things clear when you talk."

"I'm sorry, Papa." The grin vanished from Weedy's thin face.

Nulty turned and walked on.

"Always with the womenfolk, that damn Cheyenne," Nulty said, shaking his big head. "I thought riding with this new bunch might change his ways. I expect I was wrong."

"Sounds to me like he's got the right idea, Papa," said Weedy. "I wish I had women all the time tagging along with me."

"No, you don't, Earl," said Papa. "You just think you do. Too much woman changes a man in ways I can't begin to explain. Cheyenne's fondness for the fairer sex is not something to admire. It's something to repudiate."

"Something to what?" Weedy asked.

"Just don't do it," Papa said. "Men like that are telling the world they were *too soon and too often* kicked away from their mama's teat."

"Indelicately weaned?" Big Dave added.

"There you have it," said Papa. "I couldn't have said it better." He stopped at the porch steps. "Don't get me wrong. I love women as much as the next man. All's I'm saying is there's something to pity in the man who has to dangle on the strings of *every* woman's heart. Too much *woman* makes a man want to wash himself, change his clothes, his socks. Soon he's scraping the black from under his thumbnails—sends his whole natural state a-skelter."

"One of the women is Silvia Darnell," Weedy tossed in.

For a moment Papa stared at him as if stunned. Then he reached a hand up and absently combed his thick fingers back through his wet hair.

"Why didn't you say so in the first place?" he finally said.

Chapter 22

When Cheyenne and his men rode up the trail past the lookout boulder above Dutchman's Gulch, he knew Papa Nulty's gunmen had already spotted them coming and taken the news to their boss. Turning quarterwise in his saddle, he looked back at the wall of smoke and high-reaching flames on the long, rugged hill line. From his position he could see, even with his naked eye, that every pass had been closed by the fire. For how long the passes and trails would be closed, he had no idea. But for now, there would be no one coming upon him by surprise.

You've never been as safe in your life, he told himself.

Beside him rode Silvia Darnell. A step behind her on her other side rode Caroline Udall, silent, brooding. On his other side rode Gilley Maclaine. Silent? Yes, but brooding, he didn't think so. In fact, he had no idea what went on in her head. As it turned out, he told himself with a sense of regret, he never did.

But this was no time to reflect on what had happened between them and try to set things right. He had tried to kill her; she had tried to kill him. *Let it go at that*, he advised himself. Things happened between people. Maybe a different time, a different place—

"It looks like you're taking us right up to the shack in the trees," Silvia said, cutting into his thoughts.

Cheyenne looked at her, surprised.

"How do you know about the shack?" he asked. "Have you been here before?"

"Heavens no!" Silvia cocked her head as if repulsed by the thought. "Thank goodness I'm a hostage," she added. "I'd hate for anyone to hear that I came here of my own accord, especially in my present company."

"Then how do you know about the place?" Cheyenne asked, trying to ignore her jab.

"I've heard stories," Silvia said. "This place is not secret, you know. Every two-bit thief in the territory knows about it. It's a place to come when a man can't afford anything better for himself."

"Oh, I can do better," Cheyenne said, nodding back toward the feed bag of money tied behind his saddle.

"Of course you can," Silvia said, sounding skeptical. She looked at the money, then back at Cheyenne, shaking her head now as if she pitied him. "To you this is a lot of money. To a man like the colonel, this is just *one* night's pay. Just think, while you're out there scratching around for your next little bag of stolen money, the colonel is stacking this much aside every night— probably wondering what to do with all of it."

Cheyenne stared at her, tight-jawed.

Silvia smiled mockingly and said, "That's why gals like me never spend any more time than we have to with men like you—*you're too cheap*."

"Yeah? You don't mind raising your skirts, taking our money," he said.

"Of course," said Silvia, "and that's all it means to us, we raise our skirts and take your money. How hard is that?"

Cheyenne fell silent.

Silvia raised her brow with a bemused expression.

"Oh dear, now I've gone and hurt your feelings," she said, feigning sympathy for him. "I'm so sorry."

She had hurt his feelings. Cheyenne gave her a look that did nothing to hide it.

"I didn't *really* need a hostage, Silvia," he said. "I brought you along hoping something might happen between us. Hoping we could both find something to—"

"Of course you did," she said, interrupting him with a cutting laugh. "Men like you always go around thinking simple, stupid things like that—"

"Stop saying *of course*!" he growled. This time he cut her off. "It sounds like you think you know everything about everything. But you don't."

"*Of course* I don't," she said, seeing she had pressed a nerve, wanting to press it harder. "I don't know *every-thing* about everything. But I do know *everything* I need to about you, *Mr. Cheyenne Kid*," she said, "and it took me watching you every bit of *five minutes* to learn it."

Cheyenne felt his temper start to boil. He jerked his reins hard right and spurred his horse away from the others to keep himself from losing control—the things she'd said in front of Caroline, in front of Gilley.

The three gunmen riding behind him, along with Caroline and Gilley, had seen Cheyenne and Silvia talking. They couldn't make out the words, yet they could tell the two were arguing. Now they watched as Cheyenne's horse slid to a halt a few yards away. Cheyenne sat staring back at the black, smoky horizon.

"Damn, fellows," said Delbert Pace. "Tell me it's not like this all the time." His voice sounded a little slurred from his taking a drink of whiskey every few miles throughout the night.

"It's not," Dock Latin said, staring straight ahead, embarrassed by the actions of their leader.

"Man! I hope not," Pace said, shaking his head. "This is nothing but—"

"Shut the hell up, Handy," said Royal Tarpis.

Pace fell silent, but grinned drunkenly to himself. As they rode on, Tarpis leaned a little in his saddle toward Latin.

"We've got to do something about this," he said quietly. "Else it's going to start looking bad on you and me."

Behind the two gunmen, Pace shook his head and grinned to himself as they rode on.

When they'd rounded through the pine woodlands, Cheyenne caught his first glimpse of the shack partially hidden by the trees. He saw Papa Nulty standing on the front porch as he and his riders filed in and crossed the cleared yard. Nulty wore clean but wrinkled trousers and a white linen shirt. His shirt had been buttoned all the way up against his wide, hairy neck. Big Dave Tierney and Earl Weedy stood in front of the porch at the handrail. They both stared at the women, their hats off and pressed firmly against their chests.

"Howdy, Nulty," Cheyenne said as he and the others stopped a few feet back from the hitch rail.

"Howdy, Cheyenne," Nulty said in passing. He stepped down and walked right past him to where Silvia Darnell sat atop her horse. "Howdy, Miss Silvia. Welcome to Dutchman's Gulch. I can't tell you how many times I've dreamed of seeing you ride in off the trail." He gave her his best grin. "What brings you here?" He reached up and took her hand.

"Howdy, Papa," said Silvia. "I'll tell you what I'm doing here. I was forced here against my will. I'm a hostage of the Cheyenne Kid here," she said, poking a thumb toward Cheyenne.

Nulty turned to Cheyenne with a stunned look.

"You took Silvia hostage?" he said. "What's going on here, Cheyenne?"

Before Cheyenne could answer, Silvia cut in.

"Him and his men robbed the Sky-High last night, Papa," she said sharply. "That's the colonel's money he's got tied behind his saddle."

"Jesus, Cheyenne!" said Papa Nulty. "You robbed the Sky-High? Nobody robs the colonel. He's everybody's friend."

"The colonel is a thieving, cheating son of a bitch," Cheyenne said, trying to justify his actions.

"So what?" said Papa. "Everybody I know and regularly consort with is a damn thief." He gestured his thick hand toward Cheyenne and his men. "What's that got to do with anything?" He stood holding Silvia's hand, ready to help her down from her horse.

"It's done," Cheyenne said firmly. "If you don't want

to take any of the colonel's money in exchange for the chance to hide out here, tell me now, and we'll ride on."

"Who the hell are these other people?" Papa nodded toward Caroline, Gilley and Little Foot, recognizing the Indian. "What the hell is Bagley's barn hostler doing here?"

"The women are also his hostages, the best I can make it out," Silvia said, again before Cheyenne could answer for himself.

Papa just stared at him, his brow furrowed in disbelief.

"They're not my hostages," Cheyenne said, feeling cornered, foolish, getting angry.

"So you're saying Little Foot and I can just turn our horses and go right now?" Gilley cut in. Beside her Little Foot gave her a sign, cautioning her to keep quiet.

"Try it," said Cheyenne, anger finding its way into his voice, his eyes, "I'll put a bullet in you." He took her words as a good and timely excuse for him to rest his hand on the big Colt holstered on his hip.

Papa noted that Cheyenne didn't move his hand away from the gun when the woman shut up and made no attempt to leave.

"Sounds like every one of you are worn plumb out from the trail, the fire and whatnot," said Nulty. He looked up at Silvia. "Why don't you come down here? I'll carry you inside."

"I'll walk," Silvia offered, allowing Nulty to assist her from her saddle into his burly arms.

"I won't hear of your feet touching this dirty ground," Nulty said. "Some of us are *still gentlemen*, in spite of the rigors of our harsh frontier lifestyle."

Cheyenne stared seething.

"Come inside, Cheyenne," said Nulty. "I think you need to tell me everything that's been going on."

"Want us to get back up to the lookout rock, Papa?" Tierney asked.

"Neither one of you move from here until I say so," Papa Nulty said sternly. He carried Silvia up onto the porch, then turned around and looked at Cheyenne, who still sat atop his horse. "Well? Are you coming inside, so's we can trash all this out like two civilized men?"

Cheyenne stared at him flatly for a moment, then swung down from his saddle, drawing his rifle from its boot. He looked all around, first at Weedy and Tierney, then at the two women and the Indian, then at his own men.

"All three of you wait out here. Keep the money bag close to you," he said to Latin, Tarpis and Pace. "Papa and I will talk everything out."

A few yards from the shack, Latin, Tarpis and Pace seated the two women and the Indian on a pine log and stood in a half circle around them. Big Dave Tierney and Earl Weedy stood near the hitch rail, their rifles cradled in their arms. They watched Cheyenne's three gunmen warily.

"This situation feels the way things feel right before a shoot-out," Pace said under his breath to Tarpis and Latin.

The two gunmen only nodded, staring back at Tierney and Weedy. The money bag lay at their feet, Latin having untied it from behind Cheyenne's saddle and carried it over with them.

"We need water," Gilley said, speaking for herself, Little Foot and Caroline. "It's been a long ride and we're parched." She nodded across the clearing toward the running stream. "There's no reason for us to go thirsty."

"Caroline," said Latin, "take the canteen from my saddle and go fetch it back full of water." He looked her up and down and added gruffly, "And hurry it up."

Caroline stood up dutifully and started toward Latin's horse. But Gilley took her arm, stopping her.

"Wait a minute," Gilley said to Latin, "why are you talking to her that way? Why's she being treated like a prisoner? She's not one of us."

"Oh, I don't mind being," Caroline said quickly.

"She likes to be talked to that way." Latin gave a thin smile and stepped in, took Caroline by her other arm and pulled her free of Gilley's grasp. "Am I right, Caroline?"

Caroline cast her eyes downward.

"Sort of. . . . ," she said. "I mean, I don't mind so much."

"There, you see? She don't mind so much," Latin said mockingly. He gave her a dismissing shove and said, "Go on, get everybody some water."

"I'll accompany you to the horses, ma'am," said Pace.

Latin and Tarpis watched as the two walked toward the hitch rail.

"You made a bold move, shoving that woman, treating her the way you did," Tarpis whispered sidelong to Dock Latin. "I don't want to be standing too close to you when she tells Cheyenne about it."

Latin grinned and hooked a thumb in his gun belt.

"She ain't going to tell him," he said confidently.

"You're betting your life on it?" Tarpis said.

Latin shrugged and considered it.

"Yeah, it was a bold move at that," he said. "But Cheyenne has used her all he cares to. He's got his head stuck in Silvia's bustle."

"That ain't no bustle, son," Tarpis replied with a sly grin.

"Still, with Silvia Darnell twisting her skirts at him, I'm thinking Cheyenne might pitch me his leftovers. He's got too damn many women now. I'd be doing him a big favor taking this one off his hands."

"She's got wear lines and brush cuts on her, for a fact," said Tarpis, watching Caroline Udall take the canteen down from Dock Latin's saddle horn. "But even a man who appears to have lost interest in a woman most always gets that interest back when he sees another man sniffing his hunt."

"I'll sniff his hunt," said Latin. "From what I've been seeing, our new boss is playing his string out fast. I don't owe him nothing. Neither do you. You and I might be looking for a new man to lead us if he don't draw himself in a little." He looked at Tarpis to see if he agreed.

"Or maybe just decide to lead ourselves . . . ?" Tarpis said, testing the idea.

"No, not me," said Latin. He shook his head. "I'm not going to follow myself." He gave a grin. "There's no telling where I'd end up."

"Damn, look at this," said Tarpis, seeing Delbert Pace walk back from his horse's saddlebags, carrying a fresh bottle of whiskey in his hand. "Where's he getting them from? No saddlebags hold that many bottles!"

"The son of a bitch is a magician," said Dock Latin.

"I've never seen nothing like it," Tarpis said.

Caroline Udall walked on to the stream to fill the canteen with fresh water. Pace approached, wagging the bottle of rye in front of him.

"Jesus, Handy, how do you do it?" said Tarpis, looking at the bottle as if it might be a mirage.

"No *good* drunkard is ever without a drink," Pace said, pulling the cork, smiling at the bottle. "I learned that from my pa when I was ten years old." He raised the bottle to his lips and took a deep swig.

Little Foot had sat silently, listening, watching. He stood up from the log and rubbed his palms on his trousers upon seeing the open bottle of rye raised into the air.

"You just as well sit yourself back down, Injun," Tarpis said to him. "Ain't none of this *firewater* coming your way."

"Hey, come on, now, Roy," Pace said to Royal Tarpis. "That's no way to be. When a man needs a drink, somebody ought to give him one." He stepped forward and held out the bottle. Little Foot took it with a trembling hand and turned up a long swig.

"He gets on the warpath and scalps you, Handy, it's your own damn fault," Tarpis chided.

"I have never scalped a man," Little Foot said, feeling the whiskey surge through him. He narrowed his gaze at Tarpis. "But I do know how."

"Is that a threat?" Tarpis asked, his rifle barrel rising in his hand. "Because if it is—"

His words stopped short at the sound of angry cursing coming from the shack's open front window. They had heard bickering now and then coming from Cheyenne and Papa Nulty, but nothing like this.

"Damn!" said Latin, him and Tarpis looking at each other, then back at the shack.

Inside the shack, a chair crashed. Silvia cursed and shrieked; Papa Nulty bawled out like a raging bear. At the hitch rail, Tierney and Weedy took a combative stance toward Cheyenne's men. At the log, Little Foot sat back down beside Gilley. He looked toward the stream and the trees beyond it, gauging the distance in case he and Gilley needed to make a fast run for it. Beside him, Gilley squeezed his upper arm, letting him know she understood.

"Take it easy over there!" Latin called out to Papa Nulty's two gunmen. "They know what they're doing in there."

Tierney and Weedy stood tensed, ready. But Tierney saw the killing coming if he didn't say something to stave it off.

"All right," he said, letting out a breath, lowering his rifle a little. He said to Earl Weedy beside him, "Keep your head, Weedy. We're the hired help here." He jerked a nod toward the shack. "Let the bosses sort things out."

Yet, almost before he'd finished saying the words, the fast, steady beat of a rifle firing resounded out the window, followed by Papa Nulty's bloody scream. The impact of the bullets hurled the large outlaw straight out the window and over the porch, into the dirt at the hitch rail. The horses spooked and reared and jerked against their tied reins as Nulty's body rolled to a halt at their skittish hooves. It was wrapped in a tangle of greasy checkered curtains, broken glass and pieces of window frame.

Big Dave Tierney and Earl Weedy jumped away in shock for a moment at the sight of their fallen leader lying bloody in the dirt.

Across the yard, Latin swung his rifle up to his shoulder.

"Kill these sons a' bitches!" he shouted at Tarpis and Pace as the rifle bucked and exploded in his hands.

Chapter 23

———

As soon as Cheyenne had fired the succession of rifle shots and sent Papa Nulty flying out the window, he grabbed Silvia by her wrist before she could run out the front door. Outside, bullets thumped against the front of the shack. Silva shrieked and scratched at his face, trying to pull herself from his grasp. But Cheyenne held her firmly in his free hand, his other hand holding his smoking rifle.

"Turn me loose, you crazy son of a bitch!" Silvia screamed.

Cheyenne shook her hard, then held her against a wall.

"Listen out there, Silvia!" he said. "You can't go out there. They'll kill you!"

In the yard, a gun battle raged back and forth between Cheyenne's men and Papa Nulty's. The frightened horses had jerked the hitch rail apart. They raced wildly back and forth across the yard. The long top rail still held one of the horses' reins. The rail swung back and forth like some ancient weapon as the horse circled the shack, bucking and kicking, running amid flying bullets.

"Oh my God, you saved my life, Cheyenne!" Silvia said, holding the back of a hand to her mouth. Cheyenne saw her eyes swim with gratitude and admiration.

"That's all right," he said, releasing his grip on her a little. "Just do like I say and everything—"

He let out a grunt as the ball of her slender knee slammed upward into his crotch.

"There, you bastard. For starting all this!" she shouted, jerking away from him while he bowed in pain. Gunshots still resounded in through the broken window. Bullets thumped against the front of the shack. He was right about one thing, she thought. It was too dangerous to go that way. She turned to run past him, out the back door.

Even in his stricken condition, Cheyenne wrapped an arm around her, grabbed her and held on. She turned with her nails outstretched like claws and swiped them down the side of his face. But one swing was all she got. Before she could claw him again Cheyenne managed to get his Colt up from its holster and make a swing of his own. The gun barrel struck the side of her forehead; she crumpled in his arm. He scooped her up in both arms in spite of his pain-racked crotch and headed out the back door.

As the bullets continued to fly out front, behind the shack Cheyenne spotted the frightened horse with the hitch rail still attached to its reins. He approached the animal slowly. "Whoa, boy . . . ," he whispered in a soothing voice. The horse chuffed and grumbled and stomped its hoof, the ongoing gunfight keeping it skittish.

Cheyenne got his hand on the horse's rein and untangled it from the broken hitch rail. The horse settled a little, feeling a firm hand take control.

"Where—where are we going . . . ?" Silvia said dreamily in the crook of Cheyenne's arm.

"Don't worry about it," said Cheyenne, "I've got you."

"You son of a . . ." Silvia's words trailed back into unconsciousness as Cheyenne lifted her up into the saddle and swung up behind her.

Now the money, then out of here . . . , he thought, with no remorse whatsoever for his three men here to die in the dirt while he rode off with all the money.

He gigged the horse and guided it deeper into the cover of trees. He circled out of sight and watched from cover, searching all around the yard for the bag of money. Not seeing it, he cursed to himself and swung down from the saddle. Leaving Silvia sitting slumped forward on the horse, he jerked a rifle from its saddle boot and stepped over beside a large pine.

In the yard, Caroline Udall was positioned flat behind the low log where she, Little Foot and Gilley had been seated when the shooting started. She held her hands over her ears and trembled against the hard, rocky ground.

Ten feet away, Royal Tarpis and Dock Latin lay prone in the dirt, firing round after round as fast as they could, relying on the volume of their fire to keep Tierney and Weedy pinned around the front corner of the shack. Blood ran down the back of Latin's hand from a deep graze in his forearm; Tarpis had a gaping hole in his shoulder.

A few feet from them, Delbert Pace lay sprawled in the dirt, holding two Colts out at arm's length, firing furiously. His bullet shattered the bottle of rye lying in the dirt beside him. A dark circle of whiskey wet the ground. When he ran out of bullets in both guns, he let his hands fall limply to the dirt and lowered his drunken head as if accepting defeat.

"Reloading, keep me covered," Dock Latin said to Tarpis. He jerked his rifle around and stuck round after round into it.

"Hurry the hell up, Dock!" said Tarpis, sounding worried. "I'm going down too." He kept firing, but he began spacing his shots, knowing that each shot left his rifle that much closer to being empty.

Having fallen back and taken cover around the corner of the shack, Big Dave Tierney and Earl Weedy had been able to conserve their ammunition a little better. As one reloaded, the fire of the other kept the three gunmen pinned in the dirt.

Tierney listened close, noting the wane in firing.

"They're reloading," he said sidelong to Weedy. "Here's our chance!" He levered a round into his rifle chamber and smiled at Weedy with satisfaction. "Looks like I ain't going to hell after all. Leastwise not today."

"Still, you should have repented from your sins whenst I gave you the chance," Earl Weedy said. He shot Tierney a tight, excited smile, also levering a fresh round into his smoking rifle. Sweat streamed down his gaunt face. "Okay, *sinner*, I'm ready! Let's walk them down and send them to hell," he said.

In the dirt, Latin and Tarpis were both frantically reloading their rifles.

"Holy *Jesus! Hurry up!*" Latin said to Tarpis. He had just finished reloading, but Tarpis was still working at it.

"I'm hurrying, damn it!" Tarpis shouted. Two bullets kicked up dirt in Latin's face. To the side, Pace shook his head and fell into drunken, hysterical cackling.

Seeing Tierney and Weedy move into sight and advance, firing with every step, Latin quickly turned his rifle, levered a round and shoved the stock against his shoulder. He squeezed the trigger.

Nothing . . . ! He tried levering the rifle again, hoping to kick out a bad bullet and make a fresh start. The lever wouldn't budge—jammed!

Good God! He lay shaking, jerking the rifle lever as the gunmen stopped firing for a moment and continued walking forward, as if they knew they were advancing on dead men.

Tarpis let his reloaded gun fall to the dirt and raised his hands a little. He looked up and saw Tierney's smoking rifle barrel looming only inches from his face. Next to him, Latin let his rifle drop too, and saw Weedy's grinning, sweaty face above him, his smoking rifle cocked and pointed.

"Don't shoot, please, Weedy!" he said, raising his hands from the dirt as much as he could. "You and me were never enemies!"

"Repent, repent . . . *O ye sinners, repent,*" Weedy said, grinning widely, liking the religious role he had taken on earlier with Tierney. "Lest ye burn in hell!"

"I do repent, Weedy, honest to God, I do," Latin said. Not far from his side, Delbert Pace lay hugging the earth.

"Quit fooling around, Weedy. Shoot him!" Tierney said.

"Oh, all right," said Weedy, grudgingly.

On Latin's left his heard Tierney let out a grunt as a rifle shot exploded. He cut his eyes toward Tierney just in time to see him stumble forward over Tarpis and land in the dirt as a thick red mist of blood loomed in the air behind him.

"What the—?" Earl Weedy turned quickly toward Tierney to see what was going on just as another rifle shot exploded. Latin flinched as Weedy's blood splattered down on his face, along his back. This time Latin realized the shot came from the trees along the far side of the shack. He looked through blood-hazed eyes toward the sound of the shot and saw Cheyenne step out into the cleared yard, his rifle still up, smoke curling from its barrel.

"Cheyenne . . . ," Tarpis said with relief. He pushed himself up beside Latin and reached a hand down to him. Latin took his hand and rose to his feet, feeling shaky, getting himself back under control. In the dirt nearby, Pace rose onto his knees, his arms clasped across his belly, cackling hysterically under his breath.

"Shut up, Handy!" Latin shouted. "Or I'll kill you myself."

They watched Cheyenne start toward them. But then they saw him stop and bolt back in the direction of the woods as the sound of hoofbeats raced, breaking through dry brush and undergrowth.

Inside the trees, Cheyenne stopped and stared as the horse with Silvia on it disappeared from sight.

Damn it to hell! he said to himself. She could have given him a chance. She didn't have to run away, leave him standing here like a fool in front of his men. What was wrong with these women? He could have proven himself to her, somehow, he thought. Still feeling the pain throb in his crotch where she'd kneed him, he took a deep breath and turned back to the yard.

All right. She didn't want him? *Then to hell with her,* he told himself. That was her loss—he brushed a broken pine needle from the sleeve of his forearm—not his, he thought, walking toward the shack.

By the time Cheyenne had walked across the yard to join his men, Delbert Pace had managed to get his drunken laughter under control. He'd picked up the empty Colts and stood with them in hand while he wiped his wet lips on the backs of his hands. He loaded each pistol in turn, stuck one in his holster and the other one inside his shirt, behind his belt. Two long, wide streaks of urine darkened the inside of his trouser legs.

Dock Latin had cleared and rechecked his jammed rifle when Cheyenne stepped in front of him.

"Boss, you saved my life," Latin said.

"Hell, all our lives," Tarpis put in.

"I owe you a bunch," Latin said to Cheyenne.

"Obliged, but forget it," said Cheyenne. "What do you think, that I could leave you out here to die?"

"No!" said Latin, he and Tarpis both shaking their heads vigorously. "If ever I might have had doubt," Latin continued, "I for sure know better now."

"We went the right way, going with you, Cheyenne,"
Tarpis put in. "But I reckon we already knew that."

Cheyenne nodded and said modestly, "Don't make
a big thing out of it. This is the way I ride." He looked
over at Pace, ignored the man's wet trousers and said,
"Handy, you got any more of that idiot juice?"

"I bet I can come up with some," Pace said, already
turning toward the loose horses standing huddled
near the spot where the hitch rail had been.

"Give everybody a drink on me," Cheyenne said.
He looked around the yard, taking his time, not wanting it to appear that the money was the real and only
reason he'd come to his men's rescue.

"You got it, boss," Pace said over his shoulder.

"Where's the money?" Cheyenne asked Latin and
Tarpis.

The two looked all around on the ground, then at
each other with stunned expressions.

"The woman and the Indian took it, boss," Pace
said, stopping on his way to the horses. "Soon as the
shooting started, I saw them heft it between them and
take off toward the woods."

"Damn it, Handy," said Dock Latin, "were you
going to tell anybody?"

Pace shrugged.

"I just did," he said.

Seeing Caroline Udall finally venture up from behind the log, Cheyenne let out a breath.

"Talk about it later," he said to the men. "Drink your
whiskey while we ride. We're not letting Gilley and
that crippled Indian skin us out of our money." He
reminded himself bitterly that this was the second

time Gilley Maclaine had taken his money. No matter what else happened, the minute he caught up to her, she was dead.

As the men hurried over to the horses and began sorting through the animals, Cheyenne stepped over and lifted Caroline enough to sit her back on the log.

"I was on my way back here for you, Caroline," he said. "Are you all right?"

"I'm all right," Caroline said, looking away from him. "You don't have to lie. You weren't looking for me."

"Sure I was," said Cheyenne. He lifted her face toward his on his fingertips. "Look at me, Caroline," he said, gently but firmly, forcing her attention on him. "I don't know what you think was going on between me and the dove, but it was only business. I had to play to her a little just to keep things going my way."

"I don't care," Caroline said in resignation, forcing her face away from his.

"It's true, Caroline," Cheyenne persisted. But seeing his talk was getting him nowhere, he was glad to hear Tarpis call out to him from the horses.

"Boss, we're going to be a horse short if a woman is going with us," he said.

Cheyenne gazed down at Caroline. She continued to look away from him. He could tell she was crying softly. Shaking his head, he said, "Caroline, I'm going to have to ask you to wait here for me."

"Go on," she said, "leave me here with the dead. I'll be all right."

Cheyenne looked around at the three bloody bodies lying in the dirt.

"But I am coming back for you, Caroline," he said,

sounding sincere. "Don't even think for a minute that I'm not."

"Just *go*," she said, still not facing him.

Cheyenne backed away without another word.

For the next few minutes, from her seat on the log, Caroline heard the commotions of the four men getting their horses ready for the trail. Finally, as she stared off into the woods through watery eyes, she heard the horses' hooves galloping away, splashing across the stream and fading deep into the surrounding pines.

In the silence so still she thought she could actually hear the sunlight move westward across the sky, she continued to sit and stare out at the distance where familiar brownish black smoke rose and bellowed. An hour passed . . . two hours. The smoke inched closer on the wind.

Finally she sighed, stood up and took a deep, cleansing breath. She walked to the two bodies lying almost side by side in the dirt. She stooped down, slipped a big Remington revolver from one of the dead outlaws' holsters, stood up and cocked its hammer using both hands.

A moment later, a single gunshot shattered the silence and resounded off through the woods. Birds shooed upward as one, like a handful of husk pitched onto the wind. On the woodland floor, the single rider stopped for a moment, but only for a moment. Then he batted his heels to his horse's sides and led the two spare horses behind him as he raced toward the sound of the shot.

In the clearing, Caroline stood stunned, her ears ringing loudly, a streak of burnt hair smoking across the back half of her head. She looked up from the gun lying on the ground at her feet and saw the ragged, bandaged figure and his black-smudged horses riding toward her.

"*Caroline!*" the rider shouted from thirty yards.

Although her ringing ears didn't allow her to hear the rider, she saw something familiar . . . something in the way he rode, the way he sat in his saddle.

"Segan . . . ?" she said, not realizing how loud she'd said it.

"Oh, Caroline, yes, it's me!" Segan shouted tearfully, sliding his horse and his smoke-blackened spare horses to a halt.

He stiffly climbed down from his saddle, bandages covering his face, his chest, his forearms, like some ancient mummy from the Valley of the Kings.

"Thank God!" he said, turning, grabbing her into his arms, pressing her against him. "I thought I'd never see you again."

"Se-Segan," Caroline said, standing limply against him, only catching shallow echoes of his words.

"Yes, it's me, Caroline," Segan said, holding on to her even though she offered no return of his embrace. "Nothing could keep me from finding you."

Caroline stared off over his shoulder into the woods as he babbled on into her deaf ear.

"I have burned every inch of ground behind me following Cheyenne's trail. I saw them ride away from here earlier. When I didn't see you, I knew they must've left you behind. So I came straightaway!"

Caroline only nodded, knowing he'd said something about following the trail to her.

"I stole the horse I'm riding from the settlement. I found these two wandering along a stream where somebody must've lost them. They're battered and skinned up something awful, but they'll ride. I brought them in case I found you. And now I have, thank God, *thank God!*" He squeezed her tighter; she only nodded.

He held her at arm's length, his big hands on her small shoulders.

"Things are going to be fine now," he said, "just fine from now on." But when he'd stopped speaking, she saw his countenance change before her eyes. "But tell the truth, darling," he said, "did he force himself upon you? I won't hold it against you if he did. Only I've *got* to know, for *my* sake, for *our* sake."

Caroline did not hear what he asked, but she could tell what subject he was broaching by the way his grip tightened on her shoulders.

"He never touched me, Segan," she lied, her voice raised against her own deafness. "He gave his word and he kept it." She studied his face, gauging if what she said was going to be enough. His expression changed, but only slightly; she had to give him more, she decided.

"He would have had to kill me if he tried, Segan," she said, hoping that was all it would take. And it was.

Relief flooded Segan's face. He pulled her against him again.

"Thank God," he whispered. "Thank God. . . ."

Caroline only nodded. While she stood woodenly, smelling of burnt hair, her arms limp at her sides, she did reach a hand up and carefully patted his bandaged back.

"Just take me home, my husband," she whispered, not hearing, or even caring what he'd said. "Just take me home. . . ."

Segan pulled away but kept an arm around her. The two turned and walked toward the horses. Smelling the burnt hair, seeing the big Remington that had been smoking on the ground, he gave her a questioning look.

"It was nothing," she said. "I tried to shoot myself." She raised her arm and encircled his waist, accepting him back. "But it appears I missed."

Chapter 24

When the gunfight began, Gilley Maclaine had snatched up the bag of saloon money, thrown it over her shoulder and taken off running, Little Foot right behind her, the small Indian limping and struggling to keep up with her. Inside the woods, Gilley had stopped once, only for a moment, to look back and warn him.

"As soon as they finish killing each other, whoever's left alive will be coming for this money," she said, slightly out of breath. She dropped the heavy bag of money on the ground.

"Yes, but only . . . because you . . . *took* the money," Little Foot said, gasping for breath. "If you left it there . . . they wouldn't care . . . what we—"

"I wasn't about to leave without it," Gilley interrupted, "not after what Cheyenne put me through." She wiped a hand across her sweaty forehead. "You've got to keep up, or I'll have to leave you behind."

Her words stung and shamed Little Foot. He wanted to tell her that he was doing his best to keep up, but that his withered foot would not allow it. But that would be an excuse, and even though it was a good and honest excuse, his warrior's pride would never allow him to say it, even with the whiskey he'd drunk still glowing warmly in his brain.

"You go on ahead . . . don't worry about me," he said, starting to catch his breath. "I am a warrior."

"I don't want to leave you," Gilley said.

"Go on," said Little Foot. "I stake myself out here. I will ambush them . . . and kill every one of them."

Gilley stared at him for a moment, then looked down and shook her head.

"Anyway," she said, "I'm sorry, Little Indian. But I've got to go." She hefted the bag back up onto her shoulder.

"I am not Little *Indian*," Little Foot said, correcting her. "I'm Little *Foot*, remember?" He raised his small, withered foot and wagged it a little, as if to remind her.

He was drunker than she'd realized.

"I know that," Gilley said, placating him. She left him without looking back and hurried along the rocky trail toward the smoke and flames that lay atop the hills ahead of her. How she would avoid the fire, she had no idea. But she had money, plenty of it. Something would come to her. It always did. *Keep moving*, she told herself.

As she disappeared out of sight, Little Foot squatted on his haunches and continued catching his breath. After a moment he looked around at the many rocks strewn along the trail. Good rocks for throwing, at least some of them, he thought. He sorted through the loose rocks, running his hands over them until he'd selected half a dozen that fit just right in his hand.

He stood up and gazed back along the trail, the whiskey lending him courage, and a sense of well-being he had never felt so strongly. *Let them come,* he told himself, taking a warrior's stance, one rock in his right hand, the other five cradled against his chest in his thin left arm.

As he stood waiting, he began chanting a warrior's death chant, or at least he hoped that's what it was. With his having grown up for the most part in the white man's world, there were things he knew, and things he didn't about his people. There were also chants for weddings, for giving birth, for just giving thanks to this spirit or that. But it didn't matter, he told himself. What the chant was intended for was not as important as what he felt in his heart as he spoke it.

In his heart he spoke the chant a warrior speaks before hurling himself, his life, his arrows, his only spear . . . or *rocks*, at his enemy. This was all that mattered.

As he prepared for death, be began hearing the beat of hooves coming up the trail toward him. He tensed himself and stood more firmly. His chanting quickened with intensity. The whiskey boosted his courage, but it did not create it, he was certain. The courage had to be in his heart to begin with for the whiskey to bring it out.

Either way he was ready for death when death came galloping into sight.

As the glimpse of horse and rider appeared in a glint of sunlight, his chanting stopped. He let out a fierce war cry and began hurling rock after rock. Yet, as the harsh sunlight waned and his third rock left his hand, he recognized Silvia Darnell, her gaping mouth, her terror-filled eyes as she caught a flash of a rock the size of goose egg whistling toward her forehead.

"Oh no! Oh God!" he exclaimed.

He'd killed her! he thought, seeing her roll backward out of her saddle, her arms outspread, both legs flung open in the air. She flipped off the horse's rump and slapped facedown on the ground like a limp bundle of rags. The horse, feeling the weight of its rider gone, slowed down to a halt and looked back as if in curiosity.

Little Foot dropped his remaining rocks and ran limping to the woman, who was sprawled on the hard, rocky ground. This was not at all what he'd chanted for. This was not the act of a warrior; this was the act of a drunken fool!

Damned whiskey! he cursed to himself, suddenly sober, stooping, turning the woman over in his arms. Hearing her groan, he brushed dirt and particles of pine bark from her face, her open mouth. A knot the size of the rock that had felled her had already risen on her forehead.

"*Ma'am!* Ma'am! Please wake up! Please don't die!" he said, shaking her.

Her eyes were lazily open, but severely crossed and unfocused. Drool seeped from the corner of her lips and ran down her cheek. He could think of no chant for what he'd done, nothing to be said in any language to make up for having stone-knocked the wrong person.

"*Aiiieeee . . . ?*" she groaned mindlessly, asking some strange question to which there could be no answer.

Yet Little Foot let out a sigh of relief at just hearing

her groan. When her eyes lost their glazed leer and uncrossed, he scooped her up into his thin arms and hurriedly limped back to the waiting horse.

"What hit me . . . ?" Silvia mumbled half-consciously into his shoulder as he lifted her up back into her saddle and climbed up behind her.

"I don't know," said Little Foot, "but lucky for you I came along when I did." He batted his heels to the horse's sides and sent it continuing up the trail at an easy gallop.

Less than a mile farther up the trail, Gilley stopped and looked behind her, dropping the bag of money from her shoulder. This wasn't right, no matter how she looked at it, she told herself, unable to shake from her mind the hurt look on Little Foot's face when she'd left him behind. She owed him nothing; they were not friends, partners, lovers. Nothing. Just a couple of people thrown together a few steps ahead of a wildfire, she told herself.

Still, she couldn't square what she'd done. She saw the Indian's hurt face, and she saw the way she thought the Ranger would interpret her actions, although she owed him nothing either—all right, she did owe the Ranger, she admitted. Maybe she owed Little Foot something too. She wasn't sure. . . .

"*Damn it!*" she cursed out loud.

Jerking the money bag off the ground, she dragged it roughly off the trail, deeper into the brush and pine. Moments later she stepped onto the trail again, dusting her hands together, and started walking back in Little Foot's direction. All right, she'd go back and stick with the Indian. She was angry with herself for doing it. It wasn't like her. But it seemed right. *Here I go. . . .*

"Ranger, I hope you're satisfied," she said under her breath.

But before she had gone thirty yards, she heard the sound of hooves coming up the trail toward her. She ducked away into the trees and stood watching from cover until she saw Silvia bobbing limply on Little Foot's chest.

"Now what?" she whispered to herself, stepping out onto the trail, waving the horse down.

"What happened to her?" she asked, looking up at Silvia as Little Foot reined the horse to a stop.

"She got hit by a rock," Little Foot said. "It's a long story," he added, dismissing the matter. "You didn't get very far," he said. "Where's the money?"

"I hid it," Gilley said. "Nobody is going to get it but me."

"I understand," said Little Foot. He looked back along the trail. "I thought I heard a horse coming. This is not a good place to be." As he spoke, he swung down from the saddle and handed her the reins. "You ride for a while. I'll walk."

Gilley just looked at him.

"I told the Ranger I would look after you," he said. "A warrior is as good as his word."

Again, the Ranger influencing everybody's actions, Gilley told herself. She took the reins and said, "I'll ride for a while, but then it's your turn."

Little Foot nodded; Gilley swung up behind Silvia and let her flop back against her.

"Did you . . . hit me?" Silvia asked dreamily, the

knot on her head turning the purplish color of fruit going bad.

Gilley gave Little Foot a quizzical look.

"She doesn't know what she's saying," Little Foot said quietly.

The Ranger walked through a wavering drift of silver-gray smoke. Behind him, more sinister, black, flame-streaked smoke broiled up from the valleys and hillsides. The barb walked along easily at his side, smelling the scent of cat, hearing the roar and crackle of fire, but growing less skittish toward either one under the Ranger's confident guidance.

At the edge of a high cliff, the Ranger held his battered telescope with one hand and surveyed the fiery hills that stood between him and the town of Iron Hat. Any thought of the colonel's posse catching up to him was out of the question now, he knew, seeing the raging nightmare of flames licking into the blackened sky. Had they tried earlier, they would have given up by now. Had they not given up by now, it was a good bet they were dead, he decided with finality.

He turned his lens from the direction of Iron Hat and onto the clearer trails below. Off to his right, he recognized the Cheyenne Kid and three of his men riding hard along an upward switchback trail. He scanned the trail right to left, judging the distance of a mile or less, seeing the two women and Little Foot moving along at an easy pace.

One level below, a mile between them . . . , he told himself. He felt the heat of the wildfire begin to creep through the back of his duster as he closed the telescope, adjusted the sleeping panther cub in the crook of his arm and stepped into his saddle.

"I wish I didn't have to ask you," he said to the barb, nudging the animal off the trail, down onto a steep decline of loose rock, gullies and brush.

Halfway down the steep mile, he saw Little Foot look up, spot him and begin waving his arms back and forth. Sam wanted to raise his Colt and fire a warning shot, but he wasn't sure they would understand. Not only that. He knew that firing the shot would tip off Cheyenne and his men that someone was on the trail ahead of them, maybe armed and waiting. So he held his fire and rode on, knowing it was up for grabs who would arrive first, him or the outlaws.

Luckily it was him, he thought minutes later as he stepped the barb onto the trail in a rise of dust, a spill of loose rock.

"Ranger, it is good to see you," Little Foot said, taking the barb by its bridle and guiding it out of the rising dust. Sam looked at Gilley sitting atop the horse, Silvia sitting in front of her with a wet cloth held to her swollen forehead, having come around some over the past half hour.

"What happened to her?" Sam asked.

"Hit by a rock," Little Foot said. In an effort to change the subject, he said, "I think we have gunmen on our trail, either Cheyenne and his men, or the outlaws who killed them."

"It's Cheyenne," Sam said. "I saw them from up there. They'll be here any minute." He swung down and pulled the cub from inside his duster. The little cat raised a sleepy head and blinked back and forth.

Little Foot reached out and took the cub without

being asked, and cradled it on his arm as Sam worked his own arm back and forth, getting it loosened up.

"Where's the saloon money?" he asked Gilley, as if already knowing she would be the one to ask.

"I took it and hid it," she said.

Sam nodded and said, "You seem to have a knack for taking Cheyenne's money."

Gilley smiled.

"I'm not keeping it," she said, "since it's *not mine*." She gave him a look. "I'll take you to it."

"Maybe later, *I hope*," Sam said, gazing back along the trail.

"Give me your rifle, Ranger," Little Foot said. "I will side with you. We will stake ourselves out—"

"I have no guns to spare, Little Foot," Sam said, cutting him off. Seeing the hurt look in the Indian's eyes, he said, "Besides, I need you to get these womenfolk out of sight. If these fellows do kill me, you'll have to get them down out of here on your own. Can I count on you?"

Little Foot jutted his chin.

"Yes, you can," he said. "I will even take care of this panther cub. I will raise it on goat and mare milk until it is strong enough to eat red meat. I will be honored to raise it, and even more honored to someday set it free."

Sam smelled a lingering waft of whiskey on Little Foot's breath.

"Are you drunk, Little Foot?" he asked.

"I was earlier, but not now," Little Foot said. He glanced up at Silvia, then back at the Ranger. "I think I am better at some things when I'm sober."

"All right." Sam nodded and said, "Get them off the

trail and out of sight. If this goes bad for me, head north until there's no more sign of fire."

"No, Sam, you go with us," Gilley said from her saddle. "Go with us now! Don't stay here and fight these men. Don't be a fool. They'll kill you."

A fool . . . Sam just looked at her.

"I didn't mean that, Sam!" she said quickly. "But please, just come with us! Nobody will blame you. There's four of them."

"Take her and go," Sam said just between himself and Little Foot. "I hear their horses." Sam drew the rifle from its saddle boot and checked it.

Little Foot grabbed both the horses' reins and led the women and the Ranger's barb off the trail, the panther cub asleep in the crook of his arm. Sam turned and walked toward the sound of hooves pounding along the trail toward him.

When the four horsemen rode up into sight, the Ranger stood in the middle of the trail facing them. Seeing them hesitate as they reined their horses down, Sam called out, "Cheyenne, you've had your run. Step down, it's time we settled up."

"He's got our Sky-High money. I can tell by the way he's acting," Cheyenne said to the other three. "Gilley and that Injun brought it straight to him." He raised the rifle from his lap and stood it on his thigh. "Let's take it."

Latin and Tarpis looked at each other. Tarpis said, "Yeah, let's take it." They looked back at the sound of Delbert Pace's horse stepping off the trail into the cover of brush and pine. "Handy, you *damned coward*," Tarpis called out to him as Pace slipped out of sight. Then he turned back and said to Cheyenne, "Ready when you are, boss."

Sam raised his rifle to his shoulder as the three gunmen made their charge. First and foremost he wanted the Cheyenne Kid, he thought, the simple reason being Cheyenne was the only one with a rifle in hand. The other two held pistols leveled and firing at him—bad judgment, out of pistol range, firing from horseback. What kind of leader allowed that? He took aim. Only a leader who had gone too long with too many other things clouding his mind, he thought as he felt the jolt on his rifle shot and saw Cheyenne fall backward from his saddle.

Latin and Tarpis rode forward firing their revolvers, the shots falling ten feet short, kicking up dirt.

Sam's second shot sliced through Royal Tarpis' heart and sent him rolling off his horse in a spray of blood.

Latin realized their mistake and jerked his rifle from its boot. But the Ranger's third shot nailed him dead center. He sailed off his horse and slid to a bloody stop. Sam walked forward, his smoking rifle hanging in his left hand. He stopped and stood looking down at Cheyenne, who lay against the cutbank side of the trail, blood running from his lips, a gaping hole in his chest. Cheyenne's hand was wrapped around the butt on his holstered Colt.

"Get them . . . back, Ranger," he said in a weak, rasping voice.

Sam could tell by the look on his face that the women had stepped back onto the trail and were coming forward. Without looking back he called out, "Everybody get back. This man is still armed."

He saw the relief come to Cheyenne's eyes and knew the women had fled back off the trail.

"Obliged . . . ," Cheyenne said. He coughed violently, then looked back up at Sam. Nodding at the big Colt holstered on Sam's hip, he said, "Can you help . . . me out?"

Sam paused, then nodded at the Colt in Cheyenne's holster. "Only if you could *help me* help you," he said quietly.

"I'll try," Cheyenne said. He paused, then said, "I never should have . . . tried to lead . . . hell, I done well just to follow." With all his waning strength he struggled until he slid the Colt up from its holster and managed to half raise it.

From the edge of the trail, Gilley and Silvia both flinched at the single blast of the Ranger's Colt. They stayed where they were, but Little Foot limped forward at a trot and drew to a wary halt at Sam's side, the panther cub awakening and bobbing its head on his crooked forearm.

"He drew on you?" Little Foot said almost in disbelief. He stared at the bullet hole in Cheyenne's forehead as the Ranger reloaded his spent round and lowered his Colt back into its holster.

The Ranger didn't answer. Instead he said, "Don't let the women up here. Wait until I get him off the trail. Then we'll ride back the way we came."

"Oh, you don't want them to see him?" Little Foot said.

"They don't need to," Sam said. "They've seen enough." He gazed away at the black sky and licking flames. "We're going to have to ride a long way north to get ahead of this fire. Luckily, it looks like the wind has turned in our favor. Let's hope it stays that way."

"A warrior lives his life on the turn of the wind and the rage of fire," Little Foot said. He looked at the Ranger. "Or so I have heard."

Sam nodded, reaching out and rubbing the panther cub's furry head. The cub growled menacingly even though it smelled its mother on the palm of Sam's hand—its mother's scent mixed with that of burnt gun powder, leather reins and brass cartridge casings.

"I've heard the same thing, Little Foot," he said. "I believe it must be true."

Arizona Ranger Sam Burrack is back!
Don't miss a page of
action from America's most
exciting Western author,
Ralph Cotton.

LOOKOUT HILL

Available from Signet in October 2012.

The Mexican Hill Country, Old Mexico

Arizona Territory Ranger Samuel Burrack rode up a
long, slanted hillside above miles of smelting furnaces
and mining encampments. When he'd reached a point
where he could breathe without the acidy odor of
melted copper burning his nostrils, he stopped and
pulled his bandana down from the bridge of his nose.

Clean Mexican air..., he told himself, inhaling
deeply, letting his lungs take their fill. Beneath him he
felt the stallion chuff and blow and lift its muzzle to a
cool passing breeze.

"You too, pard?" He said quietly, patting the big
Appaloosa's withers with a gloved hand. He nudged
the stallion forward, his right hand holding his Winchester rifle across his lap.

Fifty yards up the trail, he found the tracks he had
lost earlier when he'd started crossing a hard rock
ledge. Now that the ledge had given way to softer dirt
and gravel, he saw the hoofprints of the two horses

he'd been tracking all the way from the foot of the Sierra Madres. *For the last three days . . . ,* he reminded himself. Wanting a closer look, he stopped the stallion and stepped down from the saddle, rifle in hand.

Yep, it's them all right . . . , he told himself, looking closer at the sets of prints. He had seen early on where a faulty nailhead had broken off one of the shoes, leaving a shallow gap imprinted in the dirt. Soon that gap had filled with packed dirt. But crossing the rock ledge, the impacted dirt from the shoe must have broken loose. Now that the two horses had left the stone surface, he knew the empty nail hole would fill with dirt again. But that was all right, he thought. He was back on their trail.

He had come to know the hooves of these two horses. At a walk, one of them veered a little to the left over a short distance of twenty or so feet—the sign of a lazy hand on its reins. The other horse, the one with the broken nailhead in its shoe, had a splayed right front hoof. With every step this animal took, the hoof print turned a slight bit outward—hardly noticeable except to the sharpened tracker's eye.

Sam stood up from the prints and looked all around. He was not the gifted tracker that he would like to be, but he was still learning. Learning, with his fingers in the dirt. The only way to learn, as his captain would say. And his captain was right, he told himself, walking along, reins in hand, leading the stallion along the narrow trail.

Tracking required close attention to detail. Some men worked hard at learning it; others didn't. Some men pinned on a badge thinking being gun-handy was all it took to be a good ranger. But even though he'd only been a ranger for a little over two years, he'd already seen that men who didn't learn sound tracking skills soon left the trail in defeat, or worse. Some of them left in a plank box.

He'd not only learned the particulars about these two horses—how they moved and what identifying marks they left behind—but he'd also put more than just a little thought into the two men riding them. One was a quick-to-kill Missouri madman named Hodding "Hot Aces" Siebert. The folded wanted posters inside the flap of his bib-front shirt told the ranger that Hodding Siebert had been outrunning the law for over three years. Siebert knew that getting caught left nothing of his future but a hard drop at the end of a hangman's rope.

Sam knew that with such a grim reckoning awaiting him, "Hot Aces" Siebert played out his life hard and fast. He took what he wanted when he wanted it, and heaven help the man who tried to stop him. But Siebert wasn't the first killer the ranger had hunted down, nor did Sam have any intentions of allowing him to be the last. So, while Siebert's murderous regard for the rest of the world gave Sam no cause for alarm, it did hold his attention.

Sam knew that in Siebert's three years of freedom from Yuma Penitentiary, the man and his various cohorts had robbed some nine banks, three trains, and a dozen or more payrolls. At each robbery he'd left at least one dead man lying in his wake. In addition to the killings while in pursuit of his trade, Siebert was known for senseless indiscriminant killings all along the border country—an unpredictable lunatic with a gun. Especially when riding alone, left to his own devices, Sam told himself. Maybe riding with a partner would help keep him in check. He hoped so.

Real pieces of work, these two . . . Sam shook his head a little, considering these men whose dark menacing lives he'd committed himself to bringing to their bitter ends.

It was his job, he reminded himself.

The second man was Texas outlaw and escaped convict Bobby Hugh Bellibar. Another hard-case with nothing to lose, Bellibar's crimes over the past years were so numerous and diverse, Sam was certain the courts must've had a hard time deciding whether to list his heinous offenses alphabetically or in the order of their perpetration.

Sam stopped and looked out over a valley a few hundred feet below. A thin glittering river wound out of sight at the bottom of a steep hillside. He thought about the empty canteen he'd found along the trail three hours earlier. He'd known then that it wouldn't be long before they gravitated toward whatever water lay nearest them. *And there it was*, he told himself, Winchester in hand, leading the stallion behind him.

Twenty minutes later he came upon a lone horse standing to the side of the trail, its reins dangling loose to the dirt. The silvery-gray dun stood dark with sweat and lathered in white foam. Upon seeing the ranger, the animal shied away a few steps, favoring its right forehoof. *The horse with the out-turned hoof*, he thought, not surprised that it would be the first horse to falter under the weight of its rider and the rigors of this steep, rocky trail.

He let Black Pot's reins drop from his hand, knowing the stallion would stay there. First checking for any sign of an ambush, Sam eased forward, his rifle hammer cocking under the pull of his thumb.

"Easy, boy . . . ," he murmured to the silver-gray dun, picking its reins up from the ground. He examined the animal's right forehoof, lifting it up between his crouched knees for a closer look. The horse chuffed and grumbled a little as Sam pressed with his thumbs and worked the horse's hoof around with his gloved hands.

"There's nothing wrong with you that a little rest and water won't cure," Sam said. "The water's not far, but you'll have to rest while you walk." As he spoke, he loosened the cinch and dropped the saddle from the dun's back. "That'll help some," he added.

The horse looked at him, grumbling and scraping its good hoof on the ground as if in protest. Sam rubbed a hand along its withers.

"I know," he said as if the animal understood him, "but it's walk with us, or spend the night here alone, feeding wolves."

The horse stared at him through caged eyes, but then it took a wary step closer and probed its frothy muzzle toward him.

"That's what I thought," Sam said. He chuckled to himself, rubbed the horse's muzzle and drew the tired animal over beside Black Pot. He stepped back up into his saddle. "Don't worry," he said to the sweaty dun, "we'll take it nice and easy down to the water."

On the same trail, miles ahead of the ranger, Hodding "Hot Aces" Siebert lay prone on the gravely stream bank, his face and the upper half of his body sub-merged in cool rushing water. Bobby Hugh Bellibar stood beside him, holding the roan's reins loosely while the thirsty animal drank.

"Here's the hard truth of it, Bobby Hugh," Siebert said, his palms supporting him on the gravely bank. "I'm not riding double the rest of the way to Copper Gully. Your horse gave out on you. We keep riding double, mine will do the same before we're off these hilltops."

"I hear you, Aces," Bobby replied.

"This is nothing personal against you, Bobby Hugh," Siebert said, "but when riding stock gets in short sup-ply, every man has to fend for himself." He paused as if in reflection, then said, "If I had dollar for every man I shot over a horse, or *thought* about shooting over a horse, I'd be rich as a pound cake."

"I understand," Bellibar said acceptingly. "Me too."

"So, figure something out before we leave here," Siebert said with resolve; and with that he lowered his face into the clear, cool water.

Bellibar watched him drink.

"I think I got it figured," he said as Siebert finally pushed himself up from beneath the water.

"Yeah, what's that?" Siebert said, water running down from his wet hair, his clothes.

"I'm taking *your* horse, Aces," Bellibar said flatly.

"You're talking out of your head, Bobby Hugh." Siebert gave a sharp grin and turned sidelong to where Bobby had stood watering the tired roan a moment earlier. But Bellibar wasn't there, and neither was the roan.

"Back here, Aces," Bellibar said, behind him.

"Right," said Siebert, getting the gist of it. He rolled over onto his back, his wet hair hanging in dripping points down his forehead. "I expect you think you've caught me at a disadvantage," he added, cocking his head slightly.

"Yep, that's how I make it," Bellibar said, the horse's reins in his left hand.

"You make it wrong, Bobby Hugh," said Siebert, the grin still there on his wet face. "Don't you think I already thought of this before I said anything about the horse?" He gave a dark, confident chuckle. "That's why I unloaded your Colt earlier while you were dozing against that big pine. You're *jackpotted*, pard. Now I kill you and take your power."

Take my power . . . This crazy bastard.

"You're bluffing," said Bellibar. "I heard that one before—tell a man his gun's not loaded, then gun him down when he makes a move to check it."

"Already heard that one, huh?" Siebert sighed, shaking his head a little.

"Yep," said Bellibar. "It might even have been you who told it to me."

"I wouldn't doubt it," said Siebert. He pushed himself up from the ground and stood with his feet spread shoulder-width apart. He wiped his left hand across his face, pushing his wet hair to the side. His right hand stayed poised near the tied-down holster on his hip. "Only this time it's a fact, Bobby Hugh," he added, in a stone-serious tone of voice. "I've got your bullets in my pocket. Want to see them?"

"Nope," said Bellibar, his demeanor still confident,

unwavering. "I believe you did it, you sneaking son of a bitch."

Siebert gave a short shrug. There was no sign of bluffing in his eyes.

"Like I said, Bobby Hugh," Siebert said quietly, "times like this it's every man for himself. You should have listened to me."

Bellibar could tell the older gunman was ready to make his play. He saw Siebert open and close his gun hand, getting ready.

"I did listen to you, Aces," he said. His expression softened a little. "That's why I took your Remington from your holster while you sucked water."

"Nice try, Bobby Hugh," said Siebert, "but I ain't falling for it—" As he spoke his right hand slapped against his empty holster and stopped him short. His eyes suddenly took on a look of desperation.

Now it was Bellibar's turn to give a wide, confident grin. He reached behind his back, taking his time, and grabbed Seibert's big Remington.

"See?" He wagged the gun back and forth in his hand. Looking down at it, he cocked it toward Siebert's chest and said, "I bet you didn't unload it, did you?"

"No, Bobby Hugh," Seibert said in defeat. "Damn it to hell, I didn't unload it." In a flash he thought about the small Colt Pocket pistol he carried behind his back, shoved down into his belt under his shirt tail. But it was too late.

Bellibar's hand bucked, once, twice, three times, as he recocked and fired the big Remington.